J. T. CROFT

First published by Elmfire Press 2023

Copyright ©2023 by J. T. Croft

First edition

ISBN 978-1-7397277-9-6

All rights reserved.

Cover design by Fay Lane:

www.faylane.com

No part of this book may be reproduced in any form or by any electronic or mechanical means, including information storage and retrieval systems, without written permission from the author, except for the use of brief quotations in a book review.

It is illegal to copy this book, post it to a website, or distribute it by any other means without permission. This novel is entirely a work of fiction. The names, characters and incidents portrayed in it are the work of the author's imagination. Any resemblance to actual persons, living or dead, events or localities is entirely coincidental.

J. T. Croft asserts the moral right to be identified as the author of this work.

Elmfire Press

Unit 35590,

PO Box 15113,

Birmingham, B2 2NJ

United Kingdom

www.jtcroft.com

"Poets suffer occasional delusions of angelhood and find themselves condemned to express it in the bric-a-brac tongues of the human world. Lots of them go mad."

Glen Duncan

CONTENTS

Preface	vii
Acknowledgments	ix
The Exchange	1
Glow	41
Reflections	60
Nightingale	82
The Cresset Square	176
Sleep now, Adelard	204
Bric-a-Brac	255
Get Exclusive Content	269
About the Tales	270
Also by J. T. Croft	277
About the Author	279

PREFACE

Within these pages, you will find an assortment of tales, much like the eclectic mix of items found in a bric-a-brac shop. There is no singular over-arching theme guiding these stories; rather, they reflect the diverse musings of my imagination (and in the case of the title story, my father's). I offer you a medley of emotions and experiences, woven together by the threads of curiosity and wonder. Just like the curious objects displayed on the shop's shelves, each story carries its own uniqueness and charm.

I wrote this collection with a desire to explore or revisit fragments of writings that held promise but that were unfinished whether through a lack of skill at the time, or a clear sense of what it was the story was trying to tell me (if I don't know what the story behind the story is then that is deeply unsatisfying to me). An author's 'to be finished pile', much like the clutter of a house, can occupy a good chunk of their hard drive or second drawer, and a purge or donation to the nearest charity or bric-a-brac shop is sometimes in order (or enforced!).

As with all my fiction, there is a magical or supernatural

thread that binds them together. It is the essence of wonder, the allure of the unexplained, and the thrill of discovering the extraordinary in the ordinary. I offer you a glimpse into the many facets of the human experience and the mysteries that lie beyond our comprehension. It is my hope that you will find solace, intrigue, and perhaps even a sense of kinship with the characters who inhabit these tales. Sometimes the most extraordinary treasures are found in the most unexpected places.

J. T. Croft
October 2023

ACKNOWLEDGMENTS

For my father, whose creativity and imagination brought life to these tales, and of whom I am equally proud.

To my Advance Reader Team, *The Muses*:

Audrey Adamson
Siobhan Allen
Richard Brulotte
Tracey Bryant
Ali Christie
Laura Coveney
Matthew Coxall
Karen Furness
Julian Grant
Lana Kamennof-Sine
Daniel Nobles
Christine Ruiz Noriega-Hollnbuchner
Jackie Tansky

THE EXCHANGE

'All clear!' shouted the air raid warden, shuffling to the side of the East End tube station platform to allow the shuffling throng of relieved men, women, and children back to the surface.

The fading strangles of the siren wound to a whimper as Francis stumbled over the last step and into the city-wide blackout of the post-raid blitz.

'Compton Square's been hit,' cried a man from behind, and Francis stepped aside to adjust his eyes to the gloom of the wartime London night. The safe platform far below the ground had seemed a cheery cathedral of candlelight by comparison, but reality struck home – there was no mistaking the plume of distant smoke backlit by the rising glow of incendiary bomb fire.

A broad hand upon his shoulder steadied his shiver, and he glanced up into the pale and whiskered face of the landlord. 'Best get back to the pub, lad, if it still stands. *The Exchange* is always busy afterwards with folk needing to steady their nerves with a drop of best brown or something stronger. There'll be tales to tell of who was lucky, and who was not.'

'Yes, Mr Hoskins.'

They meandered their way back through the rapidly emptying streets, hindered only by the rattling, feverish bells of fire engines and paramedics scrambling with hand carts lined with bundles of bandages. As if in response, a rousing chorus of an anti-German song greeted them as they turned into the side street, raucous and defiant as the men queued beneath the sign of the weighing scales. They waited impatiently for the publican to remove his keys and open the leaded green glass-panelled door to a cigarette-incensed, sorrow-drowning sanctuary.

'Come on, Stan!' called a man, partially inebriated. 'I've got most of a pint to finish and I'll need another after that bomb that hit Mason Street.'

Hoskins rattled the key and the shield wall of thirsty men fell into the tap room to reclaim their pews from an hour before, steadying their shaking hands with the comforting, flat beer in glasses ringed with the memory of frothy heads and pre-raid conviviality.

'*The Exchange* got away with it,' said a caped man leaning on the counter. Francis began to man the beer pumps as though emptying a never-ending bilge of a sinking ship.

'Been here since Tudor times,' said Hoskins bringing out more glasses and clearing a space on the bar for more arms and hands heavy with shillings and sixpences. 'Old Gerry can huff and puff, but he won't blow my pub down while I live and breathe.'

Through the melange of frantic men, Francis filled and spilt glass after glass until the initial frenzy was tamed by liquor and camaraderie. He slumped on the bar like a spent navvy heaving with asthmatic breaths.

'I warned you about nights like this when you took the job a few months ago,' said Hoskins slapping him on the back and grinning with approval. 'You did well tonight, Francis. I think *The Exchange* suits you and you've lasted a longer time than most of your age.'

He sought for a reply but contented himself with a splay of his hands among the warm, wet puddles of beer in a gesture of gratitude. Glancing up, he saw the buttoned tweed coat of a newly entered, smartly dressed woman who politely coughed to gain Hoskins' attention.

'I've come to use...the...*operator*,' she whispered handing a letter into the publican's hand. 'My introduction from Mrs Hubert who I believe is a regular? I need to get in touch with someone—' she hesitated, searching for words, '—*behind the lines*.'

Hoskins read the letter and folded it back into his waistcoat giving Francis a nudge to wipe down the bar. 'She is and has favourable terms of access but it's highly irregular, particularly tonight of all nights, and I had closed up for the evening...'

Francis strained to hear the conversation through the 'Danny-Boy' droll of the drunkards in the far corner. His curiosity was always aroused by any mention of the room at the top of the stairs or the clientele that infrequently and discreetly passed through its locked door. What lay behind the secrecy he could not fathom, but ideas of a brothel were quickly quashed. Hoskins was a devout Catholic, and besides, Mrs Hubert and the well-dressed, middle-aged women (mostly) that came into the oldest inn in that part of town often left clutching letters, legal documents, or handkerchiefs to stem the tears from red-rimmed eyes. Similarly, thoughts of a closeted priest or German spy rapidly lost traction because apart from the visitors or Hoskins, no one went in, or out. Silence was the only squatter when Francis passed by the panelled portal during closing hours. Once or twice he had imagined voices during the thirty-minute slots allotted to those that hurried, self-consciously up the stairs, but the chatter and clamour from the lounge and tap room meant he could not be certain.

'What's up there?' he had asked when Hoskins had appeared to be in a genial mood. 'Gambling, or gangsters?'

'Neither.' The landlord's mood swung back to its customary gruffness, and he sighed, staring at the ceiling as though trying to see through the floorboards. 'Nothing but comfort and certainty, lad. Now go change the barrel on number two, and don't ask me or anyone else about it again.'

There was always the furtive and hinted-at assurances of secrecy above all else. Sometimes the women callers raced out as though desperate to be elsewhere or away from the place, returning a few days later with expectant eyes filled with trepidation. Mrs Hubert, the officious boarding house owner, two streets away, made frequent, tight-lipped appearances. Whether from familiarity with what lay beyond the door above or a natural disinclination for any emotion apart from impatience, her visits sparked little response unless it was in the depths of her tired eyes.

Men often stayed for a drink or two to drown out the shakes from what had transpired, but whether through their conscientiousness or the disapproving look from the landlord, Francis could make nothing of their hints and riddles to satisfy his curiosity. He suspected something important to do with the war was taking place in the most unlikely place possible. It made bizarre sense. Every unknown visitor he now regarded, rather enviously, as being a spy or informer, doing their dangerous bit for foreign resistance or the War Office, while he remained pulling pints and propping up old soldiers. He glanced over at an old Tommy, rich with rum, regaling embellished adventures of Gallipoli to the dusty, stuffed, moth-eaten bear next to the cigarette machine.

'I understand the need for discretion,' said the woman

imploringly, handing over a ten bob note. 'I must get a message through; it's a matter of life and death.'

Hoskins nodded sympathetically and raised his finger in front of his lips. 'Follow me, but it'll be up to the operators if they'll see you without an appointment. Don't make a habit of impromptu visits – careless talk and all that; you understand?'

The woman nodded, and Hoskins led her towards the base of the stairs.

'Keep the cattle watered, Francis. I'll not be long.'

'But—'

The landlord raised his eyebrows to end any further inquiry.

A trio of domino players in need of milk stout interrupted any thoughts of offering to escort the visitor upstairs, and when Francis glanced back, the woman and Hoskins were gone.

Several nights later, Francis emerged from the cellar, bumping into a tearful woman racing down the last few steps. Unusually, she had only been in the room above for less than twenty minutes. With an apology, he offered her a clean bar towel, which she declined.

'Are you alright, Missus? Would you like a moment in the lounge; it's quite empty and I could get you—'

'My son was just like you,' she said staring wet and wide-eyed into his face, raising her hand to brush his cheek, 'and now I know he's not missing; he's gone...'

The sound of shattered glass from the bar was followed by jeering mockery from the patrons. The momentary spell was broken. Hoskins' voice boomed in annoyance as a minor skirmish broke out. She turned, hurried out of the hall and through the smog of the adjacent snug to open the outer door, letting in a draught of turbulent fresh air into the hall and up the stairs.

The door on the landing creaked open.

His heart pounded, wondering whether to launch into a pretence of heroics by the landlord's side. No man, let alone a brace of drunkards, could match Hoskins in bare-knuckled, beer-fuelled bravado. Those foolish enough to forget the dusty, tarnished boxing trophies on the gin shelf, or the photos of him as a younger middleweight, sporting the corridor to the urinals, would soon regret it. Francis opted for cowardice and curiosity and tip-toed upwards like a footpad sensing he had only a few minutes before the miscreants would have their heads banged together and their arses introduced to the muddied pavement. Then Hoskins would call for him, or even bustle through to the cellar in a bellow, shouting to see if he had fallen asleep while cleaning out the lines.

The door was ajar, and he thrust his head through for a cursory peek. All seemed dark, a result of the furnishings, blackout curtains and heavy drapes that he registered in an instance. Light was present, but it was dim, and coming from the right-hand wall that adjoined the old typewriter factory, fire-ravaged a decade earlier and still shut up and abandoned. He glanced back to hear the raucous cheers in full vigour and stole inside.

Squinting in the dark he saw no one, but a room sparse with furniture that he had not expected. A solitary, water-stained tasselled lampshade upon a table beside the opposite windowed wall meekly shed its electric incandescence across the room to suggest two curtained booths. Blackout drapes were suspended from 'U' shaped rails on the ceiling each surrounding cracked, leather-backed armchairs facing old, oval mirrors like a dimly lit, Gothic barber shop. The right-hand cubicle had its drapes drawn back to display thin candle-lit stubs mounted and surrounding an oval mirror, dim and aged. The adjacent booth had its black, light-consuming drapes partly drawn. A muffled, mechanical tapping sound followed by the ping of a tiny bell from within, caused him to step back, ready to hide or escape back down the stairs to the more familiar darkness of the sweaty, stinking cellar. He hesitated, listening and sensing he was not alone, but no movement or further noise came from the enclosed and intimate space. He fingered back the curtain to peep into the draped delving to see an almost identical chair and mirror, this time surrounded within its ornamental frame by clusters of flickering candles, their light casting dancing shadows across the ceiling and glinting off the small silver counter bell in the recess of one arm.

The tall, oval mirrors were foxed with the haze of extreme age, their darkened glass smoky, almost opaque. Faint shadows and shapes moved within their depths and Francis rubbed at his eyes, squinting to see the room reflected – the lamp, the far wall, the chair, but not himself.

Whether to understand the illusion or create a sense of security, he stepped across to the open booth and drew the surrounding curtain, reclining into the creaking leather and catching the nipple of the bell in its arm. It rang softly before he had time to dampen it with his guilty, shaking hand.

From the smoky silver of the mirror, a shadow took form and sat down, summoned by the resonant, fading tinkle, and the reflected room vanished in a wave of darkness accompanied by the clink of curtain rails from beyond. He gathered his thoughts and gasped.

It's an old, transparent...two-way...mirror. The building next door is still being used, or at least one room is...

'Sorry to keep you,' said a gentle, muffled voice that appeared to come from the opposite side of the wall. 'I'm normally in the other booth but I'm having to man both since Mrs Peacock moved upstairs.'

For a moment Francis considered flight. His investigation had gone too far, and he was caught.

'Who are you looking to contact or receive information on their whereabouts?' It was a young, feminine enquiry, spoken with the uniformity and automation of an opening line much practised. He felt obliged to at least apologise or make one last attempt to solve the mystery – cowardice twice in an evening was out of the question. The shadow shifted as though examining something like a diary out of view in her lap. 'I don't seem to have anyone down for the rest of the evening; it might be a clerical error at our end though, not unheard of. I'll just get a little more light...'

The outline of a young woman, similar in age became clearer yet still partly obscured by the foxing of the reflecting glass as she rose, her buttoned cardigan tapping against the frame. She conducted a lit taper around the mirror on her side, setting life to hidden candles and revealing more of her pretty, freckle-cheeked face.

'Contact?' said Francis watching her sit in the foreground on what appeared to be a stool just in view leaving the empty chair of exact likeness to his own in prominent view before him. She hesitated in her tapping of an antique typewriter on a small gurney pulled from the other booth and glanced up through her dark, shoulder-length hair.

'Yes. Someone you have lost recently and need to contact?' She removed a pencil from behind her ear, chewing at its tip whilst snatching glances back through the clearer parts of the mirror.

Francis shrugged. 'I have lost no one recently that I know of.'

'Parents or a brother missing in action, perhaps?' She wrinkled her nose, much to his delight, hoping to elicit a coherent response to what sounded to her like a simple question. The typewriter thrummed as she rolled in a new sheet of paper and began to type.

'No, I'm an orphan,' he said leaning closer to catch a brief, clear glimpse where the mirror remained unspoiled. 'They found me at St Francis' church, hence my name.'

She glanced at him suddenly. 'I'm familiar with it. My sympathies, Francis. I never knew my parents either. Not knowing if they are on this side or that is something we never get used to, is it?'

'I wouldn't really care which side they are on because I never knew them, but I hope they wouldn't be German sympathisers, if that's what you mean.'

She looked bemused and ceased typing, eyeing him curiously through the glass. 'Why aren't you fighting, or are you on leave?'

'I tried to sign up but I couldn't pass the medical – I've got weak lungs. I couldn't even work down the mines and I'm no farmer.' All thoughts of Hoskins and the bar downstairs vanished as courage and confidence returned. 'What's your name, and are you the operator?'

'My name is Gwen, and yes, but I shouldn't really be having personal conversations. I thought we were done for tonight till you showed up.'

'We?'

'*The Exchange* and everyone who volunteers to keep it manned, I mean.'

Francis stared blankly into her partly obscured eyes. 'What is this place? I thought the place next door was burned out years ago, but...' he leaned back into the button-backed chair and slapped his forehead. 'It's perfect isn't it; I was right.'

'About what?'

He waved his arms around the room. 'An old pub and a

burned-out factory next door. No one would suspect it's some sort of intelligence job going on here,' he tapped his head and winked, seeing the confusion on her face blossom into a knowing smile and a solitary raised eyebrow.

'You aren't supposed to be here, are you?' she said coyly, picking up the pencil and tapping the glass to scold him. The mirror remained steady and unmoving. She shook her head with mock disapproval enjoying the cat-and-mouse game playing out.

'Don't worry,' he said. 'My lips are sealed. I'd like to do my bit though, you know, and volunteer to pass messages on or do anything to help with the situation, hush-hush-like. While I'm only a barman, you can trust me even if old Hoskins doesn't want me up here. I'd make a good spy—'

'What?' she said with a snigger. 'You have too gentle a face for that, and besides, you don't know what you are volunteering for, do you? You aren't even supposed to be here...'

'If you'd put a good word in for me, I'll happily give my life for King and...'

'You'll get yourself boxed by Hoskins, and me sacked if our betters find out. I'm supposed to report things like this,' she said blowing out the candles and growing fainter and more muffled. She hesitated at the typewriter.

'Wait, Gwen. I'm sorry, and I was only curious. I would never want to get someone like you in trouble. Let me make it up to you – I've got tickets for the Palais on Saturday – they are showing Fred's and Ginger's latest if you like dancing and...'

From the street below, the sound of crashing dustbins and the slam of the shutting outside door heralded the booming voice of the landlord.

'Lad! Where are you?'

A glance back to the mirror briefly outlined her lightly framed silhouette as she extinguished the last of the candles on her side. She withdrew the curtain behind her revealing the reflected room once more with its empty, solitary chair. Her delicate face became clearer as she pressed closely against the glass, her cherry lips and pale blue eyes fixing him with sweet interrogation. 'Been a while since I was asked out. That's very sweet of you, but you must go or we'll both get into trouble.' She furrowed her brow and nodded curtly for him to observe the approach of the landlord.

'Francis! Where the devil are you?'

Without taking his eyes off the mirror, he leaned forward until he could almost kiss the glass. 'The feeling's mutual and it's been a while since I've dared to ask anyone as pretty as you out. I get Mondays off if you'd like to take a walk instead. What time do you get off your shift, whatever it is you do? They can't keep you all night, surely.'

A thud of heavy boots entered the hall and took the first step as the landlord began his ascent.

'It was lovely talking to you Francis, even if it was just for a little while. I don't meet many people of my age doing this, they're mostly older.' She drew back leaving the imperfect antique mirror dark, with his own ridiculously rakish, blushing expression hazily reflecting from its cobweb-foxed obsidian surface.

'Damn visitor leaving the blasted door open—' muttered Hoskins on the stairs.

Francis shot out of the chair and glimpsed the chink of light on the landing. Hoskins' shadow flitted against the wall of the staircase like a giant.

He changed his mind on the booth knowing the curtain rails wouldn't settle in time, and rushed for the blackout drapes finding a recess wide enough for him to hide. Pulling his toecaps in and sideways like a hidden Charlie Chaplin he held his breath as the landlord entered the room.

The tinkle of curtain rails being pulled back accompanied the proprietor's mutterings.

'You still there, Miss Hastings?'

'Just leaving, Mr Hoskins,' came the muffled and more distant reply, 'unless there's anyone else tonight. It's been a bit of a last-minute rush, hasn't it?'

Francis thought the darkness between the blacked-out sash window and the curtains could not get any worse, but the faint slit of light at the frayed velvet edges gradually faded with each candle-extinguishing puff from the landlord, leaving only what appeared to be a single flickering candle peeping in on one side, with the brighter light from the landing on the other.

'You mean that impromptu visitor, the friend of Mrs Hubert's? Bit of a cheek but I'll not gainsay the old battle-axe; I've faced men in the ring less terrifying than her.'

Gwen laughed. 'I'll keep that off the records, shall I? She passes on a lot of information that would make us a lot busier otherwise.'

Hoskins hummed in resignation. 'No one else has been in, have they?'

The air in Francis' lungs screamed for release and he let out painfully slow breaths, sipping quietly to refill them as he crossed his fingers and clenched his eyes tightly.

'No,' said Gwen with barely noticeable sarcasm. 'No one spying or prying that would cause any bother. How's that new lad of yours working out?' Francis winced, imagining the operator enjoying an amusing revenge for his forwardness, the power to out him at any moment.

'When I can find him, and he's not asking questions,' said Hoskins with a snort, 'he's a good, honest, and hard-working sort, but—'

'Go on.'

'I don't think he'll stay. I get the feeling he's meant for

better things than East End pubs and all this dilly-dallying in the dark.'

'Why don't you tell him, then?' she said. 'There aren't many places *like this* in the country, and it might be just the thing a young man would be keen to take on if it didn't put the fear of God into him. We're always looking for people on the outside. Mrs Hubert won't live forever.'

Hoskins murmured incoherently and indecisively. 'There's so much work for us all these days, what with the war; difficult to keep tabs on everyone coming and going and keeping tongues from wagging.'

'Then get help,' she said with sincerity.

'God only knows what would happen if everyone knew about this place or the value of what's kept here; that's what worries me most. More than the crown jewels I wouldn't wonder.'

'It's what we provide, not the material cost, that is priceless, Mr Hoskins. Comfort and certainty, remember? You trusted me once and put a good word in for me after the fire, didn't you?'

Francis listened to the long, drawn-out sigh. 'I was sorry to see you go, Gwen. It was the least I could do and besides, you were a comfort after the wife left, walking old Samson and listening to my nonsense.'

Gwen softened, her voice growing clearer as her faint footsteps approached from the other side of the glass. 'I loved walking that old softie for you, and besides, you used to pay me in Liquorice Allsorts. I miss those now I'm working all hours over here.'

Hoskins laughed gently in reminiscence; a tender sound Francis had not experienced. 'I miss that dog, my dear, and....' His shuffling feet suggested the conversation was approaching its end. 'Say hello to the missus, if you see her.'

'I will,' said Gwen softly. 'But I think she'd rather hear it from you, all the same when you're ready. Goodnight.'

For a moment, the landlord made no sound, then Francis heard his footfall coming towards the curtains and he readied himself for the shock and disappointment on the old man's face. He was about to emerge and own up to the trespass when all remaining light ceased with the click of the lamp. The door closed and locked, leaving him in the void between glass and curtain while the heavy footfalls receded down the stairs.

'He's gone,' said Gwen quietly and sounding far away. 'You owe me one, my charming, honest, hard-working little spy. You'll find the catch on the window is broken. If you hurry, you can be back in the cellar from the trapdoors below the drainpipe before he catches you! Goodnight.' The crisp crackle of the pinched candle from the other side was faint, but final. Francis whispered her name, but there was no reply.

Lifting the sash behind, pale lights from across the street poured into the tiny, makeshift vestibule illuminating the stone ledge and cast iron drainpipe at arm's length distance. He drew in a breath and climbed out, pinching his fingers as he lowered the frame, and shimmied down the twenty feet of the rusty cylinder to land, flat-footed upon the heavy wooden barrel doors of the cellar. Several inebriated men, dumped and slumped on the pavement from the fracas earlier glanced over and beckoned him to come to their aid, or at least to readmit them to the bar. With just enough time, he swung into the cellar, tripping over a stack of barrels to bash his head on the ceiling beam with a yelp.

'Where the hell have you been?' boomed Hoskins coming around the corner. 'I've been calling you!'

'Men...outside,' lied Francis feeling the lump on his forehead for any sign of blood. 'Tried to get back in.' Hoskins caught sight of the developing bruise and laughed, dragging him through the narrow passageway and up the slippery stone steps into the blinding light of the hall. A scrum of men called for beer and brandy like hungry fledglings left in the nest without their mother.

'You damn fool,' he said wiping at the sensitive spot like a coach in a boxing ring while Francis winced and jittered. 'You'll live. I thought you'd had enough and done a runner. Leave the manhandling to me in future. Now get back to the bar, the whole pub has got a thirst on.'

His forehead burned as he manned the pumps and cleared away glasses, but nowhere near as hot as his flushed face and heart for the mischievous, mysterious, and pretty operator he had briefly been acquainted with. He stuck his head out into the street at several opportunities and glanced at the boarded windows and padlock-gated door of the old factory next door half hoping she would emerge so that he could see her again.

She did not emerge on that night, or any other.

'Samson?' said the welder leaning against the bar waiting for Francis to settle the head on a pint of mild. It was quiet for lunchtime, and a splendid opportunity to ask questions while Hoskins was in the parlour finishing his steak and kidney pudding. 'It was a mangy old bull terrier. Ugly it was, just like him, but it was company for him after his wife left. It put a spring back in his step, him being known for being light on his feet in the ring and all.' The man nodded towards the piano above which hung the photograph of a thickly set dog, brown and white patched with one eye and a hair lip. 'He's been grumpy or sad ever since though whether it's his missus or the mutt he misses most, I do not know; I never met her – before my time.'

'Do you remember a young woman about my age, dark

hair and blue eyes coming in to walk him?' said Francis handing over the chestnut-coloured beer.

'I don't recall anyone of that description—' the welder said, wiping the back of his oily hand across his frothed moustache, '—but there was a young kid who used to walk him. An unpredictable thing was old Samson, but it was like a kitten when she was around; she used to take him around the church on Blunden Street but that was way back, before the fire at the factory next door so it wouldn't be the same person.'

'What happened next door?' asked Francis handing the man his change.

'Old or dodgy electrical wiring they said. The place caught fire, and some folks died, by smoke mostly on account of there being only one door. The fire engine turned up and put the worst of it out and it's been empty since; no insurance you see.'

'Have you ever seen anyone go in or out?

The man shook his head and lit a cigarette. 'I live across the street, and I've seen no one. I'm surprised it hasn't been condemned; there's no roof on most of it, you can see right into the room adjoining your first floor from my attic skylight or could do before I blacked it out. Why do you ask? I wouldn't go playing or courting in there, it's unsafe.'

Hoskins emerged, sheepishly and unsuccessfully hiding a bunch of carnations from the inside of his old sheepskin coat. He nodded a greeting to the welder, elbow raised, draining his glass.

'Just going out for an hour or so, Francis. You can lock up, it's nearly afternoon closing. I'll be back at four; I've got my key.'

Both men left leaving the bar empty. Francis was alone with his curiosity in conflict. Whether to gain access to the room by the climb to the first floor in full daylight via the drainpipe or follow the landlord and his awkward, flushed face to discover who he was meeting or where he was going. He might even be meeting with those connected to the secrets above, perhaps even Gwen. Before he knew it, Francis had switched off the lights and locked the door, coat in hand, turning to see the pair part ways at the end of the street. Following at a distance, he pulled up his collar and pursued his target with all the subtlety of a poorly acted movie spy.

Several turns ahead he caught sight of the man heading into the churchyard of St Francis, flowers now held openly and shamelessly in his right hand. Keeping behind the wide trunk of a venerable yew he watched as Hoskins tracked through the rows of headstones and laid the flowers upon the dew-laden grass before a small slab of black marble. Breath steamed from his mouth in the cold afternoon air as his head wandered to gaze fleetingly at inconsequential details in the churchyard – a robin alighting on a dew-laden rose hip, the top of a Routemaster bus hovering over the high wall in traffic, and finally, courageously, a momentary glance at the headstone. A quick kiss from his fingers passed to the top of the grave and he moved on, weaving through the long grass to stand beside a memorial bedecked by spent flowers. He pulled something from his pocket and opened his fist to let the brightly coloured objects pile at the base of the stone cross, and for a moment he hung his head in respect.

Behind the yew came an old couple, arm in arm, bearing their own floral tributes, and Francis self-consciously turned around, trying to avoid appearing like a voyeur. They passed with a greeting, and he looked back to see the memorial solitary and silent. The slow, shambling landlord walked on beyond the far gate and towards the park, out of his sight, intending it seemed to make the most of the late September sunshine.

It seemed wrong to intrude on the grave with the floral

offering, so Francis wandered over to the Portland stone of the modest, stepped plinth and cross of the public memorial. He had rarely visited the church, let alone the graveyard, so was taken by surprise to read that it had been erected in memory of those that had perished in the typewriter factory. The sweetness of something familiar yet strange for this location reached his nose before he glanced down at the spent flowers and the brightly coloured baubles, sandwiched or ringed by soft black liquorice.

Allsorts...

The slow, circuitous route back to the pub ended with the familiar camel-coated, cottage loaf silhouette of Mrs Hubert banging on the wooden frame of the locked, glass-panelled doors. For a moment, he considered escape to a safe and secure distance until she left, but she turned round, her spectacle-mounted nose twitching, beckoning him like a schoolmistress.

'Where's 'Oskins?' she snapped. 'I need to speak to the operator and I prefer to deal with him.'

'He's out for the afternoon,' said Francis with a weak and unconvincing smile.

She peered through the rippled stained glass to determine the truth of the matter. 'Well, let me in, it's urgent and I haven't got time to hang around out here. She'll see me, don't you worry about that. I've got a list of names that needs passing along.'

'I'd prefer we waited until Mr Hoskins gets back,' he said. 'He's the only one with the key.'

Several men loitered behind, expectantly curious and hopeful of an early opportunity to drink and play cards. Mrs Hubert closed her eyes with a look of disgust. '*Why did the closest one to me have to be in a pub of all places?*' she murmured to herself. 'I know where the old fool keeps it so he can blame me if he's put out and my thirty years of service passing messages back and forth are not worth anything. I kept his mother company all those years while he was off knocking other men senseless around the East End, that's worth something.'

Francis looked at the small gathering of men now forming behind them, wondering if he would get in without opening the floodgates and putting the license at risk. 'I'm not supposed to open up before time—'

'*Do I look like I need a drink?*' she huffed, her eyes widening as Francis stifled his open mouth, replying from his honest but unfiltered subconscious. He shook his head while his brain caught up and engaged the appropriate gear.

'I'll just be a minute,' he said unlocking the door and squeezing her through the open door whilst he spread himself wide to prevent any entry from the disgruntled men outside. Twisting to re-lock it, he offered to take her coat, but Mrs Hubert was off like a pinball, nudging into chairs from her passage past the piano. Something glittered in her hand as she waddled through the hall and thumped up the stairs. She had found the key's hiding place almost immediately, and very close by, but Francis saw no obvious spot and he would have heard the fall board of the piano being raised and shut. The upper lid itself was surmounted by a heavy, brass carriage clock that he could barely lift one-handed when he was instructed to wipe the dust about.

In a laboured, breathless moment she reached the landing, unlocked the door and clicked on the lamp inside. The light was extinguished as he reached the end of the hall when Mrs Hubert locked the door behind her with an indignant click of the lock.

The few hopeful raps on the pub door subsided and

Francis caught the sharp striking of matches from the room above. Carefully placed non-creaking footfalls on the carpeted treads got him half the way up, far enough to show the flickering of candlelight emanating from the gap beneath the door. The sound of the counter bell from one armrest rang impatiently before the muted and muffled voices of two women began in familiar and earnest conversation. His heart leapt, knowing that even if he could not see her, Gwen was on the other side of the door, and the wall within the upstairs storeroom. The conversation was quiet and difficult to follow, so he crept into the parallel box room and put his ear to the interior wall. To his surprise, he could hear nothing but the whistling wind and an occasional pigeon flapping within the allegedly roofless room beyond.

It was a small matter to return to the door and listen at the lock, but to hear only Mrs Hubert with any clarity, rustling within the leather armchair.

'They'll be with you in a few days... no, Mason Street was hit... about eight were injured as well as killed... any update from over in France?... I see... I'll let them know... Tell the new lads that West Ham lost on Saturday... what would we do without you, my dear? Give me the casualties from this week to pass on...'

The bizarre conversation continued, and just as one train of thought led him to one explanation, another suddenly caused a wreck and left him bewildered. There were frequent exchanges of names, with the old woman requesting clarification of the more unusual or international surnames, often connected with a military rank. The muffled sounds of the typewriter tip-tapped in response to names, some of whom Francis recognised locally but had not been seen since the night of the last air raid. General chit-chat descended into gossip and he blushed, making for the stairs upon hearing snippets of the infidelity of wives spending quality time 'alone' while their oblivious husbands sought comfort in the arms of the common room below.

The cellar seemed a good place to start opening up and cool his reddening cheeks, the dark somehow comforting as he spent a half hour washing glasses and loading up bottles into crates to restock the bar in the snug. He awoke from his stock check when the main door slammed. Mrs Hubert had left.

The door was quickly and securely locked once more as the carriage clock struck a quarter to four and he looked over, seeing something was out of kilter, not in its accustomed place. The framed picture of the dog lay tilted and not as it had been before the woman's arrival or during his frequent trips back and forth between the cellar and the ground-floor rooms.

A nudge of the frame back to its vertical position released a key from its secure spot wedged between the wall and the frame. It clattered on the piano lid and Francis glanced towards the stairs and the time on the clock until opening.

'Just a quick chance before Hoskins gets back...'

The key rattled in the lock as he nervously swung open the door. The room was still lit by the lamp and several candles surrounding the left mirror frame. Light tapping could be heard followed by the familiar *ting* of the typewriter reaching the end of the line. Both cubicle curtains were drawn back, and he peered into the murky silver from behind the armchair. 'Gwen!' he whispered. 'Are you there? She's gone.'

The silhouette of the young woman peered around the inside of her frame, pencil balanced atop her pouting top lip. She opened her mouth briefly letting the pencil fall to the floor. 'You didn't kill yourself on that drainpipe then, I would have known...'

'I just wanted to see you again, that's all.'

'And?' She twitched her nose expectantly.

'And to ask if you'd given any idea to walking out with me sometime.' he said watching her rise from her search beneath the armchair like a blurred revenant among the haze of foxed glass. 'Or if you'd had a word with your superiors about me.'

'I've done no such thing on either count,' she said fidgeting on the stool, avoiding eye contact. A hint of blush coloured her cheeks, visible only to the close inspection of her face. He thought she might be wearing lipstick, her hair fixed with Saturday night precision. 'Bet you went with another girl last Saturday—'

'Did not,' he exclaimed. 'I asked you and I've been hanging around the place waiting to ask you in person without this mirror in the way.' She glanced over and shrugged, chewing at the recovered end of the pencil. Her feet tapped on the floor excitedly, emulating her quick piano fingers on the typewriter forte. 'I bought you flowers but—'

She turned covering her hand to her face to hide her smile. 'But what?'

'When you didn't come or go for three days, or go in, I put them in a vase in the snug.' He sighed. 'Hoskins pinched them a few hours ago and took them to the churchyard.'

Outside, the roaring and singing of men coming back from the football almost drowned out her reply.

'That was very kind, Francis,' she said turning a sad, muted smile towards him. 'But I don't think this is going to work and I can't lead you down the garden path. I can't go to the talkies or the park with you, not tonight, not ever.'

'If you got me a job, I could work on your side and there'd be no problem unless that is—' he faltered and looked at his scuffed shoes through his grubby fingers. How did he ever think someone as perfect as Gwen could ever consider walking arm in arm with him in public? '—you'd rather not be seen with—'

'An honest, good-looking and hard-working fella with sad, sparkly eyes and a lock of chestnut brown hair that keeps flopping over his brow?' she said, suddenly regaining her composure and looking away to hide her true feelings. Francis had seen this ruse in femme fatales at the pictures and pushed his luck.

The home crowd bustled and banged on the outside door for admittance, drowning out the opening creak of the door behind him.

He glanced at her bare ring finger. 'Then why not? Have you got someone you are sweet on, perhaps one of them spies or other? If only I was in uniform...'

'It's not that,' she said. 'It's because I'm—'

The door swung open, flooding the room with daylight. Francis whirled around to see the backlit silhouette of Hoskins, his shaking head illuminating before the flickering candles. The landlord drew in a long breath.

'Because she's dead, lad.'

Francis held out his hands, disregarding the absurd statement, fumbling with apologies and sheepishly studying the floor. To his surprise, Hoskins sat down in the opposite chair, beckoning him to do likewise. 'I came in through the snug,' he said. 'Saw the door was open. Well, now you know.'

'I don't know anything,' said Francis. 'I meant no harm, I was only—'

'Gwen's dead, Francis. Everyone on that side of the mirror is dead. It's called *The Exchange* for a reason.'

She turned to meet his gaze, the sunshine in her smile hidden by a cloud of sadness as she nodded, biting her lip.

'But the two-way mirror, and next door, and the secret messages for the war effort—'

'Look closely, lad. It's the same room, only we aren't in it. We use them to pass messages between the two sides from those seeking comfort and certainty until both parties are ready to move on. She's here in this room but on her side where things are the same, but different.'

Hoskins rose, lifting the mirror from its clip with some effort, and placed it on the floor. He knocked on the darker, unfaded wallpaper where the frame had once hung to prove there was no trickery. Turning the glass towards him, Francis gasped. The image remained unchanged – the room reflecting the armchair with no shift in perspective. 'Gwen is the operator for this exchange and she makes appointments, provides a connection in many more ways than you think, and does the secretarial work for those present – all from this room mirrored in the afterlife.' Francis leaned forward to touch the glass, leaving his print upon the surface as Hoskins continued. 'We can't reach them and they can't reach us, beyond talking; do you see?'

'How is this even possible?' said Francis, glancing back at the mirror. Gwen rose and stepped aside, disappearing out of view and into the other booth, reappearing a moment later in the mirror clasped in Hoskins' left hand. She rubbed at the fingerprint from beyond with the cuff of her blouse without success reinforcing the landlord's point.

'It's true,' she said. 'That's why I can't walk out with you, no matter how much I want to.'

The landlord lifted the mirror back to its place on the wall with a heave. 'There's no satisfactory answer to how it works, or I'm none the wiser. Alchemy, old lore, divine intervention, or magic who knows? I've been meaning to tell you once I had faith, but never found a good time. I feel I can trust you, Francis. This must remain a secret, known only to a few.'

'But why?'

'Because there are only a few of these things left and we can't take the risk of them being stolen or destroyed. Just how would you go about getting the whole of London in here?' He stooped to place a hand on Francis' shoulder. 'You can barely keep them out of the cellar after I've chucked them out on the street. It should go on as it always has, since before medieval times, as I understand.'

Gwen returned to sit in the mirror before him. 'It was Mrs Hubert, she forgot to lock the door. I'm sorry.'

Hoskins shook his head. 'She caught me as I was halfway up the street and it's my fault for not seeing the signs. I hope you won't need to mention it to anyone on your side, Gwen. I'm certain the lad won't talk, not unless he wants to lose his job *and* his teeth.' Hoskins raised an eyebrow, but it was the clenched hand of the middleweight about the armchair that encouraged a quick response. Francis was certain the threat was only intended metaphorically regarding his pearly whites and wouldn't really have been carried out, but he had made his mind up already.

'*... he's a good, honest, and hard-working sort...*'

'No, of course not, but I don't—can't believe what I'm seeing and hearing. I followed you today to the church, you took my flowers—' Avoiding the open mouth of the landlord, he turned to see Gwen dabbing the corner of her eye with her sleeve.

'*Liquorice Allsorts*,' he said. 'You died in the—'

'Yes,' she said. 'And there's no need to be worried about me or anyone on this side. It's just like living was but not with the people you once knew or loved. That's where the mirrors, the operators, and the Exchanges around the world come in,' she said settling her gaze on Hoskins' face. The landlord's eyes meandered around the room with a look of overwhelming sadness, as they had done in the churchyard a few hours earlier. She continued.

'To help both sides come to a resolution so they can move on with their lives or—' She raised her eyes to the top of her head and made a thumb towards the ceiling, '—move on to the other place.'

'Your wife,' said Francis recalling the action at the grave. Hoskins shifted on his heels.

'She's on the other side, isn't she?'

Hoskins nodded, making for the door and escape from emotional entanglement. He hesitated and looked back, allowing some of his simmering grief to rise to the surface. 'Some of us choose not to use the option to communicate even when we have it — it's too painful when you can't have someone utterly that you loved for thirty years and never told them. Not really told them, I mean.

'I've been very selfish, haven't I, Gwen.'

She shook her head. 'She misses you in the same way. I think all it would take is a few moments to let go, for both of you. She's ready to go upstairs, Mr Hoskins and I'll be here to hold both of your hands, so to speak when the time is right.'

Francis stared deeply into her compassionate eyes. Gwen was no ordinary typewriter factory girl turned secretary for the dead, here was someone with empathy and warmth that no earthly counsellor could rival. She caught the look and smiled, understanding the wordless compliment.

A thunder of fists on the locked door downstairs broke the silence.

'Time to let the rabble in. Don't be long, you two, and lock the door behind you when you come down, Francis. You can keep the key – you'll be assisting me with the clientele from now on, especially Mrs Hubert.'

Francis rolled his eyes at the penance and Gwen stifled a snigger.

'Good luck,' she said. 'First appointment is with Mr Smith from the Commonwealth Office at six-thirty tonight, Mr Hoskins. Several merchant seamen came over last week and it will confirm what he fears.'

He nodded and paused at the door not turning to speak. 'A word of advice for both of you. Keep things professional; it's not good to get involved with someone you can't touch or hold.'

Knowing the true business upstairs kept Francis far busier and more emotionally drained than he had expected in the weeks following his discovery and impromptu induction into the strange world between the living and the dead. Despite this, he felt a renewed sense of purpose, buoyed by the important work and trust of both Hoskins and the operations team on the other side. His sadness ebbed and flowed, filled during those quiet moments when he was alone or during fleeting interactions with Gwen, knowing that she was always out of reach. Their gentle but formal back-and-forth interactions would never be enough to satisfy his heart and he sighed, trying to let go of the pretty, speckled woman who looked the same age but had died when he was still only ten years old. He wondered what it must be like for her to see people age, as she remained the same.

Francis recovered himself at the graveyard one Sunday afternoon, a pocket full of liquorice ready to lay as a tribute, but made the painful decision to let his feelings go. It was enough, now, to spend a few moments with his head bowed before offering the sweets to a small group of children playing nearby on a heap of mounded rubble. He thought Gwen would approve.

Later that evening, as he lit the candles and dusted down the upstairs room, he caught her, mirroring the movements of his cleaning and the preparations for the appointments to come.

'Your side or mine?' she said squinting at a blemish in the

glass unconnected with its age. Her face became clearer, and he fortified himself against any notion of further amorous intent.

He approached the glass, breathed upon the surface and rubbed at the spot. 'Mine.'

Her face reappeared, and for a moment, they locked eyes. The landlord's parting words on that fateful night strengthened his resolve, and he sniggered, breaking the tension, and releasing the knot in his heart.

'Is this what spies get to do while they are in training?'

The muffled, reciprocating laughter from beyond death's mirror dispelled all words unspoken, and they were just two young people again talking.

'I feel such an idiot for asking you out,' he said putting away the cloth. 'But I've got room in my life for a friend if you're interested?'

Gwen nodded, her bottom lip trembling. 'So have I. I'm glad we got over the—thing, you know? I'm glad you brought it up because I've been squirming after our last brief goodbye.'

'Hoskins is right, of course,' he said, clicking on the lamp. 'Damn silly idea trying to carry on with someone you can't knock about with.'

'He's right about most things, and I'm glad we've cleared the air on that. It's been hard thinking about letting someone go; that's usually an issue with the living.'

'What's it like?' asked Francis. 'Why do some people move on, like your Mrs Peacock, while others can't or don't?'

'Imagine a waiting room at a station,' she replied scratching at her head. 'People that have died take a while to arrive, sometimes a few weeks before they show up, and they leave when their train arrives, so to speak. For most, it's when they are reconciled with their past life, and find—'

'Comfort and certainty?' offered Francis.

Gwen smiled. 'Yes. Love binds people to the world of the living, and those that aren't ready to say goodbye remain here, just as they did in life but with no wants or hurts, apart from the parting with loved ones.'

'What about you?' he said. 'If it's not inappropriate to ask. You said you were an orphan like me — is there someone on this side that is preventing you from leaving like all the others you help?'

'It's called the *yearning*,' she said, puckering her lips. 'It's difficult to describe, but those that don't form emotional attachments in life spend a lot longer here.' A sharp pang of concern on his face caused her to rephrase the answer. 'It's not a burden, and I quite enjoy helping people, it's just my luck though—'

'What do you mean?' he said as she shook her head and rolled her eyes.

'The only guy to ask me out was ten years too late.' She blushed.

'You mean you never truly fell in love?'

She shrugged. 'Outside of typewriters, cats, and Liquorice Allsorts, no.'

'Can you fall in love on the other side?' he said, sensing a sharp pain of regret if he would never see her again. 'Would that help you move on?'

'It happens occasionally, but most folks or those too young to get involved, just move on regardless; they fade away when the time's right. I guess it's just not my turn yet.' She leaned close to the mirror picking a cleaner section to pick out his face. 'You did the right thing to the wrong girl, Francis. Don't hang around waiting for the right time, because you never know when your time is up. You have my permission to go find someone else to go to the pictures with, alright?'

'Tell me about Hoskins' wife,' said Francis checking his watch and changing the subject. 'If it's not confidential.'

Gwen pulled the drape around her and sat down in the armchair. 'We've only got a few minutes, but alright.

'She died of a heart attack not long before the fire. I don't see her as often as I used to in the beginning. She used to make appointments to use this exchange to contact Mr Hoskins, but she stopped making them after a while.'

'Why hasn't she gone upstairs, then?' Her face revealed a complex of emotions. 'He didn't want to see her?'

'He only saw her once, soon after she died, but he wasn't ready and struggled with it. It happens a lot on the first meeting until the emotions settle, but in his case, he couldn't bear it. It's common with men, especially tough ones with soft insides.'

She stabbed at the typewriter keys punching out staccato letters on the page, mulling over her thoughts.

'It feels like we are really close to something,' she murmured. 'That night you found out, he was teetering on the edge ready to give in and let his grief take control.'

'You think he could be persuaded, by someone like me?' he said.

'Maybe, but you could just as easily push him back. My heart tells me that if he doesn't come to terms with her death one way or another, she'll move on, and he'll regret it for the rest of his life.'

'He'll see her again though, won't he, when he dies, assuming there's no downstairs...' He had given little thought until now as to the alternatives.

'He'll be alright,' she said. 'For all his faults, but regret could leave him here for a long while.'

'I'd better get downstairs myself otherwise—' He was interrupted by the chilling sound of the Medusa across the city. He rushed to the window, raising it to peer into blackness as the air raid sirens wailed to their full, mournful cries. One by one the powerful searchlights at the docks scoured the skies with wandering columns of light searching for targets for the guns at Hyde Park. A warden in the street below banged on doors, calling out to get to Anderson shelters or the subway station. What few lights could be seen blinked out. The man glanced up at the window.

'Oi! Shut that window up and get away, you fool. You'll make yourself a target letting light out like that.'

'It's a raid,' said Francis catching her worried expression from the mirror. 'Don't worry, there's nothing around except West Ham United and that's not worth bombing unless you are a Millwall supporter.'

'Francis!' called Hoskins from the base of the stairs. 'Put out those candles and get down here – I need you to help old Tom to the station; he's had a skinful. I'll follow after I've locked the place up, including the cellar doors – The Tanners Arms got looted during the last raid.'

'I'll let our side know,' she said, fading as he extinguished the candles and switched off the light. Her face was pushed up against the glass struggling to see him as he made for the door.

'Be careful.'

'Hold on to the rail, Tom, and watch your step as you go down,' said Francis, looking back over his shoulder from the Underground entrance towards The Exchange.

You.... not comin'?' slurred the old-timer.

'I'll be down in a moment, I'm just waiting for Mr Hoskins.'

A wave of humanity rushed forward hearing the one thing more frightening than the air raid sirens.

The distant thunder of German bombers.

'Keep calm, don't panic!' called a marshal. 'Plenty of room down below. Hurry now, nice and steady.'

Francis moved aside, taking several steps back to the road.

'You, sir!' cried the Marshal. 'Get down below.'

Ignoring the man he scanned the oncoming faces, catching a punter he knew to have been in the bar less than an hour before. A small terrier shivered in the crook of one arm.

'Have you seen Hoskins?'

The man nodded. 'He was still at the pub locking up when I came by about fifteen minutes ago; he was having trouble locking the cellar doors. I went home first to pick Bertie up—'

Francis raced through the tide of warmly wrapped, torch-bearing humanity, pushing past until the side streets became clearer, deserted by light and life. He rounded the corner, out of breath hearing the roar of the Luftwaffe ever closer, and caught the pub sign tremble in the stiffening breeze. All lights were out, and there was no time left to get back to the station.

Sounds of scattered gunfire preceded the whistling of falling bombs, screaming like fireworks towards the ground to explode with devastating sunbursts. A quarter of a mile ahead and above, he saw the dreadful black Valkyries ride towards the East End, and the first blinding flash as the first of their incendiaries struck the ground in the distance.

Racing for the door, he found it unlocked and dashed into the tap room, illuminated by a glowing amber light from outside.

Another bomb landed, louder, closer...

'Hoskins!' he screamed, barging open all the internal doors. 'Gerry's coming!'

Beyond the cellar door, he flicked on the light and caught

sight of the landlord unmoving, face down with the back of his head bloodied from a fallen empty cask nearby.

Hoskins was unresponsive as he turned the man over. A quick pulse check was inconclusive – he could barely contain the adrenaline-fuelled panic flooding his whole body.

Stay here or get out?

Francis grabbed the man's legs and opted for the latter, gripping the moleskin trousers and wrenching him in backward spurts with strength that he never thought he had. A blast from what sounded only a few hundred yards away blew out the windows, showering them both with glass as they emerged into the fiery glow of the ground floor. Falling debris peppered the roof and flaming lumps of timber rained down into the street.

'The street's been hit, and nearby houses are on fire!' he said to the limp body beneath. With arms burning, he made it to the snug door and out to the side entrance away from the terraced houses, their second floors aflame. Hoskins groaned as Francis dropped his legs, seeing the factory next door being set alight with rivulets of descending sparks.

'You're alive!' he said heaving the man onto his back. Delirious, he whined and clutched at his head trying to get up for a standing count like a floored boxer.

'*Mirror...*'

The smell of acrid smoke was growing, not only from the fiery tempest whipped up from the breeze in the narrow alleys, but from his immediate surroundings. The snug was filling with black smog.

Something was alight within the pub.

'*Gwen...*' muttered Hoskins. '*The Exchange...*' The landlord twitched and fell silent, unmoving.

A distant ringing of firemen grew clearer as the roaring bombers grew more remote

and Francis coughed, dragging in the air to his asthmatic

lungs. The adrenaline was still coursing through his veins, but his breath was short and shallow as he dragged the landlord towards a place of safety and propped him against the glass-strewn, locked cellar doors. He put his hand on the drainpipe to steady himself and looked up to the drape billowing through the blasted aperture. Faint wisps of smoke licked the top of the wounded window.

... there are only a few of these things left...

With his temporary newfound strength in body and purpose, he climbed, dragging himself up and across onto the ledge with no idea if a way down was possible through the pub. Splintered shards bit into his hands as he grabbed the sash and forced it open with a desperate cry. The room was denser with smoke than he realised and he choked, getting down to the floor where there was more air. Part of the ceiling had collapsed and a pile of debris was burning in the corner setting the drape of the first cubicle alight. It flamed intensely and through the miasma, he saw the mirror crack in response to the sudden, buckling heat. Gwen banged on the inside of the glass shouting for him to get out. Gulping air he raced to the other mirror, seeing her appear, begging him to leave it behind and escape. He shook his head and lifted the frame from its mighty hook. The weight knocked him back, and he lay dazed, the mirror upon him, her face tearful as she screamed at him to get up.

The smoke filled the room and from the corner of his eye, he saw the second drape writhe like a genie wreathed in flame. Gwen's fists beat upon the mirror from beyond the glass, and the grave, and he saw it splinter with the force of her blows, shooting her beautiful face into a myriad of abstract pieces. His legs would not obey and he knew he was knocked out in the ring, wheezing for any oxygen that had not been consumed by fire. The approaching fire engine clanged outside, and he relaxed with ever shallower breaths. The pub would be safe, they would all be safe.

She looked so pretty as he lost consciousness even with her mascara running down her cheeks. So vulnerable, so alone, so lovely.

He wondered which of the many cherry-red lips he should like to kiss first, the faint taste of liquorice upon his own as he closed his eyes.

The radiant light that woke him cast glorious glimmers of morning sunlight across the bedroom ceiling. He coughed, more out of habit than necessity, and half pushed up on his hands from the comfortable mattress to peer out of the clear window. A serene quiet lay about the street like the Sunday morning of a holiday when an entire week of rest and recuperation lay ahead.

Dressing in the mirror he abruptly paused at his top shirt button, reminded of his ordeal, trying to make sense of the situation. Had someone brought him home after the fire? What about the pub, Hoskins, and Gwen? The clock on the far wall showed a quarter to eleven, and a panic set in – he would be late to open up if there was anything left of The Exchange.

The outside air seemed sweeter than of late, rustling the early fiery colours of autumn in the great Spanish Plane Trees. It revitalised his step, and he tentatively broke into a gentle run shielding his eyes from the bright reflections of blue sky and the new day in the pavement windows, adorned with flowers and tied-back chintz. The pub stood, externally intact. What chaos and debris he had expected had been removed and for a moment, he wondered if he had dreamed the whole thing. A line of people, chatting in polite conversation, queued outside. He slowed, barely out of breath, and reached the sparkling green glass-panelled door.

'Not open yet,' said a man. He coughed politely. 'There's a queue you know.'

'It's alright,' said Francis trying the door to find it open. 'I work here and I'll be with you as soon as I find out what's been going on.'

Closing the door behind him, he turned to see the bar clean and tidy, with no odour or bitter taste of smoke. He wondered how long he had been asleep if sleep it had been. Perhaps he had spent time in the hospital?

'Mr Hoskins?' he called. 'Anyone?'

'You're early,' said an older, unfamiliar voice from the snug. 'Be with you in a jiffy.'

Not waiting to settle his bearings or the sense that something seemed different, not worse, just different, he took to the stairs and entered the open room at its top. The candlelit darkness was a melancholic interlude after the pleasant daylight and he squinted to acclimatise to the room, noticing nothing untoward or out of place, just as it had been from his remembrances before the raid. The roof had been repaired but at what speed and at what cost he could not fathom, and the notion that he had been ill for some time returned. Had it been a few days, a few weeks?

The right-hand booth had its drapes drawn concealing the mirror, the armchair, and the murmur of low voices that emanated from within. The left-hand booth stood empty and a glance at the candle-strewn mirror displayed several new cracks on its smoky, mottled surface. He sat down and rang the bell on the armrest.

'Half a minute,' came a muffled voice. 'I'm still opening up.'

Francis' initial joy at hearing the voice of the landlord suddenly turned to the anxious preoccupation of picking out the details of the familiar silhouette in the damaged mirror. The sound was not coming from this side of the glass. Hoskins came closer, on the other side of the divide, and peered through, his eyes widening as he caught his breath.

'Francis! My God, you're there—'

He realised he had failed to save the man despite his efforts. 'Mr Hoskins, you're on the other side! I found you lying by a loose barrel. Please—'

Hoskins shook his head. 'You did the bravest thing any man could and don't you worry about me. I've been well looked after this past month since you left.'

'A month?' said Francis incredulously. 'I didn't realise I had been so ill. What happened?'

A clear, gentle tapping of the typewriter accompanied the landlord's reply. 'The firemen and wardens pitched in to stop the place from going up, but it was a bit of a mess, as you can imagine. There was a gas explosion not long after and it took half the terrace along Drovers Lane with it. We had help sorting out the roof with a tarpaulin until the roofers showed up and some of the regulars took turns getting the place back on its feet; first day today funnily enough – fancy that...' Hoskins sat down. 'I'm so sorry about what happened, you shouldn't have gone back in and I blame myself, Lad, and I don't know whether to cry or be overjoyed to see you; The place and I are going to miss you...'

'Was it the bang on your head that did for you?' asked Francis. 'Tell me you didn't suffer.'

The landlord frowned. 'Only the hospital food, and the knowledge that you were gone.'

Francis smiled. The typewriter tapped and the sound of paper being torn from the roller brought him back to the question he most wanted answers to.

'I saved the mirrors for you, didn't I?'

Hoskins nodded. 'You did, though whether that is worth a

man's life is something I have wrestled with these past four weeks. Thank you for dragging me out of danger and for helping me come to a resolution. Life's too short—'

'You are going to talk with your wife?'

'Already done so,' said Hoskins with a wring of his hands. 'It was difficult, but with Gwen's help I got through it and we are back on speaking terms so to speak.' Francis caught his first glimpse of a broad, selfless smile that banished all gloom from the man's face. 'She even brought old Samson along.

'Enough about me, are you alright?'

'I'm fine,' he replied. 'I've never felt better. How long was I out till the ambulance arrived?' The sound of the curtain rings pulling back the drapes from the other side heralded muffled footsteps receding towards the door.

'Is that Gwen?' said Francis, changing tack and desperate to make sure she wasn't upset or angry with him before she left the room. 'Tell her I'm sorry if she was worried about me this past month.'

The landlord tilted his head to the opposite booth. 'You can beg forgiveness for yourself. You are in for an eternity of being reminded about it.'

He gripped the arm of the chair as the drapes alongside him parted to reveal the pretty, dark-haired operator. Seated within touching distance, clear and present in the room, unblemished by any mirror. She smiled, relaxing the nervousness in her brow, and rose to her feet from the stool, smoothing down her floral patterned dress.

'Hello, Francis. I heard you were coming over today.'

With sudden understanding, he looked back to the mirror.

'I'll leave you two alone for a bit,' said Hoskins from the side of the living. 'She's better at explaining these things than I. Best let the rabble in; there was another raid last night over towards Wembley and there'll be a few names to pass on no doubt.'

'Am I—?'

'Yes,' she said kneeling before him and taking his hands tenderly. 'You closed your eyes, and you left the world you were born into. It's been four weeks, but you are here now.'

Her warm hands calmed his lifeless, beating heart, but it continued to drum with her closeness. 'I don't feel any different, in fact, I feel amazing.'

'I told you there is no suffering or want while you are here.'

'The waiting room,' he said. 'All the windows aren't blacked out—I'm with you on the other side?' He clasped her hands tightly as she nodded.

'Bombs can't reach us here, Francis. You've left all that behind.'

The voice from the room below manifested itself at the door behind. 'I've managed cover from an Exchange over in Canterbury,' said an elderly, silver-haired lady peeping around the door. 'He's just arrived. You'll never guess, but they have their mirror in a confessional booth! Do you still want to take your time off today?'

Gwen nodded, returning to tug at his arms, pulling him to a stand. Her fingers wove between his. 'Yes, please, Annie.'

The woman grinned and retired down the stairs.

'It's a lot to take in, and you'll have a lot of questions,' she said releasing a hand to brush back a wayward lock of his hair. 'I've been expecting you for a month you damn, brave fool of a spy. What took you so long? Trust you to keep a lady waiting.'

'What happens now?' he asked sensing that everything would be alright.

She leaned forward, so close that he could almost feel the tremble in her cherry-red lips as her nose brushed his. 'I've put a good word in for you here if you're interested, but for now, we should go for that long walk in the park and I can explain everything.'

'I guess I should ask you out proper, all things considered,' he said, closing his eyes to prepare for any hint of rejection.

She pecked him on the cheek and took his hand. 'Yes. All things considered, I think you should.'

GLOW

After the taxing morning, Dr Samantha Carter found solace in her lunchtime run. The days of rain had put her on edge and had made it difficult for her to exhaust the kilometres she was aiming for, as well as mentally burning off the mounting piles of paperwork. Her watch buzzed as she passed by the small boating lake of the nearby park.

'Pace 5:08 per km...'

'Not bad for a woman in her early fifties,' she thought.

Pushing her body beyond her normal routine felt good, and she breathed deeply to maintain a steady heart rate. Thoughts of Dr Thomas' phone call echoed through her head; his words replaying repeatedly as he tried to convince her to join his private practice.

'You can dictate your hours if you like...no more silly overtime for the same salary as a taxpayer psychiatrist. You've done your bit, Sam – think about it...'

Samantha pondered in time with the plod of her feet: *'I came into the profession to serve the many, not the few yet here I am feeling burnt out with more people to see in less time. It was already hard enough with mental health issues pre-COVID, and I can't abandon the National Health Service now, not yet.'*

As she rounded the corner towards the children's play park, something made her cautious. A dishevelled man leaned against the railings keeping the kids in check, his eyes flitting back and forth between her and the childminder sitting nearby on a bench guarding the tiny backpacks and soft toys, completely unaware of his attention or presence as she stared at her phone screen.

The man noticed Samantha slow down and shifted his attention to a small boy playing by himself against the far wall. Her heart leapt when he suddenly jumped over the fence and ran towards the child beneath a large tree growing from an old, iron-stained stonewall that bulged from the recent rains.

'Hey! What are you doing?' she called out, her voice trembling.

He stopped and turned, a dreadful and urgent expression fixed on his face. 'No time...he's gonna die if I don't act!'

Samantha heard the childminder's phone drop to the ground and watched her rush to the gate, shouting with dread. The kids on the playground turned to see what was happening and the boy, who had been playing with a fallen branch beneath the venerable oak, stopped and spun around. Just then, the tree began to tip toward him, shifting and groaning ominously. As if it was alive, the old tree rocked and tilted until its gargantuan root broke right through the brick wall, splintering the air with wooden shrapnel as it toppled forward showering the air with grenades of clay and root-flung stones.

A loud crack snapped through the air just as the man lunged forward and plucked up the child like a rugby ball, narrowly avoiding being buried beneath the avalanche of stones, dirt, and branches that covered the spot that they had occupied seconds before. The tree shivered to a quivering silent rest broken only by the whimpering aftershock of tiny voices on the other side of the playground.

Samantha joined the childminder and charged into the rubber-padded zone as the children scrambled for safety. The stranger stumbled for a moment before regaining his footing and released the hysterical boy to tumble his way through the no-mans-land of clay clods, back into the open arms of the childminder.

'It's okay,' said Samantha as the toddlers huddled around them like worried lambs. 'Everyone's going to be alright.' A small group of dog walkers approached, attracted by the calamity and the sudden act of foresighted heroism.

The man caught his breath and bent over, hands on his thighs with the sudden explosive burst of speed and effort. He glanced up, catching Samantha's eye, and she saw the look of relief on his face melt into watery eyes as he hurried around the opposite perimeter to leave.

Untangling herself from several tiny hands she jogged over to intercept his path, her initial fear replaced with admiration. The man had seen the wall was about to crumble, and his actions had saved the boy's life. She felt embarrassed for her initial suspicion as she stammered in her shock for the right words.

He dithered, looking for a subtle way to bypass her. She couldn't tell if time and stress had taken a toll on his looks or if his condition and life choices had been unkind. His hair was dark and unmanaged; wild locks falling across his brow streaked with silver. The barber-less beard on his face was untrimmed, adding to its rugged appearance. He had seen a lot, from the deep wrinkles in his forehead making him appear worn out from the longer term rather than from the temporary effects of physical exhaustion. His anxious expression softened into a gentle but tired smile.

'I wasn't here for what you think...I need to go.' His voice was deep and gravelly like he'd spent years shouting and fighting through life.

'I'm sorry for calling out,' she said. 'I thought you were going to...' She abandoned all manner of dreadful thoughts. 'Thank you for saving the boy – you were both nearly killed.'

He nodded, glancing at the growing crowd pointing in his direction, before jumping over the railing and scurrying away with his head down and hands inside the pockets of his old grey hoodie.

Samantha could not shake off the oddity of the encounter, or his nonchalance of being metres away from a premature burial. People just didn't act that way in her professional and personal experience unless they were in shock. She turned towards the onlookers who were babbling above the gentle, soothing words rippling out like calming waves about the large mock lifeboat wherein huddled the sobbing children. A final shifting of the collapsed bank slipped onto the play area sending a last set of stones clattering and clanging against the side of the nearby carousel.

Samantha heard the chatter as the watch buzzed to remind her that her own playtime was over. They all said the same thing:

The poor man always had an uncanny knack for being in the right place at the right time.

Samantha took a deep breath and opened the next patient folder on her laptop. The practice had reassigned non-critical additional consultations caused by a colleague who was ill. She glanced at the first file in anticipation of her next appointment:

John Anderson suffering from mild psychosis and paranoid delu-

sional disorder with hallucinations of people dying and causing fear, anxiety, and panic; limited success using CBT and a range of antipsychotics. The patient has suffered significant post-traumatic stress triggered by...

There was a gentle knock on her consultancy room door.

'Come in,' she said automatically, only noticing the time discrepancy when she glanced at the desktop clock. She hastily stacked her papers as a tall man appeared between the doorway – tired and dishevelled. His faded grey hoody had worn away its expensive branding and the once fine leather shoes, now cracked and unpolished, had seen better days. She took a moment to fully register the familiar face as she rose to greet the unsung hero from the play park.

'Mr Anderson?' she said, her brow furrowing as the figure from the encounter a week ago became clearer. 'I'm Dr Carter – please take a seat.'

John forced a smile, though his face remained strained. He moved slowly to sit in a chair by the window and fidgeted with his hands in his lap. His eyes were drawn irresistibly to the large window overlooking the street below, but he quickly averted his gaze, shifting the chair so the outside remained out of his peripheral vision.

Samantha flipped through John's case notes, taking brief moments to introduce herself. He kept his head low, nervous as though awaiting judgement like a schoolboy before an irate headteacher.

'You did something truly admirable last week,' she said trying to make him feel at ease.

His eyes met her eyes briefly, his expression unreadable.

'It's what I do now,' he said rubbing circles into his pale, red-rimmed eyes before burying his hands between his thighs.

'How are you feeling today?'

'The same, if not a little worse. The meds don't work as I told Dr Peters, it's not something that can be controlled with drugs.' John's gaze flicked to the window once more before he averted his eyes. 'I wish to God they would, and I could get some sleep and go back to how things were before I started seeing the glow.'

Samantha drew up her chair. '*The glow?*'

He looked away, embarrassed by his words. 'I see this light around people that tells me something bad is going to happen to them. It's crazy; I know.'

'Is that why you ran towards the little boy in the play park, you saw the wall collapsing?'

He shook his head. 'I didn't know it would be the wall – I thought maybe a branch would snap or something. I only knew whatever would happen was going to occur right there and then.'

'You had a sense, a premonition brought on by a glow around the boy?' Noble vigilantism was not uncommon in those suffering mental health issues, she thought, though a visual stimulus of this nature was highly unusual.

'Yes,' said John widening his eyes. 'I can handle seeing it in the old folk as they are near their time, but it's the kids and toddlers that are going to have accidents or worse that upsets me the most. The police have cautioned me about loitering outside the schools and nurseries but I'm only trying to save them – that kiddie was lit up from the moment I caught sight of him, I was only waiting for the flash.'

Her eyebrows arched together in confusion. 'I don't understand. Can you describe what you see?'

John shifted uncomfortably in his seat as he described the strange phenomenon. 'It's like an aura or halo that grows more intense as danger nears until there's a blinding flash at the pivotal moment.' He paused for a breath before continuing. 'At first, I thought it was some kind of blessing, but now I know it's a curse. I wish I'd never tried to help that poor fella on the bridge two years ago, and I hate myself for even thinking that. I've been burdened with it ever since, just like he was.' He lifted his shaking hand scarred with cuts and puncture wounds. 'When I'm going to hurt myself, though, I don't see it — only around other people.' He held up his palm to deflect her response. 'I don't do it anymore; it was just to test my hypothesis.'

'Do you want to tell me about what happened, from the beginning?' said Samantha ready to deflect the topic if he became distressed.

He had sunk deep into the chair, his eyes dark with what seemed like a lifetime of sorrow. Samantha's gaze remained fixed as a flash of painful memory clouded his gaunt features, and she nodded slowly to encourage the words to flow.

'They say memory is fallible, but I tell you, Dr Carter, that I recall that night by the river with a clarity and regularity that would astound you.

'I had been celebrating my company's flotation on the stock market when I chose to walk home.' He hesitated; hands clasped in a knotted, tense ball of flesh. 'If only I'd taken a taxi...'

'Go on,' said Samantha, rising from her seat to fill a glass of water from the table behind her desk.

'It was late, or real early depending on your point of view when I reached the bridge over the river. A guy was standing on the edge, gazing down into the inky water far below. His face was lit up by the faint orange light coming from the street lamp and I didn't need any glow to tell me he was ready to jump.' John emptied the proffered glass of water and toyed with the tumbler between his fingers. 'There wasn't a soul around as he lifted a foot over the ledge to part with his own.'

He stole a glance and snorted with irony. 'I talked him down – not a psychiatrist, just an entrepreneur with no special people skills. He was hurting really bad inside and spouted nonsense about premonitions and glowing people. '*I can't save them all,'* he said as I held him till he stopped weeping, *'There are too many of them'*. I thought he was mad but listened until he calmed down; I didn't want a dead man on my conscience.'

'Once you engage with someone,' said Samantha, 'it puts pressure on you. It's why so many walk away. You didn't, and I can see this is having a heavy psychological influence on you.'

John winced. 'It's like I am experiencing what he had to go through, and I don't think I can handle it much longer. Perhaps it's just inevitable.'

'You are a strong and compassionate person,' Samantha replied, catching onto the subtle suggestion of suicide. 'What you did took a lot of courage and strength that most people wouldn't be able to muster. Give yourself credit even though you may not feel you deserve it.'

John nodded silently. 'I felt invincible when I helped him get in the cab. I was the last person to help him.'

'You saved him,' said Samantha furrowing her brow.

'Only for a few more days. I saw his picture in the papers the following weekend - he'd walked in front of a bus; it was no accident.'

John tugged at his clothing. 'I used to be so successful: fancy home, wife, cars, business growing exponentially, but ever since I saw the glow for myself, it's all changed, all gone. It's not fair - all I did was try to help, and now here I am broke from constantly being on guard, and alone.' He rubbed at his eyes. and hung his head. 'I'd give everything I have left for a good night's sleep - I see those poor, unaware people glow more keenly in the dark.'

'We need to get you in the right physical and mental state,' she said. 'The lack of sleep could be making your other symptoms worse, such as depression or intense anxiety, plus it is also leading to more social isolation, which isn't good for you.'

He cleared his throat awkwardly, and she detected a whiff of whisky on his breath. 'There is only one thing that helps when it gets too tough,' he whispered.

'Alcohol is not the answer, John. Have you considered that this glow you see only exists because you were told about it and your guilt for not saving him a second time has reinforced the belief? Dr Peters thinks your current state of mind is linked to the incident – a post-traumatic response to—'

'Yes, yes - I know,' he said running his hands through his hair before gripping the worn knees of his designer jeans. 'I'm paranoid, delusional, suffering from PTSD, and I see hallucinatory visual stimuli. I could be suffering from all these things, or I could be telling you the truth.'

'I believe you are telling me the truth, that you believe you see this glow.'

'That's not the same as you believing it's true,' he said. 'I've read every peer-reviewed text on psychology and personality disorders from the past four decades trying to figure it out. I'm a smart man not prone to *woo-woo*, Dr Carter. Freud doesn't get into curses and the supernatural otherwise I'd have something to work with.'

Samantha leaned forward in a show of empathy. 'Let me tell you then, as you seem rational - between Freud, you, and I, that this is a false belief no matter how believable and authentic it may seem. From experience, I know that it's not possible to help everyone all the time. Your guilt is fuelling and reinforcing the belief each time you get a positive result.'

'I get nothing else,' he said. 'I've lost count of the hits and I've yet to start counting the misses.'

'It's not uncommon and comes from a place of goodwill, but you must take a break from trying to save humanity.'

'I daren't,' said John. 'Not even for a day. I tried in the beginning, did my damndest to shut it out but the woman I abandoned is now in a wheelchair. I see her sometimes and I want to rush over and ask for her forgiveness for not being present when she fell down the car park stairs damaging her spine.'

'It was just an accident, John, a coincidence; it could have happened to anyone. Don't be too hard on yourself. It's a common delusion to think you are the only one who can complete these missions of mercy.'

John stared at the clock on the wall ticking away the remaining minutes of the consultation. 'If only I could go back,' he mused. 'Why couldn't she have been there that night at the bridge instead of me? She's always moaning to me about it being her pitch, but I guess she can sleep with it. Maybe that fella wouldn't have died and passed on this damn thing to me if she was there – it wouldn't have made any difference to her.'

'She?' asked Samantha.

'Toffee Anna – one of only a few people I've bumped into that can see the glow.' He glanced nervously at the window. 'The dotty homeless lady with the tartan trolley bag outside.'

Samantha walked over to the partially opened window blinds and peered outside. She recognised the old woman beneath the lamp post immediately as she tossed crumbs from a brown bag to a flock of pigeons. It was a small town.

'Is she still there?' he asked.

'Yes, but she's watching pigeons, not you or the building. Why do you call her Toffee Anna?'

John released himself from his tense protective huddle as she closed the blinds, darkening the room. 'On account of all those sweets she chews while she watches, waiting to help the glowers she comes across. When Anna's not at the bridge, she distracts the kids with toffees, stopping them from rushing across the road. She's watching me now.' His voice grew louder and tenser with each word. 'I don't want to end up like her –

destitute and alone. It's not possible to save everyone; there just isn't enough time. She knows how to live with the glow, but that's only because she's been seeing it for so long. I can't cherry-pick folk to help on bridges or pelican crossings as she does. Now she's trying to save me when the time comes, and knowing she's following me is making things worse.'

'I'm going to get you fast-tracked,' said Samantha returning to her desk and waking up the laptop. 'I can pull a few strings, get you a full MRI and physical examination including your eyes and I'll discuss a new care programme with the team. In the meantime, I want you to rest, and I'll give you something that will help you sleep, just for a week.

'No more saving the world until then, John,' she said. 'Doctor's orders.'

Samantha awoke with a start, her eyes burned and ached from the long hours spent in front of the laptop. Her dreams were a jumble of half-remembered images—people, thousands of them, marching beneath a bridge until they were swallowed up by the murky river below. She felt powerless to help them, but the figures seemed oblivious to her calls and walked on without looking back.

She opened the window in her bedroom, letting in the warm morning air. August had been beautiful this year—fine days followed by gentle evening rain that cooled off everything and made Samantha's soul feel re-invigorated. But it had also been marked by a strange deterioration in her vision —fuzzy blurs around people and bright flashes that she could never quite focus on. After consulting an optician, Samantha was told she had astigmatism and was prescribed glasses. But when she put them on, nothing changed—the fuzzy halos just moved and shifted into different shapes like a 3D image out of focus.

Outside, Samantha watched as a cyclist pedalled past her window, blurring and shifting around his edges. She rubbed at her eyes, trying to clear away the haze that seemed to surround him; the shadows of nearby buildings only made it worse, amplifying the strange brightness that seemed to cling to him. Pulling on a robe, she shuffled into the kitchen and switched on the kettle. A cry of alarm was cut short as she heard a clatter of metal against metal, followed by the sharp screech of sudden brakes. She rushed to the window to see people rushing to assist the cyclist, lying like a splayed rag doll before the dented bumper of a car that had turned into the street unwittingly into his path. The driver got out and rushed forward, head on hands as the man on the floor rolled himself over, rubbing at his elbow and screaming obscenities in shock. Pulled to his feet, he limped towards the buckled, expensive-looking two-wheeled machine several yards away, bleeding from the knee but otherwise not severely injured. The rider got out his phone and lifted the bicycle to a wobbling upright position on the pavement to take down details from the shaking driver.

Samantha blinked as the surrounding haze dissipated, her mind latching onto John Anderson's words:

'It's like an aura or halo that grows more intense as danger nears...'

'How is John Anderson doing?' Samantha asked her colleague as they stood in front of the coffee machine at the practice.

Dr Peters pressed a button for a cappuccino, pursing his lips and shaking his head. 'You haven't heard?'

'Heard what?' she said above the sound of the percolating coffee.

'I didn't want to mention it — since you were the last one to see him — but I was back from sick leave when you made your recommendations, and I signed off on them...'

'Chris? What happened?'

The doctor bent down, staring into the tray forlornly as no coffee appeared. 'He jumped from the town bridge three weeks ago.'

Samantha massaged her eyes, trying to comprehend this unexpected news while struggling with a fog that seemed to surround the young doctor.

'Are you ok, Sam?' he said, facing her with an expression of concern.

'Oh yeah, just something wrong with my eyes; it's fine, don't worry about it. I'm sorry.'

Dr Peters turned back to face the machine, speaking to an empty cup. 'You'd think we'd get used to it by now: such a good man, so many people attended his funeral—those who couldn't let go of him yet.'

'I'm glad,' Samantha said, blinking rapidly to clear away her blurred vision. 'John told me he felt alone...how wrong he was.'

'Yes, it was something to see. It seemed like most of the town had turned up for his funeral; kids, teachers, everyone. There were so many people that some had to stay outside and fill the path to the car park. It was overwhelming, with all the "Thank you" balloons, and messages.'

As she tried to take this in, something bright filled her vision—her colleague hunched before a steam nozzle. She blinked as the light engulfed him and without thinking, lunged forward to pull him away from the blocked pipe. The pressure shot out a shower of scalding steam just as he tumbled back into her arms. Hastily, she lifted him to his feet and switched off the coffee maker before any more damage could be done.

The doctor brushed himself off and smiled at her. 'Well, that was close! I owe you one.'

Samantha could feel her heart racing beneath her shirt and put on a smile to disguise her fear. 'Just luck. Can you leave a note on it? I'll let the practice manager know it needs repair.'

Dr Peters hurriedly made her way around the corner, entering the deserted ladies' toilet. Her hands felt clammy as she tightly gripped the rough surface of the sink basin. She stared into her reflection in the mirror, her fear and anxiety slowly dissipating for a moment until it was replaced with worries about what could have been. As she splashed cold water over her face, the foaming cascade from the arching bridge of the tap meandered across the bowl. The flow spiralled down into the depths of the drain like a river ebbing away into nothingness.

The reflective, golden waters beneath the bridge sparkled in the evening light, rippling off of the orange-rimmed cloud formations above. Samantha stood on the overlook, oblivious to the Sunday night traffic humming past her. The town was starting its evening ritual of winding down and taking its inhabitants to sleep. She crossed her arms as lamps along the pavement began to flicker. Though September nights were cold, they weren't nearly as chilly as the murky waters beneath her. Out of the corner of her eye, an elderly woman made her way slowly towards the bridge's centre. A sweet smell of caramel carried on the breeze mingled with the spicy aroma of the white bouquet in Samantha's hand.

'I'm not planning to jump,' she said, turning to see the old lady, standing her tartan trolley bag on the empty pavement and picking her teeth with the remains of something sticky. 'It's Anna, isn't it?'

The lady smiled with a nod, revealing deep wrinkles on her face. 'You are the lady that tried to help John, aren't you – one of them psychologists?'

Samantha nodded with a smile. 'Close enough. I only learned a week ago, but I thought it was high time to pay my respects.' She hesitated. 'He told me this was your pitch, and I hoped I might have a chance to talk with you.'

Anna leaned against the railing of the bridge, joining Samantha in gazing at the slow-moving current below them. A piece of driftwood floated away into the faster-flowing water.

'I was the last person to help him, Anna. You know what that means, don't you?'

Anna looked to the horizon, her ancient frame stooped and supported by a battered trolley. The wind whipped her grey hair across her face, and she swatted it away with an aged hand before placing it on Samantha's shoulder. 'Don't feel guilty, lass,' she began in a quavering voice. 'If anyone feels that way, it should be me. He ran off up the street and I couldn't keep up with him; not with my old bones and this trolley.'

'I don't think you understand me, though I do feel responsible for not being able to have done more,' said Samantha slowly, her voice quivering. 'I see what he saw, and what you see, Anna.'

The old woman shuffled and sighed; her bright, coal-coloured eyes glistened with the connection. 'You see the glow?'

'Yes. It started around the time he...' Samantha spun round and put her back to the river.

'So it continues, it seems,' Anna whispered sadly. 'Fewer

and fewer of us souls in the right place at the right time, and not a moment's peace if you let it get too much of a hold.'

'Why do we see it, and why me?'

'A question without a satisfactory answer,' said Anna digging into her pocket and offering a foil-covered sweet in her grubby, fingerless gloved hand. 'It takes some getting used to, that's for sure. I've been here close to sixty years since I tried to save a woman with a child, but they were taken away anyway.' A deep sadness filled her creased face for a moment before she continued, 'It helps if there's someone else who understands, don't you think?'

Samantha took the wrapped, golden penny and rubbed at the crackling wrapper before answering. 'Yes, but I'm not sure I believe it, I'm still waiting for the results of a neurological scan and I've been talking with a psychiatrist out of town.'

Anna nodded slowly before continuing. 'They won't find anything, believe me. It took two years before I accepted what happened in this very spot. For donkey's years after that, I couldn't speak to anyone else until I found the others who had been through the same thing.' Her eyes misted over as she whispered half to herself, 'That's true loneliness, that is.'

'John said you had found a way to live with it, but that he wasn't strong enough to continue,' Samantha noted sadly as she looked at Anna's worn-out shoes and the bag with wheels. 'Is this what happens if I don't take the other option – I become like a lifeboatman on dry land trying to save an ocean of souls?' She blushed at her rude comment.

Anna blinked and followed her gaze, then opened her bag to show Samantha all the items inside: bandages, ointments, neck braces and even a portable defibrillator.

'Where did you get these things...?'

'I have money and live in an apartment in the old part of

town; I don't sleep on the streets. I've got some spare clothes in the bottom and pepper spray so that no one bothers me while I'm out watching at night. These old rags might have seen better days, but they are warm and they don't make coats or shoes that last like these.'

Samantha smiled. 'You're very resourceful and invisible—no one really sees you, or what you are up to.'

Anna chuckled and tapped an index finger against her lips. 'Just like kindness itself. Only you, the pigeons, and a few others in the same boat as us two know the truth.'

'Are you suggesting I get myself an alter-ego?'

Anna shook her head and sealed the bag. 'No, you know how to talk to people without hesitating, even though you blame yourself for John Anderson. It took me time to learn that. Just be yourself.'

'But doesn't it get too overwhelming not being able to save everyone who ... well, you know?'

'That glows? Not anymore. When it gets too much, just close your eyes; look away from the people around you—pigeons are good—and take a few minutes to calm your mind. The glow won't come back unless you're searching for it, or unless it takes you by surprise.'

Anna looked down into the bunch of flowers. 'They're pretty.'

Turning to the river Samantha tossed the fragrant bouquet into the air and watched it settle and bob upon the surface of the river until it was out of sight. 'Will you help me, if I can't find any answers?'

The old woman nodded and dug inside her pocket, producing an orange jelly baby. 'Just don't make the same mistake as I did and follow me around if I start glowing. I couldn't bear it.'

'That's your final decision, Sam?' said the voice at the end of the line.

'It is, Frank,' said Samantha, sipping at her latte by the window of the quiet coffee shop. 'I appreciate your offer, but I've made my mind up. I'm taking early retirement.'

'We'll be sad to see you go, but I understand the stresses and strains. You'd be welcome back if you change your mind and all that free time gets to you. What do you plan on doing?'

A young woman, tearful and upset came into the shop setting the bell ringing. Samantha's gaze followed her to the corner seat opposite as she retrieved her phone and broke down into sobs upon viewing whatever was displayed there.

'Frank, I plan to focus on improving my health,' Samantha replied while still keeping an eye on the woman who was now placing some coins on the table in front of her.

'I'm planning to do some volunteering or care in the community.'

'Then our loss will be their gain. Come by tomorrow and we can finish settling your affairs here. It'll be a hard goodbye.'

'Sure thing, same here,' she said before ending the call. At that moment, a waitress sauntered up to the distraught woman's table.

'Do you mind if I just sit here for a bit and have a glass of water?' asked the troubled-looking lady, glancing down at her meagre change on the table before adding: 'I don't have any place else to go – you can keep this as a tip when I leave...'

The waitress glanced round at the quiet room and nodded. 'We close in twenty minutes, but I think that's fine.'

'That'll be all I need,' she said gratefully, grabbing at the retreating arm. 'Thank you for your kindness.'

A glance sideways confirmed Samantha's suspicions. The clear outline of the distressed woman across the room blurred in and out of focus and began to shimmer, brightening with each repeated glance. She pulled out a small brown bottle with a label indicating its contents, laying it on the seat next to her. Sam couldn't help but look at her laddered leggings as they jittered with the uncontrolled movement of her feet.

'It's like an aura or halo that grows more intense as danger nears until there's a blinding flash at the pivotal moment.'

The woman opened the container and placed several pills in her palm, closing it quickly as the waitress returned carrying a glass of water. She grabbed it and raised her fist to her lips, one trembling hand gripping tightly around the glass. The glowing light around her became incandescent.

'My name's Samantha,' said the newly retired psychiatrist, sitting down beside her and offering her hand to stop the overdose. 'Let me buy you a coffee and you can tell me what's on your mind.'

REFLECTIONS

The late afternoon sun dipped toward the horizon, its golden light filtering through the leaves of the old oak tree in Amy's garden. Luna sat beside her on the grass, their shoulders touching as Amy wove a crown of daisies for Luna's wispy blonde hair.

'Finished,' Amy said with a smile, placing the fragile crown atop Luna's head. 'Now you're a fairy queen.'

Luna's heart swelled. She loved their games of make-believe, transporting them to magical worlds where anything was possible. All that mattered was that they were together. 'And you're my faithful lady-in-waiting,' Luna said.

Amy giggled. 'What shall we play today?'

'How about princesses in a grand castle?' Luna suggested. Castles were her favourite. She could imagine the stone walls rising into the sky, pennants snapping in the wind high upon the battlements.

'Yes!' Amy sprang to her feet, already envisioning their grand adventure. Luna followed, caught up in Amy's enthusiasm. What new dangers and mysteries would they face today in their fortress of dreams?

As Amy raced ahead toward the gardener's old shed that served as their castle keep, Luna jogged to catch up to her, smiling. However vivid their imaginations, the best part of their games was simply being by Amy's side. Luna's devotion to her friend was as constant as the sunrise, and she would follow her anywhere, real or imagined, as long as they were together.

After all, that was what best friends did. Luna's world began and ended with Amy, and she wouldn't have it any other way.

The next morning, Amy woke to sunlight streaming through lace curtains. She yawned and stretched, then climbed out of bed to get dressed for school.

While Amy ate breakfast, Luna perched on the back of a chair, swinging her legs. She hummed a little tune as she watched Amy spoon porridge into her mouth. Luna enjoyed observing Amy's daily rituals; they were comforting in their familiarity.

'Do we *have* to go to school today?' Luna asked when Amy had finished.

Amy nodded. 'I suppose so. At least we'll have lunch and playtime together.'

'And we can continue our adventure in the mystical wood after school,' Luna said brightly. The copse adjoining the house was not so very large, though just broad enough to conjure a witch or dragon's lair within.

Amy smiled at that. 'I'd like that.' She collected her satchel, and they set off together down the lane toward the village school.

Other children were arriving as well, waving to friends and chasing each other along the sidewalk. Amy joined a group of her classmates, chattering excitedly about a new doll one of them had received as an early birthday gift.

Luna trailed after them, for the moment forgotten. She

didn't mind that the other children monopolised her best friend at school – they only saw her for part of the day. As long as she was with Amy, that was enough.

At the schoolhouse door, Amy turned to Luna. 'No making me giggle again today. Miss Perkins will tell Mother and I'll be sent to bed with no supper.'

'Very well,' Luna said. The lessons were boring, full of things Luna was uninterested in or already knew by instinct.

Amy smiled gratefully and followed the other children inside. Luna settled into the free desk-side chair beside her companion and propped her head into the palms of her hands. In the quiet, Luna's thoughts drifted. She thought of following Amy through the village as she ran errands with her mother, of long sunny afternoons playing make-believe in the meadow behind Amy's house. Her favourite times were when she could accompany Amy's family to visit her grandparent's farm, where there were kittens to play with, sweet apples to pick from the orchard and no shortage of adventures to be found. Her elbows wobbled on the old wooden desk as she tipped her head to glance hopefully out of the window at the promising day to come, content knowing that their grand adventure would continue.

The day droned on until released to mirth by the ringing of the school bell. The schoolhouse door creaked open, spilling laughter and shouting into the yard once more. Amy emerged with the tide of children rushing out to freedom and the afternoon ahead. The schoolyard emptied, the laughter and shouts of children fading down the street. Luna closed her eyes, tilting her face up to feel the warmth of the sun. A light breeze carried the fresh scent of newly mown grass from the surrounding fields.

'I'll never understand why we have to learn French,' she said, falling into step beside Amy as they headed out of the schoolyard.

'Mother says it's important or will be, one day,' Amy said with an impish grin. 'But the day's not over yet. Are you ready for an adventure on the way home?'

'Always,' Luna said. The sun seemed to shine brighter, and the world was aglow. Any day with Amy was sure to be an adventure.

They wandered down lanes dappled with shadows, past hedgerows alive with birdsong. A light breeze carried the scent of honeysuckle and ripening apples. They wandered the overgrown path, Amy chattering away about the odd plants and fantastical beasts they encountered in their game. Luna added details and spun stories to match Amy's inventions, crafting a whole new world around them.

When they came across a pond glinting dappled green in the woods, Amy gasped. 'A secret lagoon! We have to see what's in it.' She kicked off her shoes and socks, rolling up the hem of her skirt as she waded in.

Luna sat on the bank, content to watch her friend splash and peer into the water. A frog plopped from its sunning spot on a lily pad, startling a laugh from Amy.

'There are tiny fish in here, and water bugs skating across the surface!' Amy leaned down to get a better look, overbalancing and tumbling into the pond with a splash. She came up sputtering and giggling, hair plastered to her face.

Luna grinned at the sight of her sodden, mirthful friend. No matter what adventures they found, she would always treasure moments like this most of all.

Luna helped Amy out of the pond and onto the bank, where Amy shook out her skirt and rung water from her hair. 'What an explorer I turned out to be!' she said with a self-deprecating laugh.

'The best explorers often meet with mishaps,' Luna said. 'It will make a grand story to tell your parents when we get back, but don't tell them it was me that encouraged you into there – you did that all by yourself!'

Amy's eyes lit up at the prospect. Together, they spun a tale of raging rapids and near-death encounters with imaginary beasts, having a grand old time embellishing the details.

By the time they headed home for tea, they were tired, muddy, and still giggling over their exaggerated retelling of the afternoon's adventures. Luna felt a surge of affection for her friend, who brought so much laughter and magic into the world.

They were an unlikely pair, Amy with her bright eyes and rosy cheeks, Luna more ethereal and pale. But in all the ways that mattered, they were two peas in a pod. Constant companions through all of Amy's explorations and games, sharing a bond as deep as the secret lagoon in the woods.

Luna knew, even at her young age, that she would follow Amy anywhere. Their friendship was a fixed point, a light to guide her even in the darkest of nights. And though Amy would grow and change, Luna hoped she would remain by her side, a faithful friend to share in life's grandest adventures.

The years passed in a blur of laughter and joyful memories. Luna was always there to listen when Amy confided her hopes and fears, to offer comfort after a scrape or tumble, and to join in the fun without a care for how silly they must appear. Their explorations took them further afield as Amy grew more independent, but Luna was never far from her side. She watched as Amy learned to ride a bicycle, climbed ever taller trees, and made new friends at school. And she was there to soothe Amy's tears when those new friends were cruel, helping to bolster her confidence until she shone as bright as ever.

Though Amy's interests began to change, her devotion to Luna never wavered. They still spent long afternoons spinning tales of adventure and magic, escaping into worlds of their own creation. Luna knew, deep in her heart, that their friendship was forever.

The sun dipped behind the thick clouds, casting a soft, melancholy glow upon the English countryside. Luna stood beside Amy, her small hand gripping her friends as they gazed out over the rolling hills. The scent of damp earth and fresh grass hung in the air, mingling with the faint whispers of change.

'Darling,' Amy's mother called from the living room window, 'come inside for a moment. We have some exciting news to share.'

Amy glanced at Luna with a curious smile as she led her into the warm embrace of their home. Inside, Amy's father was waiting, puffing on his pipe, his eyes filled with both pride and a touch of sadness. Luna, sensing the importance of the moment, clung to Amy's arm and waited with bated breath.

'We received a letter today,' Amy's father began, clearing his throat, 'from a very prestigious boarding school in Switzerland. They've offered you a place, Amy.'

'Switzerland?' Amy asked, her voice filled with a mixture of excitement and trepidation.

Her mother nodded, her voice gentle yet firm. 'Yes, my dear. It's a wonderful opportunity for you to grow and learn, to become the young woman we know you're destined to be.'

Luna's heart tightened in her chest, her gaze flitting between Amy and her parents as she struggled to process the news. She could sense the unspoken words that lingered in the air: it was time for Amy to leave her past – and Luna – behind.

Amy, however, seemed to take the news in stride, her face

lighting up with enthusiasm. 'I knew I'd be going away next term, but I didn't know it would be so far. Can Luna come with me?' Her parents exchanged a glance, uncertainty flickering across their faces.

'That would depend on her parents,' her mother said slowly. 'Perhaps they haven't received a letter from her own application yet? You must remember that the focus will be on your education and there will be less time for childish things, but you'll make new friends – and they have horses...'

Amy's eyes widened. 'Will I be learning to ride?'

Amy's father took out his pipe. 'And a good many more useful things I hope, what with the expense.'

Luna's heart thudded in her chest, her grip on Amy's arm tightening as she stared at the girl who had been her entire world for so many years. She wanted to rejoice in her friend's happiness, to support her as she had always done. But she couldn't shake the gnawing fear that threatened to consume her, the creeping realisation that life was pushing them apart. The prospect of losing Amy – of being left behind – weighed heavily on Luna's fragile spirit.

Amy's mother rushed to capitalise on the expectations of her daughter. 'I'm sure Luna will be here to welcome you back during the holidays. We are so very proud of you.'

'Of course,' Amy replied, giving Luna a reassuring smile, 'my studies come first. But I'm sure we'll always find time for each other, isn't that right, Luna?'

Luna hesitated for just a moment, her thoughts a whirlwind of dread and uncertainty. Then, with a small nod and a forced smile, she agreed. 'Yes, of course. We'll always be together, no matter what.'

Over the next few days, Luna watched Amy's excitement continue to grow. She couldn't help but notice the way her friend's eyes shone brighter each time they discussed Switzerland and the boarding school that awaited her there.

'Imagine all the things I'll learn,' Amy enthused one afternoon, sprawled out on the grassy hill beneath their favourite tree.

Luna nodded, trying to muster enthusiasm. But deep down, her heart ached. She couldn't shake the feeling that their time together was slipping away like grains of sand through an hourglass.

'Must you go?' Luna asked softly, her voice barely more than a whisper.

Amy looked at her, puzzled. 'It's an incredible opportunity, Luna. I can't pass it up.'

'I am a bit nervous,' Amy admitted. 'But Mother says it's also a part of life, and that we can't hold on to everything forever.'

Despite Amy's comforting words, Luna's heart remained heavy. As the days passed, she tried to come to terms with the reality of their situation. But every time she pictured Amy leaving for Switzerland, she felt a knot tighten in her chest, her breath catching in her throat.

'Is growing up truly necessary?' Luna asked one evening, as they sat beneath the stars, watching the fireflies dance around them.

'I wish it wasn't, Luna,' Amy reiterated. 'But I think we all have to grow up eventually.'

'Even me?' Luna questioned, her voice wavering.

'Even you,' Amy confirmed, reaching out to take her best friend's hand in hers. 'You'll grow and change in your own way, just as I will.'

'I don't feel the same way. Wouldn't it be better if we could stay like this forever?' Luna persisted, her eyes pleading as she searched Amy's face for answers. 'We've been so happy together, haven't we?'

'Of course,' Amy agreed, giving Luna's hand a gentle squeeze. 'But think of all the new experiences and adventures we'd miss out on if we never grew up.'

Luna's heart sank as she listened to Amy's reasoning. It was getting harder for her to cling to the hope that things could stay the same. But she couldn't let go just yet; she needed to try one last time.

'Can't your parents see that our friendship is more important than some fancy school? We need each other, Amy. I'm scared that if you leave, I'll lose you forever,' Luna admitted, tears brimming in her eyes.

Amy reached out to hold Luna's hand, her own eyes glistening with unshed tears. 'I'm scared too, Luna. But we can't let our fear hold us back from growing and becoming the people we're meant to be. Besides, we'll still have holidays together, and I'll write to you every week.'

Luna sighed, her gaze drifting to the stars above, their shimmering light illuminating the early tendrils of doubt that threatened to invade her thoughts. She knew Amy was right; change was an essential part of life, but that didn't make its approach any less terrifying.

'I've got a surprise to cheer us both up,' said Amy with a wink. 'We are going to the country for a week before school starts.'

Luna perked up and asked the inevitable. 'Can I come?'

'Of course, silly. Didn't I say "we"? Father and mother were against it at first, but I stamped my feet and got my way. It's a grand old place by all accounts with big lawns, a massive lake with an island—'

'Are there pirates on the island?' asked Luna.

Amy shrugged. 'If you want them to be. As long as we have a nice time, I don't really mind.'

'Promise me you won't forget about me when you're off exploring the world,' Luna whispered, her voice trembling with the weight of her emotions.

'Of course not,' Amy swore, pulling Luna into a tight

embrace. 'You'll always have a special place in my heart, no matter where life takes me.'

Silently, Luna held onto Amy, allowing herself to be enveloped by the warmth of their friendship. With each passing moment, she fought to come to terms with the inevitability of change, striving to accept the bittersweet reality that lay before them.

And although her heart ached at the thought of losing Amy, Luna knew that the memories they had shared would forever remain etched upon her soul – a testament to the enduring magic of childhood, and the unbreakable bond between two friends.

The old Bentley purred up the winding gravel drive of the Grand Lake Hotel, coming to a stop under the pillared portico. Luna squeezed Amy's hand, her heart thumping with excitement and trepidation.

Through the windscreen, the hotel stretched before them, three floors of pale Cotswold stone and mullioned windows overlooking velvet lawns and colourful flowerbeds. Beyond, the lake glittered under a pale blue sky, tiny wavelets lapping at the shore.

Amy turned to Luna with a smile. 'Isn't it lovely? Just like I told you!'

Luna returned the smile, though it felt brittle. 'It's perfect.'

She wanted to share in Amy's delight, but her joy was tinged with sorrow. In a week, Amy and her family would drive away from this place, off on their grand adventure to Switzerland.

Amy's father turned off the engine and the four of them climbed out of the car. Luna drifted along in their wake as they made their way into the hotel. The oak doors swung open to reveal a marble-floored lobby and a sweeping staircase.

'Welcome to the Grand Lake Hotel,' the receptionist said. 'How may I help you?'

'Reservation for the Waite family,' Amy's father said.

The receptionist smiled. 'Of course, Mr Waite. We've been expecting you.'

Luna hung back as keys and instructions were exchanged, drinking in every detail of the place that would become so dear to her in the coming days. She would have to store up memories to sustain her after Amy left.

When the Waites headed up the staircase to find their rooms, Luna drifted along behind them. Amy chattered excitedly about everything they would do together – swimming in the lake, hiking in the hills, playing in the gardens. Luna made enthusiastic noises, though her enthusiasm was not reflected in the sinking feeling inside.

Amy's room was large and airy, with pretty floral wallpaper and a view of the gardens. 'Isn't it perfect?' Amy said again, throwing her arms around Luna.

Luna hugged her back tightly. 'It's lovely,' she said.

'I'm so glad you came with us,' Amy said. 'This is going to be the best holiday ever!'

Luna swallowed the lump forming in her throat. 'Me too,' she whispered. She already dreaded the end of this perfect holiday when the time would come to say goodbye.

But for now, she pushed those thoughts away. She was here with her best friend, in this beautiful place. She would enjoy every moment and store memories to last her a lifetime.

When Amy's parents called them down for dinner, Luna followed Amy downstairs. The dining room was as grand as the rest of the hotel, with rows of tables set for the evening meal.

'Are you hungry?' Amy whispered to Luna, eyes shining in the golden light of the chandeliers.

Luna smiled. 'Starving.'

No matter that she felt no appetite. For Amy, she would pretend. She would cling to each moment and make this holiday last forever, if only in her memory.

The next morning, Luna woke as the sun streamed through the curtains of Amy's room. Amy was still sleeping, curled up under the blankets.

Luna got up and went to look out the window. The gardens below were waking up too, dew glistening on petals and leaves in the golden sunlight.

Beyond the gardens lay the lake, a perfect mirror reflecting the blue sky. A few birds swooped low over the water, sending ripples across its surface.

It was breathtaking. But a melancholy feeling crept over Luna as she gazed at the scene. This perfect, idyllic place underscored the fact that she didn't belong there. She was out of place, an ephemeral visitor in Amy's world she couldn't truly inhabit or pursue.

When Amy stirred, Luna turned away from the window. She plastered a smile on her face, pushing aside her troubled thoughts.

'Good morning!' she said brightly.

Amy yawned and stretched, returning Luna's smile. 'Morning! It looks like a perfect day. Shall we go for a walk by the lake after breakfast?'

'That would be lovely,' Luna said. She was determined to enjoy every moment with Amy, despite the ache inside. She couldn't bear to think about how fleeting this time was, or how she might never come back here again.

All too soon, it would be time to say goodbye. But not yet.

Luna grasped Amy's hand, clinging to the feeling of warmth and solidity. Not yet.

There was still time.

At breakfast, Luna noticed Amy's parents exchanging pointed looks across the table. She caught snippets of their hushed conversation when Amy wasn't listening.

'She needs to start focusing on her studies,' Amy's father said sternly. 'No more of these fanciful games once the holiday is over. It's time for her to grow up.'

Amy's mother sighed. 'I know, dear, but please don't be too harsh with her. She's still just a child.'

'She'll soon be a young woman,' he replied. 'In a few months, she'll be distracted easily enough by more appropriate pursuits for her age.'

Luna's chest tightened at their words. She glanced at Amy, who was happily munching on toast and jam, blissfully unaware of her parent's disapproval.

How Luna wished she could freeze time at this moment, prolonging their perfect holiday together. But she knew, deep down, that it couldn't last. Amy's parents were eager to clip the wings of her imagination, to steer her towards a life of dreary responsibility and duty.

There would be no place for Luna in that life.

After breakfast, they went for a walk by the lake. Luna committed every detail to memory: the crunch of the gravel path under their feet, the laughter and chatter between them, the warmth of the sun on their skin.

When Amy spotted a family of ducklings paddling on the lake, Luna didn't have the heart to tell her what she had overheard. She simply squeezed Amy's hand, blinking back tears, and enjoyed her friend's delighted laughter.

They stayed by the lake for hours, then went boating with

her father who seemed to have relaxed and drew in great breaths as he sculled across the still water. Luna knew these simple moments of joy and adventure were fleeting, as ephemeral as herself.

Like the ducklings on the lake, the day slipped swiftly through her fingers. All too soon, the evening was falling, shadows lengthening across the ground.

Luna gazed at the sunset, a riot of pinks and oranges reflected on the rippling surface of the lake. She took a deep breath, absorbing the scents and sounds around her.

This place, and this day, would remain locked in her memory forever.

Even after Amy was gone.

As dusk descended, Luna and Amy returned to the hotel. In Amy's room, they curled up on the bed together, Luna resting her head on Amy's shoulder.

'I don't want to leave,' Amy whispered. 'I don't want to go to Switzerland. I want to stay here with you.'

Luna's heart ached. She stroked Amy's hair, wishing with all her might that she could give her friend what she wanted.

'I don't want you to go either,' she said. 'But your parents—'

'I don't care about them!' Amy cried. 'You're my best friend. You always have been. I don't want to lose you.'

Luna swallowed the lump in her throat. She knew, with a certainty that caused her pain, that Amy would move on. She would make new friends, immerse herself in her studies, and gradually forget all about the imaginary companion of her childhood.

It was the natural order of things. The way it had to be.

But not yet. They still had this night, and tomorrow, to share.

Luna held Amy close, breathing in the scent of her hair, feeling the warmth of her body and the beat of her heart.

'You'll never lose me,' she whispered. 'I'll always be here. No matter how far apart we are, or how much time passes, I will always be your friend.'

Amy sniffed, wiping her eyes. 'Promise?'

'I promise,' Luna said softly.

And in that moment, she meant it with all her heart.

The day before the end of the holiday, Luna paced around their cluttered bedroom. The walls, covered with posters and mementoes of countless adventures shared with Amy, bore witness to the deep bond between them. The afternoon sun cast a warm, golden light into the room, illuminating every cherished item and casting shadows that danced as the breeze rustled through the open window.

Amy dozed, sun-blushed and sleepy from an attack of marauding pirates near the wedding pavilion. They had beaten them back this time, and perhaps for the final time. Lying beside her on the bed, Luna stared at the ceiling, trying to comprehend the impending loss of her dearest friend. A sense of dread and emptiness settled heavily in her chest, making it difficult for her to breathe. She knew that soon, she would have to face the world without the only friend she had ever known, by her side. The thought was terrifying.

'Will I ever be ready to let go?' she pondered aloud, her voice barely audible above the whisper of the gently swaying curtains.

The quiet hum of the room seemed to answer her, though she knew it was simply her thoughts echoing back to her. As she lay there, surrounded by the memories of their friendship, Luna realised she had to evolve and adapt to survive without Amy. It was a daunting prospect, but one that she could not avoid any longer.

Her fingers entwined in the frayed edges of a well-loved comfort blanket, one she and Amy had spent countless hours pouring their dreams into. The intricate stitches told stories of laughter-filled days, whispered secrets under moonlit skies, and unbreakable promises shared between two souls. Each thread seemed to breathe life into Luna's understanding that her existence was not about proximity, but the love and memories she shared with Amy.

'Even if we're not together,' Luna thought, as her eyes traced the patterns on the quilt, 'we'll always have this connection.' She clung to the knowledge like an anchor in a stormy sea, allowing it to ground her amidst the whirlwind of emotions that threatened to engulf her.

She picked up a faded stuffed bear, limp from a lack of stuffing and repaired with many stitches, the one Amy had slept with since she was small, and tears pricked Luna's eyes. She wondered how the bear had felt when Luna had arrived to take its place in Amy's life, and whether the grief of parting would ever truly heal. 'I understand, now,' she said. 'But it doesn't make it any easier.'

The last day of their holiday found the two friends perched on a weathered bench by the lake, the sun dipping low in the sky and casting its warm, tangerine hues across the rippling water. The world seemed to have softened into a dreamy haze, as though time itself was reluctant to intrude upon this moment of farewell.

A gentle breeze whispered through the grass, carrying with it the sweet scent of wildflowers that dotted the shoreline. The sound of water lapping against the pebbled shore and birds singing their twilight songs formed a soothing symphony, filling the air with the peaceful essence of nature.

'Isn't it beautiful?' murmured Amy, her voice barely audible above the rustle of leaves.

'Quite,' Luna agreed, her eyes fixed on the ever-changing

dance of colours that played out upon the surface of the lake. The serenity that surrounded them was a bittersweet reminder of all the shared laughter and secrets that had taken place in this ethereal world, one that had brought them so much joy and yet now threatened to pull them apart.

'Remember when we built that raft together that summer?' Amy asked, a wistful smile tugging at the corner of her lips, 'We thought we could sail to the other side of the river.'

'Only to sink halfway through,' Luna chuckled softly, though a hint of sadness lingered behind her mirth. She knew those memories, precious and rare, belonged to a time that was quickly fading from both their grasps.

'Seems like forever ago, doesn't it?' Amy sighed, a faraway look in her eyes as she gazed out across the water, absorbing the tranquillity that lay before them. Luna could sense the undercurrent of uncertainty within her friend, though she remained silent, choosing to let the stillness speak for them both.

As the sun dipped lower, casting a warm glow on their faces, Luna looked sideways at Amy. The girl's eyes were pensive, her fingers absentmindedly tracing patterns on the wooden bench beneath them. At that moment, Luna could see the weight of a thousand unspoken thoughts swirling within her friend, threatening to engulf her.

'Sometimes I wonder,' Amy began hesitantly, her voice barely above a whisper, 'what it'll be like when we're all grown up. What if everything changes?' The vulnerability in her words tugged at Luna's heart, for she too was frightened by the prospect of the unknown looming ahead.

'Change is inevitable,' Luna replied gently, reaching out to place a comforting hand on Amy's shoulder. 'I see that now. But that doesn't mean we can't hold on to what we cherish most.'

Amy's eyes flicked towards Luna, a mixture of affection and trepidation shining within them. 'I just can't imagine my life without our adventures. Without you.' She paused, swallowing hard as the enormity of her confession settled between them.

'Nor I,' admitted Luna, offering her friend a weak smile that did little to mask her fears. She thought back to their countless escapades – treasure hunts through the woods, tea parties beneath grand oak trees, and whispered confessions beneath star-studded skies. Each memory only cemented the realisation that their idyllic world was slipping away, irrevocably altered by the passage of time.

'Promise me something?' Amy asked suddenly, her gaze locked onto the water's edge where the last remnants of daylight shimmered against the rippling surface.

'Anything,' Luna answered without hesitation, her loyalty unwavering even in the face of uncertainty.

'Promise me that, no matter what happens, we'll never forget each other or the times we've shared,' implored Amy, her eyes glistening with unshed tears.

'Of course,' Luna whispered, the weight of the promise settling heavily upon her shoulders. She knew all too well that, as Amy ventured forth into the world, there would come a day when their paths would diverge, and she would be left behind – a relic from a time long past.

As they sat side by side, watching the sun dip below the horizon, Luna silently vowed to treasure each remaining moment with Amy. Although the future was shrouded in mystery, one thing was certain: she would carry the memories of their friendship in her heart, even if it meant saying goodbye forever.

As the sun dipped lower in the sky, casting a warm glow over the lake, Luna couldn't help but feel her heart tighten. It was as if a thousand tiny knots were being pulled together, each representing a memory shared with Amy. They had grown up side by side, their imaginations weaving a tapestry of adventures that now hung delicately between them.

'Will you be alright, Luna?' Amy asked, her voice tinged with concern as she noticed the distant expression on her friend's face.

'Of course,' Luna replied, though her words lacked conviction. Her fingers toyed nervously with the hem of her dress, betraying her true emotions.

'Maybe we can write letters to each other,' Amy suggested, trying to ease the sadness that had descended upon them both. 'We can share our stories, even when we're miles apart.'

Luna nodded, managing a weak smile at the thought of continuing their friendship across ink and parchment. Yet deep within her, she couldn't escape the feeling that their connection was more fragile than ever. Like the lake's surface, it seemed only a breath away from shattering into a thousand iridescent fragments.

'Look,' Luna murmured, pointing towards the water where the setting sun cast its final golden rays. The lake mirrored the sky above, its depths concealing untold secrets and uncharted territories. At that moment, it served as a poignant reflection of the journey that lay ahead for Amy – a journey that would take her far from the shores of their childhood sanctuary and into the vast expanse of the unknown.

'I'll miss you,' Amy whispered, her eyes misty as they traced the ripples that broke the stillness of the lake.

'Me, too,' Luna mused. 'Life is full of change and unpredictable currents that carry us to new places.' She hesitated, then added softly, 'But some things will always remain constant – our memories.'

'Always,' Amy agreed, her expression a mixture of sorrow and determination. 'No matter where I go, you'll always be with me, Luna, even when I'm ninety-two.'

As Amy and Luna entwined their fingers together one last time, a magical connection seemed to flow between them. Their hands were clasped tightly as if neither wanted to admit that they would soon be parting ways. They stood side by side on the edge of the lake, gazing down at the shimmering water as it rippled in response to the gentle breeze that swept across its surface.

'Look,' Amy whispered, pointing to where their reflections danced upon the water. 'We're still together here.'

Luna's eyes filled with tears as she watched their mirrored images. The moving waters seemed to foreshadow the changes that lay before them both – the transition from innocent childhood into the unknown realm of adulthood.

A lone figure emerged from the shadows of the trees, drifting closer to where Amy and Luna stood. It was a young girl, perhaps two or three years younger than Amy, with wispy blonde hair and pale blue eyes that seemed oddly sad and knowing. She offered the two friends a gentle, sympathetic smile.

'It's time,' the girl said, her voice feather-light. Luna's grip on Amy's hand tightened for a moment, then relaxed. A tear slipped down her cheek as she turned to face the blonde-haired girl.

'You're like me, aren't you?' Luna asked softly. The girl nodded.

Amy turned, searching in the direction from which Luna was now focused. Only the wind in the trees betrayed any movement.

'Who are you talking to?'

Luna swallowed hard, glancing back at Amy. 'It's alright,' she whispered. 'There's someone here to help me. She's—' Her voice faltered for a moment. 'She's like me, I think.' The girl nodded again, a world of sorrow and empathy held within her pale gaze.

Amy's eyes widened with understanding.

'It's time to let her go,' the girl said gently, placing a hand on Luna's shoulder. 'Say your goodbyes and know that I am here with you as I have cared for others during their first parting.

Luna turned to look into her friend's face, remembering every detail to last a lifetime. 'You must live your life and embrace all the joy and wonder that awaits you.' She smiled at Amy. 'Do not be sad for what has passed. Simply cherish each memory and hold our friendship in your heart forever.'

Luna turned back to Amy, tears spilling down her cheeks. 'It's time,' she echoed softly. 'But I will never leave you, not truly. Our friendship will endure, eternal as the waters, deep as the lake.'

Amy pulled Luna into a fierce embrace, weeping against her shoulder. 'I love you,' she whispered. 'Always.'

When at last they parted, Luna offered Amy one final, watery smile. Then she took the other girl's hand, and together they looked into the water to see nothing but an empty rippling mirror. The waters before her were dark and deep, but there, reflected on their surface, was the memory of Amy's smile — a reminder of the love they shared, and the promise that could never be broken.

'It's your first time, isn't it?' said the girl softly, squeezing her hand.

Luna nodded, sprinkling tears into the water.

'I remember my first, and that was over a hundred years ago.'

'How do you cope?' said Luna wiping her eyes with the back of her hand. 'When they grow up and leave you?'

'You don't,' smiled the girl. 'If you did, you'd cease to exist. You live because the real ones remember you.'

'What happens to me now?'

'You grow.' The girl led her away from the water's edge.

'You change and find someone else to befriend as we all do. Come with me, I'd like you to meet a little girl that has just arrived – the only friend she has in the world is a faded cloth rabbit.'

Amy watched her friend disappear from view, and turned away from the lake at last, wiping her eyes with the back of her hand. Her parents were waiting by the car, concern etched into their faces.

'Is everything all right, darling?' her mother asked gently.

Amy nodded. 'Yes,' she said. 'It's time to go.'

Her father placed a comforting hand on her shoulder. 'We understand this is difficult for you,' he said. 'But it will get easier, in time. You're growing up into a fine young woman, and there are so many wonderful adventures ahead of you. Imaginary friends are for children.'

'I know,' Amy said. 'But it hurts to say goodbye, nonetheless.' She took a deep, steadying breath, and climbed into the backseat of the car. As the engine started with a rumble, she gazed out the window at the darkening sky, at the first pinpricks of starlight beginning to emerge.

Somewhere, she knew, Luna was gazing up at those same stars. The distance between them couldn't dim the light of their friendship, nor fade the memory of the joy they'd shared. They would always remain together, bound in the solace of imagination, kept safe in the stillness of the dreaming lake.

NIGHTINGALE

CHAPTER ONE

The fog draped London in its misty embrace. A tall, thin man wearing a tailored black coat made his way through the dimly lit gas lamps along the Victoria Embankment, their warm light glinting off of his silver-handled umbrella.

Inspector Thomas Perry scanned the pavement with sharp, pale blue eyes. His body was well proportioned, and his dignified jawline gave him an air of nobility, though he no longer had any claim to a title. Despite being in his early middle age, many years of service had carved deep lines into his fair countenance.

Perry strode with purpose, the ringing sound of his polished shoes echoing on the stones. He was known for solving cases that other officers had given up on, for finding clues where there seemed to be none. The Yard's best depended upon his perceptive instincts, even though many conservative thinkers still questioned his eccentric methods.

He crossed the Thames, skirting around small alleyways

filled with people walking into pubs and gin shops in less reputable parts of town. The clatter of horse carriages and the buzz of chattering pedestrians filled his ears, yet even amongst all this commotion, he could still sense a pervading atmosphere of dread and distress hanging over the city like a fog. It was as if the very walls were speaking, sharing whispers of past wrongs that had yet to be avenged.

A gust of wind hit him, carrying along a scrap of newspaper which caught on his leg. He glanced down and read the headline: *'Grand Soiree: A Night to Remember featuring Miss Charlotte Bloom, the Nightingale of Knightsbridge. Final dates announced!'*

'It certainly was,' he whispered with a smile, remembering how she had captivated her audience when he attended the show. 'You had everyone in the palm of your hand.'

He brushed the pamphlet aside and continued his journey, his face stern enough to part the crowd in front of him, like a ship cutting through turbulent waters. His tailored suit, crisp and immaculate despite the dreary weather, spoke of a certain professionalism that few could match. Those who considered attacking him would likely be dissuaded by his intimidating presence; it was clear he had skills that few could challenge. He held a silver-handled umbrella, a sign of both practicality and style rumoured to contain a stiletto made of Italian steel.

His thoughts strayed back to cases he had solved in the past. There was the infamous Lady Whitmore murder, where he had exposed an intricate web of deceit and betrayal within the upper echelons of London's high society. Then there was the elaborate financial fraud scheme orchestrated by the cunning Albert Chamberlain, which had taken months of relentless investigation to unravel.

As Perry entered the dimly lit halls of the police headquarters, he was greeted by the familiar faces of fellow officers and clerks, each busy with their burdensome tasks. His attention shifted to Superintendent Gregory who was deep in thought, poring over a pile of documents.

'Inspector, a word,' Gregory said without looking up. His gruff tone betrayed his annoyance at being interrupted.

Perry moved into the small office. 'What can I do for you?'

'This alleged assault and battery business you are pursuing against Lord Kempton – I've had the Lord Mayor breathing down my neck about it all week. The two of them play Bridge.' Gregory finally glanced up, his eyes hard as flint. 'He wants this case wrapped up quickly and quietly, and if possible, not at all. I want you to put it aside for the moment, understand?'

'With all due respect, sir,' Perry said, 'I need to conduct this investigation without fear or favour. If that means upsetting a few aristocrats along the way, then so be it.'

Gregory slammed a fist on the desk, causing the pile of papers to slide onto the floor. 'Blast it, Perry! Must you always be so obstinate? This is a sensitive matter, and we have to proceed with delicacy and care. Is that clear?'

Perry did not flinch. His unwavering gaze and steady tone betrayed nothing of his simmering frustration. 'I understand the pressures from above, sir, but I have to find the truth. No one, no matter their status, is above the law. If Lord Kempton is guilty of beating that poor woman's face into a pulp, he must face justice.'

Gregory folded his face into his hands with an exasperated sigh. 'I'm surprised you are willing to go that far against one of your own.'

'My own?' Perry asked, raising an eyebrow at Gregory's insinuation.

Gregory gestured vaguely with one hand. 'You know—the ruling class. It appears you want to be unpopular with everyone.'

'I suppose I should take that as a compliment,' Perry replied dryly.

'If you weren't so damn good at sniffing out rats for the terriers to chase,' said Gregory, nodding over his shoulders at the desk of busy policemen, 'then we would have parted company long ago.' He rubbed his cheeks and hunched forward, staring into the inkwell. 'This has been a horrible day.'

'The Mayor?' said Perry, leaning forward to offer a sympathetic ear.

'The least of my worries, not counting you. Sergeant Higgins chased a group of men attempting to rob a jewellery shop over in Marylebone today; one man ran straight into an oncoming tram; not a pretty sight. Higgins is taking it pretty hard, but it was bound to happen eventually; he's been on the force for twenty years now.'

'I can have a word with him if you like.'

Gregory shook his head. 'Best not just at the moment. The man who was killed was Charlie Flynn's son.'

'Colm Flynn?' said Perry stiffening back into the chair. 'There'll be hell to pay.'

'That's what I'm afraid of. It's been a horrible day, and tomorrow will be worse – mark my words. I thought you had best to hear it from me. Don't get involved – it's well known there is bad blood between you and that gangster, not to mention the fluid truce and tenuous unwritten agreement between his operation and our looking the other way.'

'You're aware of how I feel about that,' Perry pointed out. 'We had the means to close him down and throw him in jail multiple times.'

'But we would have lost various leads into even more serious matters from his informants.'

'We shut down his rivals for him – I'd say that was much more convenient for him than for us.'

Gregory massaged his jaw, 'I was of that same opinion back when I was your age, but now that I'm sitting behind this desk, the world ain't so black and white.'

'There will be a reprisal,' said Perry. 'Flynn may be a ruthless criminal, but his son meant more to him than any life sentence that could be given out.'

'Charlie Flynn will be going through pure torture right now and when he calms down from trying to beat the walls and the people responsible into dust, we may well find a few of our own in the Thames, too.'

With an exasperated sigh, Gregory waved a dismissive hand. 'Just get on with your investigations, Perry. But tread carefully, and leave Kempton alone, or the consequences will be severe, for everyone.'

Perry rose and gave a curt nod, then turned on his heel and strode out of the office.

Outside, the air still lay thick with the November smog. The inspector's mind raced as he pondered the complexities of the situation and the Kempton case. He noticed two small flags, limp and damp from the fog, hanging above a millinery boutique. It seemed to him a reflection of the social class divide: two men at opposite ends of this spectrum—an underworld boss and an apparently untouchable lord—who seemed to get away with any kind of crime. The heavy fog seemed a fitting metaphor for the elusive clues that evaded him, and the frustration gnawed at his insides. He could almost hear the ticking clock in his mind, each second bringing him closer to an unspecified deadline. Yet, even as these thoughts swirled around him, Perry couldn't shake the feeling that something ominous loomed on the horizon. The air seemed heavy with a tension he couldn't quite place as if the very fabric of the city was bracing itself for a storm.

He turned into an empty street; his mind calmed by the familiar cut through to his home. In his quieter moments,

Perry's thoughts often wandered to his family's decline, a factor that had pushed him into police work. He was an outsider in both stations – neither fully accepted by his upper-class roots nor the working class where he now belonged.

With each step, he drew nearer to his sparsely furnished apartment near Waterloo. Its modest dimensions and simple furnishings were a far cry from the grand house of his youth. A single bed, a cluttered desk, and a bookshelf laden with classic literature awaited him within its walls.

As a man of few indulgences, Perry took solace in the small comforts afforded to him: a glass of absinthe after a long day, the soothing purr of his Persian cat, and the escape provided by the works of Dickens, Brontë, and other literary greats. He paused at the entrance to his lodgings, taking a deep breath as he steeled himself for yet another night spent poring over evidence and witness statements. The scent of damp earth and the distant hum of horses' hooves filled his senses, grounding him in the present.

He shivered as the fog chilled his skin and trekked up the worn, carpeted stairs to his second-floor residence. With each step of the weathered wooden steps, Perry was aware of the fact that justice depended on him.

As the door to his apartment creaked open, Perry's thoughts turned inward once more. He couldn't help but wonder what his life might have been if fate had not intervened so cruelly, stripping his family of their status and forcing him into this solitary existence. Yet, despite the gnawing self-doubt, the Inspector remained steadfast in his pursuit of justice. The shadows of London were a labyrinth of danger and deceit, but he was determined to navigate its twists and turns, to bring peace to the city's tormented souls in an attempt to soothe his own. And as the fog swirled outside his window, the relentless ticking of his mental clock drove him onward and away from sleep.

He moved around an octagonal side table bedecked with an ornate ebony and ivory chess set, the sole reminder of his once privileged upbringing, and the only thing he could carry during his mother's exile to a distant town to live among even more distant relations. At least they were free, though tainted, by their father's addiction to gambling, and incarceration for debt. Three hundred years of power and prestige brought low in three hundred card games. He lifted a black knight into a position to offer an exchange of pieces; tomorrow, playing as white, he would decide its fate.

Perry gazed out from the gloomy apartment windows at the thick fog oozing below, masking the city's darkest secrets. Flickering gaslight shadows ran along the faded floorboards. He felt the pressure of unsolved cases weighing down on him like the heavy atmosphere outside.

'Algernon,' he whispered affectionately as his Persian cat wove around his ankles, purring softly. 'Did Miss Hemmings downstairs feed and comfort you while I was gone?' The simple gesture provided Perry with temporary peace from his busy mind's eye. 'Yet another night trying to catch apparitions,' he sighed quietly as he glanced at the clock on the mantelpiece marking each passing second.

His mind raced with possibilities and connections, the clues weaving themselves together like the threads of a tapestry. But for every mystery that unravelled, another seemed to take its place, taunting him with its unanswered questions. His eyes fell upon the spines of the classic literature that lined his bookshelf, seeking solace in the words of authors long departed. Yet even the comfort of their tales could not quell the storm brewing within him.

As he moved towards his cluttered desk, the feeling of rough paper under his fingertips gave him back his determination. 'Time waits for no one,' he said to himself, gripping the silver umbrella handle tightly as he prepared for what lay ahead. The night chill in his palm reminded him of the darkness lurking beyond his door – darkness which he intended to conquer.

After a few hours, he nestled into his worn armchair by the fireplace, its fabric moulding comfortably around him and the Persian purring on his lap. He opened The Odyssey, its yellowed pages and musty smell giving him a sense of comfort. His thoughts wandered to the passage with Odysseus and the Sirens:

'Whoever draws too close, infatuated by their song,

Never sees his loved ones again, never returns to his homeland joy.'

He gazed into the crackling fire. Many times he had narrowly escaped the lure of oblivion, the temptation to lose himself in the depths of a case and never resurface. He thought of his spartan rooms, the solitude of his life that stretched endlessly before him. Home and loved ones seemed as distant to him now as a faraway island veiled in mist.

With a shake of his head, he returned to his reading, eager to lose himself in the familiar tales. The case would still be there, waiting, when he emerged from the sea of stories that had kept him company through many a long night. Duty would call him back, as it always did, to the unravelling of mysteries and the relentless pursuit of truth. His eyelids slumped; his ears oblivious to the sound of someone on the stairs outside.

'Inspector,' a voice called out suddenly, shattering the silence. It was accompanied by a single rap on the door. The sound echoed through the small room like a gunshot, sending Algernon scurrying for cover beside the desk.

Perry's heart raced as he tensed, his hand instinctively reaching for the pistol that lay hidden within the top drawer of his armoire nearby. The unexpected intrusion left him feeling exposed and vulnerable – a sensation he loathed.

'Who's there?' he demanded, his voice steady despite the pounding of his pulse in his ears.

'Constable Davis, sir,' came the hesitant reply from beyond the door. 'I've been dispatched by Superintendent Gregory. There's been...a murder, sir. In a nearby park. He requests your presence immediately.'

The words hung heavy in the air, laden with both dread and anticipation. With each beat of his heart, Perry knew he was being drawn deeper into the shadows. And as he reached for the door handle, an icy shiver ran down his spine, heralding the beginning of a fresh case, but he grabbed his coat and umbrella and strode to open the door.

'Take me there at once.'

As the constable led him through the empty streets to the waiting cab, Perry's mind raced with the possibilities. A robbery gone awry, a crime of passion, a premeditated act of violence? He would have to examine the scene to determine the motive.

The park loomed before them, shrouded in mist and moonlight. An eerie stillness hung over the landscape, the rustling of leaves and cooing of roosting pigeons muted by the thick autumn smog.

By the boating lake, several bobbies milled about, warding off a small crowd of curious onlookers. In the centre of it all lay a lifeless figure sprawled face down on the bank, pale limbs askew against the damp grass.

Perry tightened his gloves and knelt beside the body, his pulse quickening, wondering if the attacker had intended to drag the victim into the water and had been disturbed.

'No identifying calling cards or belongings on her person,' said the Constable. 'We don't yet know who she is, sir.'

Perry twisted the woman's face into the light of the constable's torch and gave a sharp intake of breath.

'We do now,' he whispered. 'I want this kept as quiet as possible to avoid any speculation and to protect the woman's reputation, at least until we inform any family. It's Charlotte Bloom, the vaudeville actress, and we will never again witness the like of her unique talent in this world.'

CHAPTER TWO

Inspector Perry stood at the edge of the park, the damp grass clinging to his boots as he surveyed the grim scene before him. The lifeless body lay sprawled beneath a gnarled oak tree, her fiery red hair splayed around her like a crimson halo. Charlotte Bloom, the Nightingale of Knightsbridge, had been brutally murdered.

'Inspector, sir,' a uniformed officer called out, snapping Perry from his thoughts. 'The Superintendent has been informed of your initial findings but awaits a formal identification before making this public; he would like you to concentrate wholly on this case immediately. Mr Rook, the undertaker, has been dispatched and has been allowed to assist you whilst the coroner is indisposed.'

'Very good,' Perry replied, making his way toward the body. His heart twisted with a mixture of dread and determination; another woman's life snuffed out by a merciless killer; another talented flame extinguished from an empire still reeling from Queen Victoria's death two years prior. He couldn't afford to let emotions cloud his judgment, not now when lives hung in the balance.

'Her throat was crushed,' the hastily dispatched doctor

informed Perry as they both crouched beside Charlotte's body.

Perry's eyes narrowed as he studied the bruising on the actress's neck, noting its unique pattern. A familiar cold fury began to simmer within him. The same marks had been found on three other women's bodies in the past year. He needed to find answers quickly before the site became clouded by time, the killer's traces obliterated by the feet of gongoozlers and gawkers.

'Thank you, Doctor,' Perry said, straightening up and rolling down his sleeves. His blue eyes scanned the surrounding area, taking in every detail, searching for anything that might lead to the killer's identity.

'Inspector,' the same constable from earlier approached once more, his voice hesitant. 'I've questioned one or two of the first to arrive – the rumour is that this might be the work of the Shadow Strangler; people are frightened.'

'Rumours won't solve this case, Constable,' Perry snapped, irritation flaring in his chest. He didn't need distractions or gossip; he needed facts and evidence. 'Let's focus on what we know and find the person responsible.'

Perry felt a creeping sense of urgency. If this was the work of the Shadow Strangler, then the killer was growing bolder with each attack, and there was no telling when or where they would strike next.

The incessant ticking of the clock in the undertaker's parlour grated on Perry's nerves, each second a reminder of the urgency pressing down upon him.

'Mr Perry,' Samuel Rook greeted him as he entered the white-tiled, windowless room. Rook was a short, wiry man with a bald head and a thick moustache that seemed to quiver with every word. Standing among the coffins and embalming tools, he appeared as much a fixture of his macabre surroundings as the instruments themselves.

'Rook,' Perry nodded, his eyes scanning the room. 'You've seen the marks on Charlotte Bloom's body; I fear that you have encountered them before.'

Rook's expression darkened as he thought back. 'You know I have, Inspector. On two other women I prepared for burial in the past year.' He paused, visibly pained by the memories. 'Such a tragedy. She was a talented actress; her loss will be felt deeply.'

Perry clenched his fists at his sides, the cold fury rising within him again. To think that this monster had taken the lives of at least three women, snuffing out their potential and leaving their families bereft. 'I need to stop this from happening, Rook. I cannot bear the thought of another life lost to this madman.'

'Nor can I,' Rook agreed, his voice strained. This shared sadness, this common drive for justice, bound them together in their pursuit of the truth. Though they came from different worlds, their work brought them together repeatedly, each recognising the other's dedication to the cause.

Perry's face was ashen as he asked, 'Have you discovered anything about the murder weapon?' His mind raced with possibilities.

Rook hesitated before replying as if weighing his words carefully. 'I believe so if you have the stomach for it.'

Perry frowned as Rook took his silence as an affirmation to proceed. The undertaker padded over to an ice-filled barrel and pulled out the partially decomposed, dripping carcass of a large piglet.

'Breakfast?' said Perry, watching as the man heaved the heavy lump onto the marble surface of a side table, and unthreaded the chain of his pocket watch from the slit in his waistcoat lapel.

'The chain-like marks and studs are certainly distinctive. I believe the garrote may be something quite personal.' Rook wound the pig's neck with the silvered chain, threading the bar through the larger ring above the winding mechanism and drawing it tight.

The dead pig's tongue lolled from its mouth as Rook applied a surprising amount of force for such a small man. Perry felt his stomach churn uneasily at this unnatural sight, but he steeled himself and focused on observation. The undertaker twisted the chain causing the bar to bite into the pink flesh. 'See how the marks of the winding crown form studs from the tightening?' said Rook releasing the porcine cadaver back to the slab and removing his watch back to his pocket.

'Just like on Bloom's body,' he declared, swallowing hard, 'and the other women. It's the same man then.'

Rook nodded solemnly; the gravity of their task was apparent in every line of his face. 'The Shadow Strangler.'

Damp air clung to Perry's skin as he stared at the stiff corpse of the actress laid out on the undertaker's table. Almost at any moment, he expected her to rise from her pretence of death like an Act Three Shakespearean heroine. Rook, standing beside him, shared a sombre glance. 'The chain could not be made of silver – it wouldn't withstand the force.'

'How about gold?' said Perry. 'Nine carats?'

Rook stuck out his lower lip. 'A possibility, but you saw what my modest steel device accomplished; you are looking for a gentleman, or a scoundrel without the means to purchase a fine watch.'

'That doesn't narrow it down very much in this part of

London,' Perry said, trying to keep his voice steady. 'Did you find anything else?'

Rook hesitated, then cleared his throat. 'I'm afraid so,' he murmured, and Perry could hear the pain laced in his words. 'From the bruising upon her thighs and buttocks, there is reason to believe that the killer may have...violated her before or shortly after death. It was a similar situation with the other victims.'

'Dear God,' Perry whispered, feeling his stomach churn. The horror of the situation only intensified with this new revelation. His mind raced back to the previous women— similarly desecrated, their dignity stolen even after their lives had been taken.

'Each woman had auburn or red hair and green eyes,' Perry said, turning to Rook. It was times like these he found solace in their mutual respect, the understanding that they both sought the same goal: justice for the innocent.

'It's possible the killer has a specific type in mind.' Rook replied, his gaze never leaving the body.

'Thank you, Samuel.' The gratitude in Perry's voice was genuine. He knew the level-of-detail Rook provided was invaluable in his investigations. They had worked together on many cases, each time combining their expertise to uncover the truth.

'Of course, Thomas,' Rook nodded. 'I still feel I owe you, especially after what you did for my sister.'

Perry remembered the case—the violence inflicted on Rook's sister by her husband. He had helped to bring the man to justice, and since then, Rook had been unwavering in his support.

'You've paid me back many times over with your insights; let's focus on finding this monster,' Perry said, his voice firm and determined. 'Together, we'll put an end to this nightmare.'

'Agreed,' Rook replied, his eyes meeting Perry's with a shared resolve.

As they continued their examination of the body, each additional detail they uncovered only fuelled their determination. A cacophony of footsteps echoed through the mortuary as Perry paced back and forth, his brow furrowed in deep concentration. His gaze kept drifting back to the lifeless form of Charlotte Bloom, her once vibrant features still beautiful, her neck now marred by the cruel handiwork of the Shadow Strangler.

'His brazenness is alarming,' Perry continued, staring at the blue-black, bloodied line on the porcelain skin. 'Each time he strikes, he grows bolder, more confident. This time it was in a public park.'

Rook nodded solemnly, his hands clenching into fists at his sides. 'You'll find him, Thomas, I have faith in you.'

Perry turned to face his long-time ally; the weight of their shared responsibility was clear in the lines etched across their faces. He knew that Rook's keen eye for detail and unwavering dedication would prove invaluable in their pursuit of the truth.

Perry's frustration simmered beneath the surface; a smouldering fire held at bay by sheer force of will. His removal from the Kempton case gnawed at him, an injustice he couldn't reconcile with his sense of duty. To make matters worse, the death of Colm Flynn had left the police force reeling, vulnerable to dangers both known and unknown.

'Damn it all,' Perry muttered, rubbing his forehead with one hand as he paced the length of Rook's office. 'They strip me from the Kempton case, and now we're dealing with a serial killer and the fallout from Flynn's son's death.'

Rook, ever the empathetic companion, nodded solemnly. 'I understand your frustration, Thomas. What happened to Colm was particularly harrowing.' He hesitated, swallowing hard before continuing. 'It is why I have been allowed to help you so early – Mr Grimes, the temporary and acting coroner, was incapacitated following his visit earlier today.'

Perry raised his eyebrows in surprise. 'I've never heard tell of Grimes having any weakness of the stomach.' He rapped on the marble surface. 'He's harder than any work of stone.'

'Me, neither,' said Rook swallowing hard. 'I am also not a man that succumbs easily to my work, but Colm's face... When the tram struck him, it was nearly unrecognisable as human. I've done my best to reconstruct it with wax, for the family's sake, and considering who his father is. Mr Grimes may struggle to remove the image from his mind, even when his stomach settles.'

'It's what Flynn will do next that will determine who lies before us in the coming days, and who examines the bodies.'

Perry's heart clenched in his chest as if gripped by the same chain that had taken Charlotte Bloom's life.

'Thomas,' Rook said cautiously, his voice barely audible above the low crackle of the gas lamps. 'There may be a way of finding the killer through unorthodox means.'

Whether it was the subtle quavering of the undertaker's voice or the look away from Perry's probing glance, the inspector made his inquiry.

'You mean illegal?'

Rook plucked at his moustache. 'That depends on your outlook or religious persuasion. There's something I've been meaning to tell you, but it may affect your opinion of me. It is a secret likely to shock you; you may even think me mad unless I show you.'

Perry looked up; eyes locked on Rook's apprehensive expression. A sudden chill crept down his spine. For a moment, the face of the familiar, quiet man transformed in Perry's mind into the evil visage of a killer. Perry blinked several times, and the thought passed leaving the gentle face of the undertaker once more.

'Speak your mind, Samuel,' Perry urged, bracing himself for the impact of Rook's words and gripping the handle of his umbrella. 'You know that you have my confidence, as you hold mine.'

Rook hesitated, wringing his hands and glancing around the dimly lit room as if seeking an escape from the burden of his secret. His breath hitched, and Perry could see the internal struggle etched across his features.

'Thomas, I believe... I can give you the name of the killer.' Rook's voice trembled, betraying the gravity of his revelation. 'But not from my lips.'

'Then whose?'

Rook glanced down at the woman's body. 'From hers.'

Perry frowned. 'She was dead in the park with no pulse; she couldn't possibly have revived...'

'Yes, she was dead, but I have a way that will restore her to life for a brief period...'

Perry stared at the undertaker's wavering lip. 'Samuel, you are not yourself this evening. The toll of two dreadful injuries has caused you to become fanciful.'

'It is the truth, Thomas, and I only reveal it to you for your past kindnesses, the unburdening of my secret, which I have never divulged to you, and in remembrance of another who fell victim to the same murderer.'

Perry tensed, his gut churning with a mixture of anticipation and dread. How could this be possible? What hidden truth had Rook uncovered that could lead them to the identity of the monster who had committed such unspeakable acts?

'Samuel, are you sane?' Perry asked, his voice a mere whisper, lest the walls themselves might be listening. 'I see no lightning conductor or rack of potions, my friend. Even if you could do as you claim, how can we trust such information?'

'Because,' Rook replied, his voice steadier now, 'the dead always seek vengeance, Thomas, and that is the purest form of truth. The restoration will only work on those recently deceased, and before the body breaks down. I could demonstrate on the beast if you need proof, though there is always a price to pay.'

'What do you mean?'

'Just this: whatever fate has caused my ability to do this exacts its price, and I offer this opportunity only if you ask it of me.'

'Even if it were true, how did you come by this talent, and why haven't you used it before?'

Rook spread his hands on the table's cold, polished surface. 'To answer the latter question, first – through grief or foolishness – I know not which, I already have.'

'On whom?'

'My wife,' said Rook slumping his shoulders. 'She lay here ten years ago, twisted by cancer and I couldn't let her go.'

The silence in the room was broken only by the dripping of the tap into the porcelain sink upon the far wall.

'Your wife died, Samuel. You told me you buried her.'

'I restored her through my selfishness and within twelve hours, she was lying here again.' Rook shook with the memory. 'They all do unless what is done to them is returned in like fashion to the agent of their death yet how does one affect the universe for robbing a life prematurely through cancer?'

'This is not the order of things,' said Perry softly. 'No matter how hard we want these things to be.'

'I would be dead now for the man that restored me – I am living proof and I have not told a living soul.' Rook scoffed. 'Not only did I end up acutely appreciating what it is like to be dead for a short while, but I have ever since been drawn to life's ending seeking answers and finding only more questions.'

'I will listen to this fable out of friendship,' said Perry, 'but then you must rest, and I will ask a doctor to visit you.'

Rook turned away and folded his arms. 'I was in my early twenties when I was struck down in the street by an Egyptian nobleman riding a wayward horse. I woke what seemed hours later in his care in a fine drawing room on the other side of London. He was distraught and confided that his guilt and honour would not cause a man to die at his own hands when he had the power to change places. Restored to life, he explained I had only hours to live. I thought him mad, as you think of me, but all I wanted to do was escape the opulence of his Richmond house.'

'You say that the dead can only be restored for a short time — how is it you still live decades later?'

'Within one sunrise to sunset,' said Rook. 'If the killer or person responsible for one's death is found and the ritual reversed, then the latter dies, and the former takes his life's share; I believe the Orientals call it Karma. Despite my objection, and the hours ticking away till he was frantic with remorse, he laid lips upon mine and died instantly, falling to the floor. I felt a sudden change as though returned to my previous life, I remember the longing for the previous feeling to return as I clutched my broken skull, bilious with the pain that was not present before. I ran, not knowing what he had given or taken from me.' He turned and Perry saw the familiar scar and hollow near the back of the undertaker's head. 'It took four months to fully heal. Not until I parted with my dead wife, and I laid my lips on hers did I realise he was telling the truth.'

Perry shook his head in disbelief. 'And what manner of ritual is this that restores life?'

'I know not, only that he rambled a lot regarding his Egyptian heritage; some secret passed down from antiquity I gather. It is but a single kiss,' said Rook, turning to stare fully into Perry's eyes. 'The transfer of a single breath is all that is required, bestowed by one that has tasted death and been restored. The Egyptian called it *The Breath* and must also have died at one time to bring me back.'

'You are making me nervous, Samuel,' said Perry, gripping the handle of his umbrella. 'If you feel the urge to kiss dead people, then I need to inform my superiors...'

'Before you do,' said Rook suddenly. 'Think of Mary Webster.'

'The prostitute killed in like fashion six months ago?'

Rook nodded. 'I want her avenged, Perry, even if you put me into an asylum. Don't think I was foolish to fall in love with her because of her obvious charms – it was deeper than that. The feeling was mutual, but I was too late to protect her that night she was murdered. I should have told you then about *The Breath*, and maybe she would have returned the favour to the Shadow Strangler, and we would be together still.'

'I'm so sorry for your suffering, Samuel, but—' Perry said gently as he started to move toward the door, only to be met by the hideous and unholy screech of some unhinged, crazed siren. The piercing scream assaulted his ears in the tile-enclosed room. Instinctively, he whirled around, pulling the nine-inch blade from its sheath inside his umbrella handle. His arm trembled as he held the point of his dagger in front of him. He glanced past the tip and noticed Rook struggling to restrain the pig on the bench—it was thrashing and squealing horribly, maddened by the pain of its missing front legs and rear shank. Rook gagged and wiped his mouth with the back of his upper arm.

'What have you done?' said Perry inching forward. 'Tell me this is some sick parlour trick.'

Rook steadied himself and continued holding the creature down as tears streamed down his face. 'I'm telling you the truth, Thomas—now please put it out of its misery.' Perry's mind raced while trying to make sense of Rook's words. In his haste, Rook ran to grab a knife from his instruments and slit the animal's throat, silencing its screams forever.

'I'm sorry you had to see this,' said Rook, wiping his sweating forehead with the back of his hand. 'Charlotte Bloom is unharmed save for the scar on her neck. I leave the decision to you, and what to do with the secret I have just revealed. I do so for Mary Webster and hoping you will bring the killer to justice before he strikes again; it is not only the victim who suffers – remember that.'

Perry's mind reeled with the possibility. If true, this could be their only chance to stop the Shadow Strangler before he struck again. But how could he rely on such unconventional means? How could put his faith in the words of the dead?

'Samuel,' Perry said firmly, his resolve hardening, 'if you can truly bring me the name of the killer from Charlotte Bloom's lips, then I still need evidence. The testimony of a dead person is not admissible in court.'

'Very few know the identity of the woman lying here at present,' said Rook, wiping his knife and placing it back with precision in the porcelain tray. 'It will be as if she never died, and you were mistaken with your initial identification.'

'There is no murder without a body.'

'Unless we tell her and she returns *The Breath* to the killer, then you will have a body by sunset this evening. You might also have the killer in chains.'

'Whoever did this should face justice, not vengeance,' said Perry looking down upon the serene face of the Knightsbridge Nightingale. 'Not to mention the moral implications of bringing someone back.'

'Tell that to Charlotte Bloom, Mary Webster, and the other women. Should they not at least have the choice? Should the world be robbed of everyone taken before their time?'

Perry nodded solemnly; his eyes filled with a grim determination that mirrored Rook's own. He thought of the actress, her voice, her talent, all brushed aside by wickedness. 'Very well,' he said, sheathing his blade into the umbrella's stem. 'But she should not know of the manner of her resurrection.'

'But that's monstrous, Thomas!' said Rook. 'You must give her the means to fully live past the setting of the sun. If you catch the killer, he will surely hang—'

'I do not make the laws,' said Perry. 'But I am bound by them, and I cannot be a party to pre-meditated murder, however justice is framed. I daresay the strangler deserves death, but he will face it at the end of a noose.'

'Those terms are not acceptable,' said Rook. 'At the very least she should know the truth of why she lies in a mortuary, and not a hospital upon her return.'

With that, Rook turned away, leaving Perry to grapple with the enormity of what was to come. As the gas lamp flickered and danced across the room, casting eerie shadows upon the walls, Perry couldn't help but feel that he was on the precipice of a horrifying truth – one that would test the limits of his understanding and challenge the very fabric of their reality.

'...the world ain't so black and white.'

Perry shook his head imperceptibly, in conflict with his reply. 'I will take responsibility for this, but my conviction stands. If we find this killer before sunset, they must face justice for the sake of all those whom they have taken, and not at her hands. I owe that to their families. Bloom is dead and must return to that state under the natural order of things.'

The undertaker sighed with resignation. 'On your conscience, Thomas.'

Rook's lips almost seemed to buzz as he touched them against the delicate blue skin of the actress, a spark of electricity that jolted every inch of Perry's exposed body with an unearthly chill. The actress' skin reacted, prickling with hundreds of goosebumps as her chest heaved and spluttered with life-giving breath.

Perry reached forward to clasp her ice-cold fingers in his own, desperately willing the warmth back into her veins as her colour slowly returned. But no sooner had she stirred than a warning echoed within Perry's core like a gunshot: before nightfall, he would have to face an enemy more powerful than any other – death itself – or watch the innocent be claimed by its cruel hands yet again.

'You have until sunset,' said Rook. 'Whether she dies again is now in your hands.'

CHAPTER THREE

Perry's gaze lingered on the woman before him, her fiery red hair cascading over her shoulders like a waterfall of embers, her green eyes glinting with life that had been snatched away and then returned. Charlotte Bloom, her once lifeless body sprawled in the park, now lay resurrected in the dimly lit mortuary.

He swallowed hard, his throat tightening. When Rook had told him what he intended to do, Perry had not truly believed it was possible. And yet here was the proof, as stunning and undeniable as the woman herself.

Charlotte Bloom's eyes fluttered open, pale green irises peering up at the ceiling. She blinked slowly, long lashes brushing against her pale cheeks. Her hands curled into fists at her sides, and she let out a soft moan.

Perry leaned forward, watching her closely. His heart thudded in his chest, torn between anticipation and dread. What would she remember? What had she glimpsed during that moment between life and death?

He wet his lips; his mouth dry. 'Miss Bloom?'

Her head turned towards the sound of his voice, the jewels of her emerald eyes focusing on his face. For a moment, she simply stared at him, confusion etching fine lines into her forehead.

Then her eyes widened, and she sucked in a sharp breath. A tremor ran through her body as she scrambled into a sitting position, hands braced against the cold marble behind her. Rook hurried to hide the pig's carcass, sloshing it back into the barrel of ice.

'Where am I?' Her voice was hoarse and ragged, as though she had been screaming. 'What is this place?'

'You're in the mortuary of an undertaker,' Perry replied gently, attempting to provide comfort in his words. 'We found you in the park after the attack.'

'Attack?' Her eyes widened and Perry could see the fear beginning to set in. She rubbed at her neck. 'I remember... someone grabbed me from behind. Their grip was like iron...' Her voice trailed off as her gaze fell to the floor.

'Can you recall anything else?' Perry pressed, his own heart aching as he watched her struggle to piece together the fragments of her memory.

'Only darkness.' Charlotte shuddered, wrapping her arms

around herself as though the memories chilled her very soul. 'So still...deep darkness.'

The room seemed to close in around them, shadows creeping closer as the weight of time bore down upon their shoulders. Perry knew the clock had started and even now they were running out of it.

'My name is Perry; Inspector Thomas Perry, and this is my...associate, Mr Rook,' he began, his voice firm but gentle. 'We need your help to find the person responsible for this and bring them to justice.'

'Justice?' She echoed, her eyes meeting his with a mixture of determination and fear. 'Why am I in a mortuary?'

'Charlotte,' Perry began, struggling to find the right words. 'This is going to be difficult to explain. You didn't survive the attack. You were...brought back.'

'Back?' Her voice cracked with disbelief, and Perry could see the terror in her eyes as the meaning of his words sank in. He watched as her hand covered her mouth, stifling a sob. 'I...died?'

'In a manner of speaking. Please remain calm,' he whispered. 'You are in no danger here.'

She dragged her eyes back to his face, trembling. 'In a manner of speaking? I remember being choked – what have you done to me?'

Perry hesitated. How could he possibly explain what had transpired here today? The truth would only terrify her more.

'We have managed to...resuscitate you,' said Rook nervously.

'We have brought you here to keep you safe until the culprit is found,' said Perry. It was not entirely a lie, but omitting key details still left a bitter taste in Perry's mouth. Charlotte searched his face, looking for any hint of deceit. Finally, she gave a jerky nod.

'I must get home,' she said, her voice strained. 'My agent

will be worried.' She clutched at her arms, shivering in the sleeveless undergarment. 'Where are my clothes?'

Rook retrieved her dark gown and accoutrements from a nearby drawer.

'My purse?' she said, sorting through the bundle.

Rook retrieved a small notebook, opening to the centre pages. 'I have recorded everything on your person at the time of your arrival; there was no purse.'

'Call me a cab,' she said.

'I'm afraid that is not possible,' Perry said. 'Not until we have caught the man who did this to you.'

Charlotte paled, shrinking back against the wall, dressing in haste to hide her modesty. Her eyes glistened with tears, and Perry had to fight the urge to comfort her. This was not a kindness he could afford her. Not when her life depended on finding her killer.

'This cannot be real,' she whispered, pausing in the placement of her stockings to look at the bruises. 'You tell me I was dead for a short time – that the man who attacked me *killed* me? I feel strange...'

'Yes,' said Perry. 'You are certain it was a man?'

She lowered the hem of her gown and nodded. 'It was dark, but there was hair on the back of the hands that lay hold of me, and a signet ring – he wore a golden ring on his third finger – I bit into it before I lost consciousness.'

Each word was agony, but he could see no other way. The truth might destroy her, and they needed her help if they were to have any chance of finding her killer before nightfall.

Charlotte stared at him, trembling. Perry kept his expression carefully neutral under her searching gaze. Finally, she looked away, pressing a hand to her mouth as a sob wracked her slender frame.

'I don't understand,' she said, her voice muffled by her fingers. 'Why can't I go home?'

'I am afraid you would not be safe there,' Perry said. It was not a complete lie, but the deception still left a bitter taste in his mouth.

Charlotte lifted her head, eyes gleaming with tears. 'What aren't you telling me?' she demanded.

Perry hesitated. How could he possibly tell her the truth without destroying what little composure she had left? There was no easy way to say it. No gentle way to say that her second chance at life was finite.

'The man who attacked you is still at large. We believe him to be the so-called *Shadow Strangler*, and if he thinks you have survived, then he may strike again. Considering your fame it would be best to stay here where we can protect you.'

It was not a lie, not entirely. Simply an omission of the most crucial detail.

Charlotte glanced into the framed mirror above the wide Belfast sink tracing the blackened scar at her throat and began to sob uncontrollably. 'Why would a policeman insist I stay in a mortuary – what is going on?'

Rook shook his head helplessly. 'She suspects,' was all he could say. 'Tell her the truth, Perry, or I will.'

Perry opened his mouth, but no words came out. He glanced helplessly at Rook, at a loss for how to answer. How could he lie to her now, after everything?

Charlotte regarded them with a steely glint in her eye. 'I deserve the truth. Whatever it may be.'

Perry took a slow breath, steeling himself. She was right—she deserved that much, at least.

'We need to find your killer,' Perry whispered, more to himself than to the others, 'before sunset, and while you still live.'

'What happens after sunset?' she said.

Rook wiped the ends of his moustache and glanced down

at the marble-topped table. 'Because the effects of your resuscitation will cease at that point.'

'My return to life is temporary?' she said, incredulously.

'Yes,' Perry whispered. 'I'm afraid it's true. You died and only by the talents of Mr Rook have been restored.'

'You mean resurrected?' Charlotte collapsed into hysterical sobs, clutching at her chest as if she could squeeze the breath back into her lifeless lungs. Perry started toward her, but she flinched away, scrambling into a corner of the room like a frightened animal.

'No, no, this can't be happening,' she gasped between shuddering cries. 'I'm not dead, I can't be dead!'

Perry's heart ached at the raw anguish in her voice. He took a slow, careful step toward her with his hands raised in a placating gesture.

'Please, Miss Bloom, try to calm yourself,' he said gently. She flinched away again, shaking her head in frantic denial.

'Stay away from me!' she shrieked. 'Haven't you done enough?'

The accusation struck him like a physical blow. He froze in place, jaw clenching as her sobs echoed through the room.

Perry withdrew a handkerchief and held it out. 'I offer you this and your freedom, Miss Bloom, to divulge our unorthodox methods and place us in irons, or to assist us in finding the Shadow Strangler so that more women do not suffer the same fate.'

Bloom snatched at the monogrammed cloth and dabbed her eyes, glancing across at the closed door. After a moment, she wandered over to the far door, hand resting on the knob.

'We should tell her,' Rook whispered from his stool beside the barrel of ice. 'She has a right to know if it's her only chance.'

Perry came close and shook his head. 'No. Taking a life is never the answer, no matter the circumstance.'

'Even to save her own?' Rook asked pointedly. Perry shot him a sharp look and Rook held up his hands in surrender. 'I just think she should have all the facts, that's all. So she can make her own choice.'

'Choice?' Perry scoffed. 'What choice is there in telling her she has to murder to go on living?'

'Self-defence is not murder,' Rook argued. 'And it may be her only option if she walks out that door unprepared, and the killer discovers she still lives. She needs to know about *The Breath* – it's the only way she can survive past sunset.'

Perry dragged a hand through his hair, frustration warring with indecision. How had it come to this? When he took the case, all he wanted was to find justice for a woman wronged. Now he was tangled in a web of impossible choices and murky morality.

'She must find her killer and bestow *The Breath* to the one that has done this to her,' Rook explained, his voice barely audible. 'In doing so, she will pass on the curse that robs her talent of this world, condemning him to death and allowing her to live.'

'Rook,' Perry began, his voice low and urgent, 'there must be another way.'

'An eye for an eye,' Rook whispered, his eyes haunted by the weight of his own words.

'Murder for murder?' he said, his jaw tightening. 'No.'

Charlotte turned from the door. 'What are you whispering about? How dare you restore my life without my consent and then tell me I'm going to die,' she said vehemently. 'I am no longer distraught – I am angry. You are as monstrous as the man who took it the first time. Do you not care, Inspector Perry?'

'I found you in the park and it grieved me deeply,' he said. 'I have seen you perform many times, and I am not a man that openly displays emotion, yet—'

Charlotte's eyes burned with rage. 'I had hoped for many things: Paris, New York, children…'

'I am not the ultimate arbiter of justice in this world or the next,' said Perry, stumbling over his words.

'It's too late for that sentiment, Inspector. You have meddled and must now face the music, as must I – or are you too cowardly to face up to your mistakes? I will haunt you for the rest of your days – one way or another.'

Perry's face flushed with the charge and the predicament. 'If we find the man, I will face any consequences you or anyone else charge me with. The decision to restore you was mine alone and Mr Rook is blameless and was coerced. What you do in your remaining hours I leave to you and I have no right to restrain you but you have the chance to save a good many more lives by assisting me – will you help me before you haunt me?'

'I was not coerced,' said Rook. 'We are as one in this.'

'Knowing one is going to die when one has already felt its icy embrace should be easier, but it is not,' said Charlotte hesitantly. 'It seems my conscience is very much alive and kicking, however. If I assist you, then I will spend my remaining hours how I choose and I need your assurance that this monster will not escape justice. Time is precious, gentlemen.'

'Agreed,' Perry nodded. 'Do you know the name of the man who attacked you?'

'No,' said Charlotte.

'Then his description, facial features, accent, colour of hair—'

'He came at me silently, from behind,' she said, realising the gravity of her words. 'How do we find a man I never saw – I'm going to die for nothing, aren't I?'

A cock crowed ominously across the street, heralding the dawn. Perry glanced nervously at Rook. 'We start at the beginning. Can you remember anything about the attack? Anything at all?' Perry leaned forward, his eyes searching hers for any flicker of recognition.

'Only bits and pieces,' she whispered, her voice thick with emotion. 'It was crowded after the performance, and I felt the need for air – I took the shortcut through the park rather than hailing a cab. Someone came up behind me, grabbed me, and...that's all I can recall.'

'Think, Charlotte,' Perry urged, his brows furrowing in concentration. 'Any details you can remember could help us find your attacker.'

Charlotte closed her eyes, forcing herself to recall that terrifying night. She perched on the side of the table and folded her arms. 'There was a struggle,' she said, her voice barely audible. 'I fought back as best I could. But then... something tight around my neck, and everything went black.'

As she recounted the fragmented memories, Perry couldn't help but feel a surge of admiration for her bravery – not only had she fought against her attacker, but she was now determined to help bring him to justice, even at the cost of reliving her trauma. The room's oppressive silence was shattered by Charlotte's foot tapping against the side of the table leg, desperate to dredge up any memory that might help identify her killer. 'I can't,' she choked out. 'I don't remember—wait! He came at me from behind... and then... there was this golden cufflink. I grabbed at the cuff, and it came free just before I passed out.'

'Take your time, Charlotte,' Perry urged gently, his heart aching for the woman who had been robbed of her life and now faced an uncertain future. Rook watched from the shadows, his sorrowful eyes betraying his concern.

'What happened to this cufflink?' Perry probed further, hoping the detail might lead them closer to their quarry.

'It tumbled across the pathway and under... under a water

fountain in the park,' she whispered, her voice quivering with emotion. 'As I fell, it rolled away from me, gleaming in the lamp nearby before I lost sight of it beneath a drinking fountain.'

'Good,' Perry said softly, trying to suppress the urgency he felt. 'Now, think back. Can you remember anything about the man himself? His height, build, or even the sound of his footsteps?'

Charlotte closed her eyes, strained with the effort of recollection. Her breath hitched as she shook her head. 'No,' she admitted, defeated. 'It all happened so fast, and my senses were overwhelmed with terror.'

Perry clenched his fists, feeling helpless. A part of him wanted to scream, to curse the wretched fiend who'd brought them to this point. But he knew anger would serve no purpose now; they needed to keep their focus if they were going to save Charlotte.

'It will have to be enough to start,' said Perry. 'Stay here with Mr Rook and I'll keep you informed—'

Charlotte grabbed at his arm as he turned to go. 'I'm coming with you, Perry. A mortuary is no place to spend your last hours on earth, and I may remember some details at the scene.'

'Out of the question,' said Perry. 'You'll be recognised, and your fanatics may hamper the investigation, not to mention draw the killer to you when he realises you are not dead.'

'Isn't that what we want?' she said. 'At a place or time of *our* choosing?'

Perry breathed out with resignation. He nodded. 'Until then, you'll need a veil or some disguise—'

Charlotte smiled, her sorrowful face suddenly awash with hope. 'We are standing in an undertaker's Inspector; I'm sure Mr Rook has a most extensive collection.'

CHAPTER FOUR

Dawn stretched its pale, hesitant fingers over the London park, casting a ghostly light on the dew-kissed grass and the gnarled limbs of ancient trees. Shadows clung to the shrubberies, reluctant to cede their territory to the encroaching day. The air was heavy with mist, and Perry's breaths emerged in faint, wispy clouds as he surveyed the scene before him. There was little evidence from his earlier visit in the small hours that such a horrific crime had taken place apart from the trampled grass, muddied and scuffed by many boots. A mournful silence hung over the park, broken only by the distant cawing of crows and the rustle of leaves beneath his boots.

'It was here that I... first felt him upon me,' said Charlotte.

Perry turned to see her shuffle forward, fighting as though repelled by an unseen force. Her once graceful gait was stilted and uneven, a reminder of the vicious attack that had nearly taken her life. She clutched at the loaned, black lace ruff at her neck studded with a cameo of some long-forgotten client of the undertaker's. The matching fascinator and veil shielded her eyes, but he could sense the emotion welling behind them. A young couple came by, offering a good morning. The gentleman hesitated and pointed at the spot in the grass, and the woman on his arm stiffened and pulled him away without a glance at the veiled figure; the most famous woman in London.

'I'm already dead to the world, aren't I?' she mumbled as they disappeared into the distance. 'I'm unseen and can never return to my life.'

'Try not to think about it,' said Perry, awkwardly offering

her his arm and encouraging her past the difficult spot. 'The fountain is some way ahead and we believe he may have been trying to drag you into the lake but was disturbed.'

The world felt suspended between darkness and light as if holding its breath in anticipation of the secrets that would be uncovered. A chill crept down Perry's spine as he walked the gravel path, his eyes scanning the landscape for any sign of disturbance. The ornate drinking fountain stood sentinel at the edge of the path, its once elegant stonework marred by years of neglect. Moss crept over its edges, blurring the intricate carvings of flowers and vines into indistinct shapes – a metaphor for the fading grandeur of the city itself.

As Perry approached the benches lining the path, he couldn't help but feel a sense of unease, as if each empty seat held the spectres of those who had come before him. Their whispered conversations formed a cacophony in his mind, a thousand tragedies and confessions playing out in the half-light. He shook his head, trying to focus on the task at hand.

Creeping along the bushes, Perry surveyed the ground, searching for any hint of the vital clue. The thorny branches clawed at his coat, as though attempting to hold him back from the truth he sought. With every step, his heart thrummed wildly against his ribs, the pressure building within him like steam in a boiling kettle. What would he find? Would it bring justice or damnation, or would it only lead to more questions?

'Inspector,' came Bloom's voice from behind him, breaking through the fog of his thoughts. He turned to see her stooped at the edge of the path, her eyes dark with determination and lines etched deep into her forehead. 'Look there,' she whispered, pointing to a spot near the base of the water fountain. 'Do you see it?'

Perry squinted, his heart leaping into his throat as he spotted a glimmer of gold half-buried in the detritus beneath the public water source. He knelt, reaching at full arm's length to retrieve the precious, in more ways than one, object brushing away dirt and leaves to reveal a cufflink adorned with an intricate emblem. The weight of its significance hung heavily in the air, and Perry knew, without a doubt, that this was the key they had been searching for. Crafted from gold, the surface of the cufflink was meticulously polished, radiating a lustrous glow that caught the dim light with every movement. The border exhibited a subtle motif inspired by the night sky, with tiny stars and delicate swirls intertwined, at the centre of which was an intricately engraved emblem of a star. As Perry held the cufflink, Bloom drew a deep breath, steeling herself to confront the memories of that fateful night. 'It's his. The hands were fluid, almost graceful,' she continued, her gaze distant as she relived the scene.

'Do you recognise the engraving?' Perry asked softly, not wanting to push her too far. 'A patron that followed you, perhaps?'

Bloom hesitated, her brow furrowing in concentration. 'No, and it doesn't look like a family crest.' Her legs began to tremble, the pain from her injuries becoming more pronounced. She gritted her teeth, refusing to show any sign of weakness.

'My thoughts exactly,' Perry said gently, placing a comforting hand on her shoulder. 'Your courage is every bit as remarkable as your performances – here, lean on me.'

'No,' Bloom replied, her voice strained but resolute. 'I can manage; I just keep thinking of the darkness and how still everything was until Rook...'

'Do you want to talk about it?'

Charlotte sighed. 'I can't describe it – like floating in dark water under a moonless sky, but feeling nothing. It was serene, calm, lonely...What if there's nothing after death?'

'Fate is playing its part,' said Perry. 'Who or whatever

comes next has their hands in this, and that is a comforting notion. I have to think that there is some purpose to man's ability to restore life.'

She shook her head in confusion, tucking a stray curl behind her ear. 'But how did Rook discover this power to restore life?'

Perry averted his eyes and cleared his throat; he examined the inconsequential fountain to distract himself while he withheld the full truth. 'Rook found out by accident,' said Perry. 'His wife died from a tumour many years ago. He kissed her goodbye and when he looked back, she was alive again—at least until that day's sunset. I can't imagine how he felt losing her twice on the same day.'

Charlotte glanced away, focussing on a man in the distance sweeping around a gloomy, paint-flaking pavilion. 'How dreadfully sad.'

'He calls it *The Breath* and all those that are revived are blessed, or cursed, by it—' Perry caught and corrected himself, '—while they live.'

Charlotte raised a hand to hide a gasp from escaping her lips. 'Does that mean I can also...'

Perry nodded, sighing quietly before continuing. 'Perhaps.'

'I see now why you brought me back,' said Charlotte. 'Restoring those who have been killed would at least allow them to help catch those who deserve death. It could also give them a chance to say goodbye.'

'And who will you say goodbye to, Miss Bloom?' Perry asked, watching as Charlotte smiled beneath her veil, a glimmer of pearlescent teeth visible between her lips.

'My audience,' she replied in a wistful tone before tenderly squeezing his arm with one hand while pointing out the heavy cufflink hidden in his other fist. 'I forgive you both and I'm just sorry there is nothing we can do to prevent the inevitable. Do not blame yourself for my death; blame him.'

She paused for a moment, taking in a ragged breath as she recited: '*All the world's a stage, and all the men and women merely players; They have their exits and their entrances...*'

Perry stiffened with surprise at her soliloquy, and she withdrew her hand.

'What do we do next?' said Charlotte.

'I need to speak with some of my informants and let Rook and my superiors know of what I've found. I can relay a message via the police box near the main gate.' Perry puffed out his cheeks and tightened the grip on his umbrella. 'Given the time we've got left, I only know of one man that may know conclusively who this belongs to.'

'A jeweller,' asked Charlotte hopefully, 'or a collector?'

'Both,' said Perry clutching at the cufflink so tightly it left the imprint in the smooth skin of his palm, 'in a manner of speaking. The man I know has an in-depth knowledge and appreciation of such items, as well as how to acquire them without payment. His name is Charlie Flynn, and he is one of the most dangerous men in London, especially now that his son was killed in a botched robbery. Perhaps I will be joining you in the afterlife, sooner than I had hoped.'

'Forgive my rash words back at the undertakers,' said Charlotte raising her veil to look him steadfastly in the eye. 'I doubt your courage no longer if that is the only way to discover the killer's identity in time. I marvel you would put your life on the line for someone you barely know.'

'Not just you,' said Perry. 'For the other women, and one in particular whom Rook was attached to.'

Dewdrops glistened on each blade of grass, as the first rays of dawn cast a golden glow over the London park. A gentle mist swirled around the trees, casting eerie shadows that danced upon the damp earth. Perry and Bloom stood at the fountain, their breaths creating puffs of white in the chilly air.

Perry nodded and pursed his lips. 'Please return to Mr Rook and inform him that—'

'Not a chance,' said Charlotte, reaching out her hand to fasten upon his knuckled hand upon the umbrella handle. 'I was not always so privileged, Inspector. My beginnings were humble and hard though I prefer not to draw attention to the fact. I have heard of this man and his reputation. I also know he has some honour regarding women.'

'How so?' said Perry, not wishing to remove the pleasant, warming touch.

'A woman I grew up with, Lilian Fletcher, was raped in one of his gin houses. He did not take kindly to the slur on his reputation and the culprit was never seen again. The substantial contents of his wallet miraculously turned up, anonymously, the day after at her place of work — It enabled her to start again.'

'He has a sense for the chivalric and dramatic,' said Perry. 'I'll give him that, but *violence begets violence*—'

'Titus Andronicus?' said Bloom with a look of surprise. She released her hand, lowering her veil with the approach of a nanny pushing a pram. 'You are versed in the classics, Mr Perry?'

He nodded. 'I prefer Greek over the Bard. I had a privileged upbringing; it seems we meet at the intersection of two opposing pathways through life.'

'My pathway ends at sunset,' she said. 'I'm coming with you. He may only break a few bones if a woman is present, perhaps less than that if I can work my charms.'

'This is no stage act,' said Perry. 'He is astute, intelligent, immune to a woman's wiles, and extremely unpredictable. He's also grieving for the death of his son, somewhat because of the actions of one of our policemen.'

'I think you are more concerned with hiding behind a woman to fulfil your obligation to me. This is the dawn of the twentieth century and your motives are admirable but are constraining – do you not want to live, Mr Perry? I would do anything to see another dawn, clear and bright.'

'Rook warned me of a price to pay for meddling in the natural order of things; I wonder if my life may be the tariff.'

'Why does Mr Rook bring people back, then?'

'He has his reasons,' said Perry. 'Love, vengeance, justice, and grief. Are there no greater motivators on a human soul?'

Charlotte glanced across at the nanny lifting the babe from its satin-padded cocoon and pressing it close to her chest to settle its mewing cries. 'We do anything for the ones we love.' She lowered her veil, resolved.

'Are you certain you want to do this?' Perry asked, his eyes searching Bloom's face for any sign of hesitation. 'This might end up being the shortest investigation in the history of Scotland Yard.'

'We need to know who this cufflink belongs to,' she responded, her voice resolute despite the pain etched in every line of her body. 'I am dead either way.'

'Let me do the talking,' said Perry, 'if we even get that far.'

With slow, determined steps, Bloom led the way out of the park, refusing Perry's offer of support. He followed closely behind, his mind racing with the implications of their conversation.

CHAPTER FIVE

Perry helped Charlotte into a hansom cab, steadying her with a hand on her elbow as she climbed inside. She gritted her teeth against the pain in her legs but made no complaint.

'Wapping Dock,' said Perry.

The cabbie turned to study the fine clothes of his fare. 'You sure, squire?'

'Yes,' replied Charlotte. 'And it's *Inspector*.'

As the carriage rattled over the cobblestones, Perry glanced at her pale, drawn face and the lines of pain around her eyes, veiled but bright. Guilt twisted in his gut—he should never have allowed her to exert herself so soon after her ordeal.

'You need to rest and recover your strength,' he whispered.

Charlotte's lips twitched into a wry smile. 'I'm harder to deter than that, Inspector. But I thank you for your concern.' Her smile faded, and she gazed out the window at the passing streets. After hastily cutting through several side streets, the stench and seagull screeching sounds of the docks heralded their terminus. The cab halted.

'That's as far as I'm willing to go, Inspector or no,' said the cabbie. 'But I'll relay the message to your superior, as per your instructions, on my return.'

They got out, watching the only means of escape trundle away through the crates and baskets of the narrow street. The riverside was a hub for sailors, dockworkers, and various unsavoury characters, contributing to its reputation as a disreputable and dangerous neighbourhood. The narrow alleyways and dimly lit streets of Wapping provided an ideal setting for illicit activities, earning it a place in the dark underbelly of early Edwardian London.

Charlotte stared at him; lips parted in surprise. For once, she seemed at a loss for words.

'This way,' said Perry, ushering her towards a dockside building. He looked about at the tall, overhanging buildings of the wharf to see a figure retreat into the shadows of the run-down upper floor. 'Eyes everywhere; he'll soon learn of our arrival.'

They ventured deeper into the streets between wharves. Perry couldn't help but feel the weight of the unknown bearing down on them. The cut-throughs seemed to close in around him, brick and mortar pressing in like an oppressive force. Charlotte, however, walked with a resolve that was both inspiring and unnerving. Her determination and refusal to be cowed by fear or pain reminded Perry why he had been so captivated by her performances on stage.

The stench of refuse mingled with the damp air, assaulting their senses, and Perry couldn't help but notice the way Charlotte's delicate nose crinkled in response. She pressed her lips together, determination clear in her eyes. They approached the narrow, dimly lit alley that led to a dead end, and the hollow tinkling of a spinning loose bottle on the cobbles caused Perry to pivot. Three men followed, silently, purposefully, and threateningly towards them, herding the nervous sheep before them like a pack of hungry wolves.

'We need to hurry,' said Perry grabbing hold of Charlotte's wrist and pulling her towards the once grand counting house that lay tucked and trapped at the end of the thoroughfare.

The Georgian remnant of a once glorious South Sea bubble drew near, like a stark reflection of the neighbourhood's shady character. Standing weathered and worn amidst the hustle and bustle of the waterfront nearby, Charlie Flynn's nefarious centre of operations exuded an aura of neglect and decay. Its exterior, once vibrant with colour, had faded, leaving behind a patchy façade. The once-bold paint has peeled, revealing layers of exposed brickwork that have succumbed to the corrosive effects of the estuary air. The roof, dotted with missing tiles, sagged in places, burdened by the weight of time while the windows, framed by rotting wooden shutters, bore the scars of countless years, their glass panes cracked or missing, allowing only fragments of light to filter through. Only one floor remained intact, curtained to shut out the world and keep secrets tightly imprisoned within the villainous lair.

They reached the entrance, and, whether by some signal from above or the realisation that they were making for the house of one who should not be crossed, the men behind slowed and turned back to the dock.

Before them, two rough-looking men leaned on their shoulders against the flight of steps leading to a heavily studded, oak door. A towering figure with a muscular build scratched at the patchwork stubble on his misshapen head and stood straight, watching their approach. The weatherbeaten face bore the marks of countless brawls, with a prominent scar running across one cheek. His thick, unkempt beard hid a cunning smirk as he recognised the Inspector, a smile that hinted at a lifetime of mischief and illicit activities. Eyes, set deep within their sockets, gleamed with a mixture of desperation and greed, reflecting a life hardened by the grim realities of survival.

'Is that the welcoming committee?' said Charlotte, her dry humour betraying the sudden necessity to grasp hold of Perry's hand.

'The sweet-looking one on the left is Crooked Jack,' said Perry trying to stay positive. 'Lost most of his voice from a mauling in a dog fight. I've not been acquainted with the second footman on the right.'

The unfamiliar man picked at his tobacco-blackened teeth, scruffy, unkempt hair and oily complexion seemed to match his slippery nature, and his shifty eyes, perpetually darting, betray a constant state of alertness. Crooked Jack whistled to his counterpart and in an instant, the wiry man leapt up the stairs and rapped on the door in a staccato of pre-ordained entry signals. The portal opened, and he slid inside leaving the hulking, arm-folded door warden to step forward.

'You've got some nerve, Perry,' he rasped. 'Today of all days – you'll be at the bottom of the river no matter what apology or compensation you've brought to pacify him.' Jack looked across at the veiled woman with lustful eyes. 'Too bad; he's a religious man, and you aren't his type.'

'I need to speak with him, Jack. Whatever happens after that is down to him.'

The door opened, cutting off the giant's reply. The wiry man returned with a length of heavy chain.

'Boss says he's not to be disturbed, and to send them to Old Father Thames—'

Before Perry had time to think, Charlotte brushed past. 'Tell him the Nightingale of Knightsbridge is here, and that she comes to repay any debt owed by Lilian Fletcher. He once aided her and perhaps he will assist me if his honour means anything anymore. I ask only for the answer to a simple question if your master has the wit to answer it.'

The faces of both men widened with surprise, a vague sense of incredulity and humour mixed with uncertainty. Their hesitation was brief as an upstairs curtain was drawn aside and the sash window was crudely levered open. 'Bring them up,' said a strained, solemn voice, 'and see that Perry is unarmed.'

Jack roughly searched through Perry's coat, ignoring the umbrella, and pushed him up the stairs, ushering the actress forward with a mock bow of platitude. The other man rattled the chain against the rusted railing grinning to reveal his broken teeth as they gained entry to the dark hallway beyond.

A musty scent filled the air, a mix of dampness and industry. The interior was dimly lit, the flickering gas lamps struggling to illuminate the space. Dilapidated wooden floorboards creaked underfoot, carrying the weight of countless footsteps and whispered secrets. Brushed forward under the watchful care of the unorthodox butler, they mounted the stairs. The walls, once adorned with lavish wallpaper, were now stained and peeling, revealing the layers of history that had accumulated over the years. Dark corners and hidden alcoves hinted at clandestine activities that transpired within these walls, serving as a haven for illicit dealings and covert gatherings.

As they entered the cramped, shadow-filled interior of Flynn's counting house, the tension between them grew palpable. Perry clenched his fists, keenly aware of Charlotte's presence beside him, and the weight of the cufflink in his pocket, like a ticking time bomb waiting to be defused. With the gentlest of staccato knocks, Jack opened the door to an Aladdin's Cave of contraband and curiosities.

The room, hidden away from prying eyes, revealed a hidden treasure trove of stolen trinkets and ill-gotten gains. Not just ordinary items of worth, here was a tasteful and well-thought-out assortment of complementary furniture and objets d'art, expertly arranged like an antique doll house.

Charlie Flynn was a criminal. He was also a connoisseur.

The air hung heavy with the scent of aged wood and secrets, infused by rich aromatic and earthy scents of sandalwood and sage. Dim lights from coloured glass oil lamps gave the curtained room an opium den appearance, that cast eerie shadows on the walls. The soft scratching of a gramophone record, having come to its end, crackled from its finely wrought Art Nouveau trumpet as the needle delicately caressed the grooves of the inner vinyl.

In the centre of the room, an ornate chessboard took prominence, its surface adorned with intricate carvings and richly polished wood; the pieces meticulously arranged in a game frozen in time, as if waiting for the next move. The ivory and ebony figures stood in contrast; symbols of the calculated strategies employed by the owner of the room.

Behind the chessboard, a large mahogany desk commanded attention. Its polished surface reflected the dim light, revealing the fine craftsmanship and attention to detail. Piles of documents, letters, and maps littered the desk, evidence of the cunning schemes and elaborate plans that were being hatched within these walls.

Seated behind the desk, a figure dressed impeccably in an old, but finely made, frock coat embodied its master, Charles Malachi Flynn. With slicked-back hair and a well-groomed moustache, his appearance was both a mask of sophistication and authority. But there, behind the veneer of composure, Flynn's grief was palpable. He sat hunched over, his face etched and frozen with sorrow. In his hands, he clutched a buckled pocket watch. Even as they approached, Perry surmised it belonged to his son. The cherished memento, its gold casing glinting in the lamplight, served as a haunting reminder of the irreplaceable loss that had consumed him. As if sensing the inspector's eyes upon the timepiece, Flynn looked up, his face pallid, as if drained of life, with a complexion marked by the signs of relentless torment. Shadows cast by unseen demons danced across its features, lending an eerie and unsettling air. The furrowed brow carried the burden of a sleepless night, knitted tightly together in a perpetual state of anguish.

'I gave him this on his eighteenth birthday, Perry,' said Flynn, his Irish lilt now carrying a mournful and lyrical quality. 'What do you want, blueblood?'

'As a mark of respect from one gentleman to another,' he said, watching as Jack moved to close and stand before the only door to the hoard, 'to offer my condolences for the accident.'

Only a twitch on Flynn's furrowed brow betrayed any sign that he had heard. 'Nobility still has its place in the world.'

He motioned, absently with a hand towards the chessboard. 'He acquired me that Renaissance set, and that accident means I'll never be able to show him the error of his ways.' Perry glanced over at the pieces, familiar with the position but noting a risky strategy he had rarely seen.

'An aggressive variation on the Sicilian defence,' said Perry. 'Your son had a keen mind.'

'I've heard you are somewhat of a player,' said Flynn. 'But his game is lost despite having the centre ground. When you are alone and unprotected, the end can come as no surprise. Black's game is over, as is my son.'

'You underestimate him,' said Perry indicating towards the seat of the chessboard with the tip of his umbrella. 'Checkmate in six moves.'

Flynn flinched with the first outward sign of emotion, getting up and seating himself in the opposite chair. 'Show me, but if you are wrong, then your end will coincide with the fall of your king.'

Laying the umbrella upon his lap, Perry sat and examined the board at length, probing the moves and doubting his initial assessment. The first few moves seemed risky, but all led to a distraction that would position black to an unavoidable win, providing white's next move played into his hands. Briefly, Perry worried that revealing the checkmate would make his opponent resist any obvious move; at which point both the game and his life would be over.

Flynn held out his hand and hovered over his white bishop, maintaining eye contact throughout. Perry stared back, poker-faced but churning inside at the high stakes.

'*Go on*,' he said to himself. '*Take my knight; it's the strongest move...*'

The exchange happened quickly and smoothly, and Perry's hands shook as he brought out his queen. Flynn probed at the board, uncertain as to his opponent's sudden confidence, seeking any error, but blind to the trap already closing around his king. Perry's unorthodox play, four moves later, revealed the inescapable truth.

'Very astute,' he said diplomatically as both men rose without shaking hands. 'You have my attention, now why are you here?' Flynn returned to the pocket watch and caressed the crumpled object as though summoning a genie. All three wishes would be the same.

Perry reached slowly into his pocket under the watchful eye of the brute behind, tossing the cufflink onto the table. It came to rest, clinking alongside the mangled watch. 'I need to know who this belongs to.'

Time seemed to stand still as Charlie Flynn's thoughts engulfed him. His eyes fixated on the golden object for barely a moment before he replied.

'Why do you ask when you know the answer? It appears our little throat choker got careless last night.'

'You know who this man is?' said Charlotte from behind her veil.

'It's my job to know everything, my dear,' said Flynn, turning towards her for the first time. He leaned back in his chair with an air of nonchalance. His dark eyes flicked between them, taking in their anxious expressions. 'Before me stand two charlatans – the first is the son of a disgraced Lord, masquerading as one of the working classes, on a death wish with the second, a femme fatal impersonating a dead actress.' He rose sharply, slamming his fist into the green-leathered surface of the desk sending the cufflink flying once more. Like a tempest, he swept his arms across the table until he seethed and tightened his fists to gain control. 'And my son; dead...'

'The Shadow Strangler has no worth to you, Flynn,' said Perry, breathing easier after the tirade. He released his grip on the umbrella handle. 'Why do you protect the identity of such a man?'

'Because fear is good for business, and not only do I benefit from increasingly large payments to look the other way, but this powerful man isn't to be crossed even by one such as I. Divulging such information could be... detrimental to my operations, and my well-being.'

'So you would have him murder more innocent women, Mr Flynn?' said Charlotte. 'Lilian was wrong about you.'

'Lilian Fletcher was a prostitute, young lady, and no one damages my stock.' Flynn peered intently trying to pierce her veil. 'Did she not tell you or perhaps you heard it from the real Charlotte Bloom?' He spat into his hands and made a sign of the cross. 'What a charade; impersonating a dead woman is a trick not even I would stoop to. the only question I have is – why?'

Charlotte looked away.

'What makes you think Charlotte Bloom is dead?' said Perry.

Flynn gave a look of injured pride. 'London is yours by day, Inspector, but by night it is mine. I had footpads and informants following our mutual friend and they arrived soon after he had finished having his wicked—'

'Enough! said Perry, determined to head off the cruel details. 'What do you want for the information – my head?'

'I have that already, Thomas Perry. I have allowed you access to my little piece of Xanadu but I can't allow either of you to leave. An eye for an eye, Inspector.'

'Wait—' cried Perry, hearing the steps of the henchman behind. His hands clicked at the hidden device on the umbrella handle, ready to be drawn.

Flynn turned and walked over to reset the tonearm on the gramophone. The needle engaged after skipping the first few grooves. The sound of a woman's operatic performance broke the chilling silence, reverberating against the walls, each soaring note filling the space.

Above the grandeur of the aria, Flynn moved over to the chessboard and placed the protected black queen into the game's final position against the white king. 'Checkmate,' he said glancing up. 'Jack – send his head to that fool, Gregory, if that is what the good inspector wishes, and inform our contact in Istanbul that I'll be sending a new acquisition for his markets in Arabia.'

CHAPTER SIX

Perry spun round to face the giant approaching with slow relish to do his master's bidding. He could see that in Jack's eyes, this wasn't work; it was pleasure.

With one hand on the handle, and another on the stem of the umbrella, Perry prepared to draw the hidden blade and fight his way out. Crooked Jack reacted first, recoiling in confusion to the sound of another's voice joining the high arcs and valleys of the gramophone soprano. Beside them, Charlotte had hesitated for only a moment, with self-preservation forefront in her mind, before she pulled back her veil and began to sing along, her clear voice melding seamlessly and with familiarity with the recording. Perry could not deny that the melody was hauntingly beautiful, but it sent a shiver down his spine as he watched Charlotte pour her soul into each note permeating the walls of the room with a sweetness the old building had never experienced. Perry's arm held out the umbrella keeping the brute at bay as he cast a glance toward the incredulous and enraptured Flynn.

The gangster's eyes widened in shock as he listened, his gaze flickering between the gramophone and the apparent doppelganger before him. Doubt clouded his features, yet he could not deny the evidence of his ears. The room seemed to hold its breath as the song reached its crescendo, the two voices blending until they were indistinguishable from one another. As the last note faded away, the crackle reappeared like a spark of electricity. Perry felt the tension hanging heavy in the air, wondering if it would be enough to sway him. It was the actress who broke the silence once more.

'Yes, Mr Flynn. You have the Nightingale in your nest, and I should be flattered you have my recording. At the very least, I know the man who will sell me into slavery was a cultured scoundrel and I offer this final performance in memory of what you did for Lilian Fletcher, as promised outside at your door. Still not convinced?' Charlotte asked, her voice barely audible over the hiss of the gramophone. She turned to face him, her green eyes locked onto his as she revealed the livid watch chain marks encircling her slender neck. Her fingers traced the pattern of bruised flesh, and Perry winced at the raw vulnerability on display.

'By all the saints—,' Flynn muttered, his gaze fixed on the angry marks that marred Charlotte's throat before crossing himself instinctively and glancing across at an ornate silver crucifix on the wall. 'I was told you were dead by one whose words I trust the most...'

'Your information is correct,' she whispered, swallowing hard against the pain. 'But here we are. I need your help, Mr Flynn, and time is precious to me.'

Perry watched as Flynn studied the marks on her neck, his eyes narrowed in thought. He knew the criminal was no stranger to violence, but even he seemed shaken by the sight of Charlotte's injuries. It was a stark reminder of the brutality that had claimed her life, and Perry couldn't help but feel a surge of protectiveness towards the woman who had defied death itself.

Flynn strode towards the corner of the dimly lit room, shaking as he opened a small, lacquered cigar box; trembling to light the fragrant rolled leaf. He fidgeted, striving for mastery over his emotions, and wandered over to the far wall, a cloud of fragrant smoke trailing him like an ominous shadow. Perry's eyes followed him, noting the tension in his broad shoulders as he moved. Charlotte stood tall, her green eyes flashing like emeralds under the flickering gas lamps. She was determined to prove herself, and Perry couldn't help but admire her tenacity.

'After the man who strangled you finished his perversions,' he said spitting distastefully into a brass spittoon, 'Your belongings were brought to me.'

'You have my purse?'

'If you truly are the real Charlotte Bloom returned from death,' said Flynn staring her bluntly in the eye, 'and I assure you no women still living could have endured what that man did to you, then identify what we took from you,' Flynn commanded, flinging open the lid of a large, battered trunk with a heavy thud and kicking it over to spill the sentimental and precious items onto a lion-skinned rug. He gestured for Charlotte to come closer, his expression cold and unreadable. He lifted a letter opener, its sharp point sifting through the jetsam of missing and stolen items like the beak of a seagull rifling through the seaweed covering a rotting shoreline meal. 'Choose wisely; I'll cut your throat using those marks around your neck as a guide if you fail. Stay where you are Perry...'

As Charlotte approached, Perry lowered his arm and saw that the trunk was filled with an array of stolen purses – some beaded, others embroidered, many rendered in supple leather or sumptuous velvet. The colours varied from rich jewel tones to soft pastels, and each purse seemed more exquisite than the last.

Perry's heart pounded against his ribcage as he watched Charlotte carefully examine the contents of the trunk. He knew how much was at stake — not just for her, but for them both.

Charlotte's slender fingers hovered over the assortment of purses, her brow furrowed in concentration. After several tense moments, she plucked a sequined purse from the depths of the pile, its glistening beads shimmering like stars against the darkness.

'This is mine,' Charlotte declared, clutching the expensive accessory tightly in her hand. 'Inside, you will find my pomander, several calling cards including my own, and a small silver locket sent to me by an admirer.'

'Open it,' Flynn demanded, his voice laced with scepticism.

Charlotte complied, revealing the items she had described into her steady palm. Perry breathed a sigh of relief as Flynn stared at the evidence, his eyes betraying a flicker of uncertainty. He forcefully flicked the sharp blade into the pile where it wobbled momentarily like a cheap imitation of Excalibur. Flynn's doubt began to dissolve, replaced by a reluctant curiosity that bordered on fear.

'Alright,' Flynn said at last, his voice gruff with reluctant acceptance. 'I believe you're Charlotte Bloom. But that doesn't change anything. I still can't help you.'

'Can't or won't?' Charlotte challenged, her eyes blazing with determination as she held his gaze, daring him to look away.

'Both,' Flynn admitted, his expression unreadable. 'But mostly won't. I'm sorry — I have too much at stake. My life, my operation... Our mutual friend has a rather distasteful cabinet of curiosities in his upstairs London apartment. Consider yourself lucky that a trophy from you has not been collected and enshrined in the depths of his private sanctuary, accessible only through an antique floor-length mirror. Don't push your luck by digging too deep into this man's affairs — if you value your life, then you'll move on and leave well enough alone. I'm sorry, but there's nothing you can do to change my mind.'

'Nothing?' Charlotte's voice was barely a whisper, but it carried the weight of a thousand promises. 'What about your son?'

'Charlotte!' Perry hissed, barely able to contain his horror at her audacious offer.

'Colm Flynn,' she continued, ignoring Perry's protestations. 'I know he died last night, and I know you want him back alive above all else in this and every thieving room you own. I can arrange that for you.'

Flynn stared at Charlotte in disbelief, his face a mask of conflicted emotions as he weighed the impossible possibility. Perry tried once more to reason with her. 'Colm suffered terrible injuries,' he warned, hoping to impress upon them the enormity of what she was contemplating. 'This isn't an option.'

'Anything is better than being dead,' Flynn growled, his desire for his son's return overriding any lingering doubts.

'Tell me the name of my killer,' Charlotte implored, her voice cracking with emotion, 'and your son will be returned to you, alive as I stand witness. I make no guarantees of his condition.'

Flynn growled, his eyes narrowing dangerously. 'Perhaps I'll make you do what you propose instead; I am not a man to be toyed or bargained with.'

'After he killed me, he did something unspeakable,' Charlotte replied, her voice trembling as she spoke. She looked down, her hand instinctively moving to her aching legs and groin. 'I know he desecrated my body. I'll suffer the same again rather than comply if you force me, but I can and will restore your boy. You have my word on both accounts.'

Perry felt a mixture of rage and sorrow surge within him

at Charlotte's words, and he clenched his fists tightly to keep from lashing out. The room seemed to close in around them, the air heavy with grief and anger. He studied Flynn's conflicted expression, and a heavy silence filled the room as they each weighed their options. He knew Flynn wasn't a man easily swayed, but Charlotte was determined to stand her ground.

Perry felt a knot forming in the pit of his stomach. He knew the moral implications of what Charlotte was suggesting, and he couldn't help but feel uneasy at the thought of tampering with life and death. Yet, he too yearned for justice for Charlotte and the other victims.

'Charlotte, this is not a decision to be made lightly,' he warned her softly. But she remained steadfast in her conviction.

Flynn's gaze bore into Charlotte, weighing her words and gauging her sincerity. After what felt like an eternity, he spoke. 'If you can truly bring my son back... then yes, I will give you the name you seek, but I advise that justice must be swift, or we are all dead men. He is slippery as an eel and has many important officials and politicians in his pay; even if you arrest and charge him, he will go free.'

'Flynn,' Perry said, struggling with his own inner turmoil, 'you must know this path we're about to take is dangerous and unnatural. I am not above the law, even if you are.'

'Sometimes, Detective, one must embrace the darkness to find the light,' Flynn replied solemnly. 'For my son, I would do anything, and risk is part of life.'

In the dimly lit room, filled with the scent of old leather and lingering cigar smoke, Perry couldn't help but question his moral compass. As they stood on the precipice of forbidden knowledge and unspeakable acts, the line between right and wrong had never seemed so blurred.

Charlotte held her breath, awaiting Flynn's response to

her offer. Perry could feel his heart pounding against his ribcage, the blood roaring in his ears, a testament to the gravity of the decision they were about to make.

'Flynn,' Perry interjected, unable to contain his doubts any longer. 'You cannot consider this. Colm's injuries were... severe. It wouldn't be right.'

'Who are you to tell me what's right for my son?' Flynn snapped, anger radiating from him like heat from a fire. The cigar smouldered along with the maddening hope in his eyes. 'You think I don't know what happened to him? That I haven't seen his broken body before it was taken away to be prepared?'

Perry looked away, his chest tightening with guilt and sympathy. He knew Flynn's pain all too well – the agony of losing a loved one, the desperate longing to bring them back. But he also understood the dangers of meddling with forces beyond their understanding.

'Flynn, please,' he implored. 'I know you want your son back, but at what cost?'

'Any cost,' Flynn said fiercely, his jaw clenched. 'If there's even a chance, I have to take it.'

'Then you agree to my terms?' Charlotte asked, her voice steady despite the tension that permeated the room. 'You'll give us the name we seek and let Detective Perry and I go free?'

Flynn hesitated, his eyes flicking between Charlotte and Perry as though weighing the price of his son's life against their own. The silence stretched on, each second ticking away like a countdown.

'Time is running out,' Charlotte reminded him gently, and Perry saw the resolve in her eyes – the determination to see justice done, no matter the consequences.

'What has time got to do with it?' Flynn asked suspiciously.

Perry stepped forward, shielding Charlotte's hesitant reply. 'Because Miss Bloom needs to return to her public as soon as possible and I need to ensure he doesn't kill again.'

'He won't do so in a hurry,' said Flynn. 'He always takes a brief trip abroad to cool his heels.'

'He's already left London?' cried Charlotte, gripping onto Perry's arm.

'Not yet,' said Flynn. The chimes of an exquisite grandfather clock marked eleven o'clock. 'But he'll be on his way to Dover just now.'

'Please,' said Charlotte, falling to her knees. 'His name for your son.'

'Fine,' Flynn relented, his voice strained with emotion. 'I agree to your terms, but if you fail,' Flynn warned, his gaze hardening once more, 'there will be nowhere on this earth where you can hide from me, or him.'

'Understood,' Charlotte said, nodding solemnly as she was helped back to her feet.

Perry could only watch the exchange, his mind a whirlwind of conflicting emotions. He knew they were treading a dangerous path, one that might very well lead them all to ruin. Yet as he looked into Charlotte's determined eyes, he couldn't help but feel a flicker of hope that perhaps, just perhaps, they might find the justice they so desperately sought. What came after rumbled in his thoughts like a distant sound of thunder.

'Before we go any further,' Perry interjected, his voice firm and unwavering, 'I demand to know the name of the killer. I will not proceed until we have that information. You have Miss Bloom's assurances, and you have mine.'

A tense silence filled the room as Flynn's eyes narrowed, studying Perry for a long moment before finally speaking. 'Very well,' he conceded. 'The man you're looking for is Lord William Rees.'

'Lord Kempton?' The name struck Perry like a blow to the stomach, making it difficult to breathe. Lord Kempton – a man he had been warned not to investigate, a man with enough power and influence to corrupt even the most steadfast of officials. The thought of confronting him sent an icy chill down Perry's spine, but he knew there was no other choice.

'Where can we find him?' Charlotte asked, her voice steady despite the gravity of the situation.

'Kempton isn't at home,' Flynn said, a bitter edge to his tone. 'Word is, he's on his way to France this morning. I have men at the ports, but it will take days to receive his whereabouts at this late stage.'

Perry clenched his fists, feeling the anger coil within him, hotter than ever. The injustice of it all threatened to consume him, but he forced himself to focus on the task at hand. They were racing against time, and he couldn't afford to let his emotions get the better of him.

'We need to stop him before he leaves the country,' Charlotte insisted, her eyes filled with determination.

'Agreed,' Perry replied, his mind already working through potential strategies. 'But how do we lure him back?'

'Leave that to me,' Charlotte said, her voice laced with confidence despite the mounting pressure. 'You say that word of my death is already circulating. Couple that with news of a final performance from the Nightingale of Knightsbridge this afternoon and it will cause speculation the like of which the West End has never seen. Rumours travel faster than cholera in London and word may reach him before he sails.'

As Perry considered Charlotte's plan, he couldn't help but feel a gnawing unease in the pit of his stomach. The stakes were high, and there was no room for error. He glanced around the room, taking in the flicker of candlelight casting shadows on the walls, the glint of steel hidden within Flynn's gaze, and the unwavering determination in Charlotte's eyes.

'Very well,' Perry agreed reluctantly, though doubt gnawed at the edges of his mind. They were playing a dangerous game, one that toyed with forces far beyond their control. But what choice did they have? He felt the weight of the decision press down upon him. They were delving into dangerous territory, meddling with life and death in pursuit of justice, and he couldn't shake the feeling that there would be consequences beyond anything they could imagine. Perry rubbed a hand over his weary eyes. He could see Flynn watching them, the man's expression wavering between disbelief and desperate hope. It was unnerving, and he couldn't help but wonder if they were truly doing the right thing.

'Alright,' Perry conceded, turning his attention back to Charlotte. 'But how do we ensure the news reaches him before he leaves for France?'

'I have contacts,' she replied, her emerald eyes shining with determination. 'I have friends in the newspapers and other places who will help get the word out.'

'It might not be enough,' said Perry turning to face the gangster puffing on the remnants of his cigar. 'It's time that is her enemy, Flynn. Our intelligence says you and your operation have two hundred men, but I'm willing to bet it's closer to five hundred.'

Flynn stubbed out the cigar and raised an eyebrow in mock amusement. 'You have no idea, Inspector. What are you proposing I do with my hard-working employees?'

'Put them to honest work and populate every gin and ale house across this city in three hours, as well as telegraph your men at the port. Spread the news that Miss Bloom's matinee performance will be her last.'

Charlotte glanced across at the gramophone. 'I will be... retiring from the theatre after that.'

Flynn stroked his moustache, checking their faces for any deception. 'If I ever see either of you again within a mile of here, then you will both retire, permanently.' He withdrew the letter opener from the purse pile and hooked the tip of the blade through the ring of the cufflink before tossing it into Perry's waiting hand.

'Now go and restore my son to me.'

CHAPTER SEVEN

'That was some performance,' said Perry as he watched the outside world go by in the cab. Charlotte remained still beside him, engrossed in a newspaper they had picked up from a vendor in Whitechapel. A brief stop at her elegant townhouse to collect a few personal items and change into a new set of clothes was all that Perry would allow before they continued their journey.

'Perhaps a lifetime of stage fright had prepared me for that moment. I confess my insides were somewhat at odds with my outward appearance. It seems rumours of my death did not make the early edition.'

'I call it bravery,' said Perry, 'but I still think the price may be too high – what you are about to do may set off unforeseen consequences.'

'You have the name of the killer, so you had best make the best use of it,' she said, steadying herself as the cab rode a pothole. 'After I return to the undertaker's, my unpleasant part is over, and what happens at sunset with Flynn becomes your problem. In the meantime, it is up to you to apprehend him before or during my last performance.'

'You still mean to go on?' said Perry turning to see her resolved face. 'That, Miss Bloom, is bravery.'

'I do. It's all I ever wanted, and I hope that I have time for one final encore.' She pointed to a line in The Times newspaper. 'I know the exact moment I will die – sunset is eight minutes past five o'clock this evening.'

Perry struggled internally; he had the information which could bring her life back, but how could he tell her there was still hope?

But at what cost to justice and the others whom Lord Kempton had cruelly taken? There was also the problem of having the Nightingale alive and seemingly without a murder victim from the night before. He looked long at her before she glanced away to see a crowd gathering around a young boy rapidly distributing pamphlets. In the short time in her presence, Perry had grown in admiration for the woman herself, and not the actress, distant and out of reach on a stage far away. His resolve wavered.

'Charlotte, there's something...'

At that moment, the cab slowed, allowing a large horse-drawn wagon to pull into the street. A small hand thrust a crudely printed pamphlet through the window. 'News travels quickly when you know the right people,' she said, handing him the flyer for her final career performance. 'Let's hope it reaches Kempton before he scurries off to France and escapes justice. I'm sorry, you were saying?'

The cab jolted forward with an apology from the driver, causing Perry's umbrella to slip out of his hand. Whether he had been gripping it and its secret latch too firmly or not, the blade became free—much to Charlotte's surprise.

'You are full of secrets Mr Perry,' she said.

Perry's indecision passed, and he clicked the dagger back into its unassuming sheath. 'I meant to say that I think you should have this, as a last means of defence, in case you are in danger. It was my father's, but I would like you to have it.'

She frowned, turning the object in her hand. 'Swordplay is

not my strong point, Inspector – don't forget your promise to meet me at the theatre should Kempton remain at large.'

'Yes,' said Perry indicating for the driver to stop. 'I'll send word either way and we'll have men to protect you.' He opened the door to get out. 'Tell Mr Rook to meet me there at three o'clock and to escort you to the theatre.' The corners of his mouth wavered as he avoided her gaze during their parting. 'Forgive me...'

'You did what you thought was right, Mr Perry. Never lose sight of that — *We are such things as dreams are made on...*'

He nodded, mutely unable to speak up and argue with her interpretation of events or his words. With a gentle squeeze, she released her fingers from his grasp.

'Find Lord Kempton and bring him to justice, for me.'

The clock struck noon as Perry stood in Superintendent Gregory's office, bathed in the weak light that filtered through the grimy window. The room was thick with tension, and the acrid scent of burnt tobacco still lingered from Gregory's last smoke. Perry stood before Superintendent Gregory's desk, his hands clasped behind his back to conceal their trembling.

'This is preposterous,' Gregory thundered. 'Lord Kempton is a nasty piece of work, admittedly, but he is a respected member of the aristocracy. We have no evidence to suggest he was involved, and you've been warned before about pursuing him.'

Perry gritted his teeth. His nails dug into his palms. 'The cufflink–'

'How do you know it belongs to Kempton?' Gregory snapped.

'He was at the theatre last night, near the park where the body was discovered.'

'Half the glitterati frequent that theatre, and most of the scum that infests the city after dark prowl the surrounding park.' Gregory frowned, but there was concern in his eyes. 'You're walking a dangerous line, Perry. You've been warned before about pursuing the man. What makes you so certain this belongs to Lord Kempton?'

Gregory leaned forward, his eyes glinting with suspicion. 'Well? Out with it, man.'

Perry hesitated, swallowing hard before confessing, 'I visited Charlie Flynn at Wapping Dock.'

'Flynn?' Gregory's incredulity morphed into anger, his face reddening. 'You went to see that man and lived to tell the tale? Do you have a death wish, Perry?'

Perry bristled at the mention of Flynn, knowing full well that he had put himself in grave danger by speaking with him. He felt an icy knot tighten in his stomach as he recalled their encounter, but he kept his face impassive.

'Sir, I had no choice given the urgency,' Perry defended himself, though he couldn't dispel the unease coiling in his gut. 'He confirmed the cufflink belonged to Kempton, and you know his knowledge is unsurpassed in these matters. Flynn says there is a secret room behind a floor-length mirror in his apartment—'

'Even if you could prove he was at the murder scene, what witnesses will come forward to testify against him?' Gregory asked, rubbing a hand across his furrowed brow. 'We cannot rely solely on the testimony of Charlie Flynn, and I need evidence to go searching an aristocrat's property.'

'Surely, that's enough to bring him in for questioning?'

'Questioning!' Gregory snorted. 'As if he would deign to answer any question we put to him. Can you imagine the pressure I would be under trying to get approval for that? Meanwhile, you've left yourself in Flynn's debt, and for what?'

'For justice,' Perry said through gritted teeth. The same words he'd told himself to justify this devil's bargain. But in the face of Gregory's anger, they rang hollow.

'There will be no justice here.' Gregory stabbed a finger at him. 'Not if you're fool enough to trust the word of Charlie Flynn. This is flimsy evidence built on personal prejudice.'

Perry's jaw clenched. His pulse thrummed in his temples. Kempton's smirking face seemed to float in his vision.

'You're too close to this case,' Gregory said, his tone softening. 'I know Kempton's grandfather played a part in the ruination of your family by extending credit to a habitual gambler, but you can't let that cloud your judgement. We need solid evidence and credible witnesses, neither of which we have.'

'The murders fit Kempton's motive and method,' Perry insisted. 'He believes he's entitled to anything – or anyone — he desires. Including women's lives; you saw what he did to that young model—'

'*Allegedly*, Perry. The rest of your argument is conjecture,' Gregory said. 'Not proof. I'm warning you, Perry, drop this vendetta before it destroys your career – or gets you killed.'

Perry's jaw tightened, his eyes narrowing at the insinuation. 'This isn't personal, sir. This is about justice.'

'Is it?' Gregory raised an eyebrow sceptically. 'Even if we were to arrest him, who would testify against Lord Kempton? Do you truly believe witnesses would risk their own lives and reputations to come forward?'

'If you don't believe me, then at least give me men to guard Charlotte Bloom; she fits the profile of those murdered by the Shadow Strangler,' Perry argued, his voice strained. 'I believe she may be at risk.'

'Charlotte Bloom?' Gregory scoffed. 'The same woman

who is alive and performing this very afternoon after your blundering misidentification of the murder victim last night? Have you lost your touch, Perry?'

'No, sir,' Perry said through gritted teeth, doing his best to suppress the turmoil within. 'It appears I was mistaken in that regard.' He clenched his fists at his sides, the heat of his determination radiating through his veins.

Perry knew better than to reveal the secret of Charlotte's revival. The threat of being dismissed as mad or incompetent hung heavy over him, a noose tightening around his neck. Instead, he ploughed forward with his case.

'If Lord Kempton is the Shadow Strangler, we can't allow him to harm anyone else.'

'Resources are tight, Perry,' Gregory replied with a dismissive wave of his hand. 'We cannot spare the manpower for what may be a wild goose chase. Charlotte Bloom is the most famous woman in London, she's surrounded by—'

'Please, sir,' Perry pleaded, frustration and desperation weaving through his voice. 'I know I'm right about this.'

Perry stared at his superior, his nails biting into his palms. He would not – could not – rest until justice was served. Kempton had to pay for his crimes, even if Perry had to overstep the line to make it so.

'Your part in this case is over,' Gregory said. 'Now get out of my sight before I dismiss you for good.'

Perry inclined his head. 'Yes, sir.'

He turned on his heel and strode from the room, his jaw set in grim determination. Kempton would slip through his fingers again unless Perry took matters into his own hands. The law had failed. Now it was up to him alone.

CHAPTER EIGHT

An undercurrent of dread pulsed through Perry's veins as the opulent theatre bustled with anticipation. He felt the weight of the air, thick with perfumed scents and stifling suspense. The stage loomed ahead, a grand canvas adorned by gold trimmings and crimson drapes that seemed to hold an otherworldly power.

The theatre was full, every seat taken, every standing place crammed with spectators. An electric current of excitement hummed through the crowd—this was to be Charlotte Bloom's final performance and London had turned out to experience it.

Perry's gaze swept over the West End theatre, taking in its sumptuous interior. It was a place where opulence dripped from every corner: the gilded ceiling and plush red velvet curtains that framed the stage, the intricately carved balconies adorned with flickering gaslights casting shadows upon the eager crowd below. The air hummed with anticipation, the murmurs of the capacity crowd melding into a cacophony of excitement as they awaited the Nightingale of Knightsbridge's last flight.

Perry stood in the shadows, watching the audience file into the theatre. Their excited chatter and the rustle of silk skirts echoed off the gilded walls. He glanced at Rook, who stood rigid as a board, jaw clenched. They both knew what was at stake. Once the final curtain fell, Charlotte's fate would be sealed.

Perry scanned the theatre, searching for any sign of Kempton. The aristocrat's private box, draped in crimson velvet, stood empty. His gaze continued roving, combing the stalls, the dress circle, and the upper boxes. Still no trace.

Rook turned to him, eyes hollow. 'We were fools to think

we could outwit him before sunset. He either hasn't heard or fears a trap.'

Perry grimaced, swallowing against the bile rising in his throat. 'There's still time. We must keep watch and be ready to act the moment he reveals himself. His curiosity and fear of being discovered will drive him to attend; I'm sure of it.'

'And if he does not?' Rook's voice was barely more than a whisper. 'What then?'

Perry ground his teeth, fighting back the urge to slam his fist into the wall. The thought of Charlotte dying tonight, her light snuffed out forever, made his chest ache as if his heart were being crushed. He thought about her last words to him.

'I'll get him,' said Perry. 'Whatever the cost.'

Rook grimaced and clutched at his stomach.

'You didn't have to come tonight, after what you did for Charlotte,' said Perry. Reviving Colm Flynn, even for a few hours, had been a distasteful necessity. The memory of the past few hours still haunted Rook's mind.

'His injuries... they were unbearable,' Rook admitted, swallowing hard. 'It was the most difficult thing I've ever done to lay lips upon that wax mask. His men trembled with fear when they took him away, horrified by what we had done.'

'It was noble of you to spare her the trauma of restoring Flynn's son.'

'Perhaps, but I did it for her, but also for Mary Webster,' Rook replied, his gaze solemn as he looked at the Inspector. 'I couldn't bear the thought of Miss Bloom seeing him like that.'

'Indeed,' Perry agreed checking his watch. 'But at least he'll be dead soon. A slight consolation, wouldn't you say?'

'Perhaps,' Rook continued, his voice barely audible over the thrum of the crowd. 'But there will be consequences for our actions. We cannot escape them.'

The house lights dimmed, and the orchestra began the overture. Perry stood motionless in the shadows, every sense strained, waiting. Watching.

As the lights dimmed and the music began, Perry and Rook moved side stage, catching Charlotte's eye as she prepared to step into the limelight for the last time. Perry's heart leapt as Charlotte emerged, a vision in crimson silk—radiant, enchanting, undaunted; her neck clothed in a matching scarf. She carried his father's umbrella, gripping its handle for comfort as her gaze searched Perry's face, seeking reassurance that Lord Kempton had been apprehended, but all he could do was shake his head. Hope drained from her expression, replaced by a deep sorrow that etched itself into her features. She had only hours left to live.

She might die on stage, and for a moment Perry felt the full force of his guilt - withholding the information that could save her life if only Kempton was present. It was too late to explain.

The seconds trickled by, slow as molasses. The hairs on the back of his neck prickled. His hand slid into his coat, fingers closing around the familiar grip of his revolver.

'Thomas,' Rook replied, his eyes never leaving Charlotte's form on stage. 'We've done what we could. It's out of our hands now.'

Perry clenched his fists, a knot of frustration tight in his chest. He turned his gaze towards the empty box that Lord Kempton often occupied, feeling the weight of failure descend upon him. 'She'll die before seeing him arrested,' he murmured, the words bitter on his tongue.

'Even so,' Rook said softly. 'She'll have left her mark on this world. And perhaps, in her own way, she will have bested him.'

As the curtain rose, Charlotte Bloom stepped forward, a vision of poise and grace. She held the silver-handled umbrella in one hand, its glistening surface catching the dim light as she opened and lifted it above her head. She began to sing.

It was a song about rain. Perry looked around the auditorium to see eyes glistening with tears, weeping like the clouds mourning for the memory of the sun that would never shine again.

CHAPTER NINE

'Where are you?' Perry murmured as the latest recital ended. *'She has less than twenty minutes...'*

His gaze fell on the vacant seat that Lord Kempton usually occupied, reminding him of his unfulfilled promise to Charlotte and the fact that she would pass away without witnessing her oppressor arrested or accused. At that moment, Perry realised the magnitude of his actions and the profound impact it had on the lives of those around him. With each note sung, he felt the weight of his decisions, knowing that their consequences would haunt him long after the curtain fell on that fateful eve.

Charlotte closed her eyes, losing herself in the swell of strings and the melody of her next bittersweet song. She emerged, pale and beautiful in the glow of the footlights, and for a moment her gaze found his. Perry shook his head, a bitter ache forming in his chest at the conflict of sorrow in her eyes and delight in her home on the stage. He had failed her, but the show had to go on.

The music swelled as the actress moved into the light, shadows fleeing before her. At that moment, she seemed almost unearthly, as ephemeral as the notes echoing through the theatre. An angel destined to fade with the coming of dusk.

Charlotte glided across the stage, every gesture graceful and poised, brushing aside flowers and tributes prematurely strewn across the stage as though drifting through a wild-meadow in a May she would never see. Her voice was warm honey as she sang of lost love and longing, the notes resonating through Perry's chest. He closed his eyes, letting the swell of music wash over him, trying to commit each tremor and trill to memory. The performance of both their lifetimes.

Perry's heart thundered in his chest, the pulse echoing in his ears as he stood side-stage with Rook. Shadows danced across the theatre walls, cast by flickering gaslights that struggled to illuminate the grand velvet curtains and gilt detailing of the opulent space. The audience murmured amongst themselves, whispers and laughter melding into a symphony of appreciation.

Charlotte commanded the stage, her fiery red hair catching the light like a halo around her porcelain face. As she began each recital, her melodious voice soared, captivating the auditorium. Perry's breath caught; it was as if she were an otherworldly apparition, destined for greatness or doom. He wondered what he would do if she died on stage... His heart pounded in time with the percussion as Charlotte sang and spun across the stage.

There. A flash of golden hair in the theatre box to the right. Perry gripped the worn velvet curtain, his knuckles turning white. Lord Kempton gazed at the stage, a confused and uncertain pursing about his lips.

A sharp intake of breath beside him. Rook had seen him, too. Perry's fingers tightened into his palm, wishing for the silver handle of his umbrella and its hidden blade. One swift throw across the stage, straight through Kempton's black heart. It would have been some kind of justice...

No. He took a deep breath, steadying himself. Kempton would not escape the hangman's noose so easily.

The aristocrat sat, fidgeting with his hands resting upon the plush velvet railing of his box to the upper right of the stage, trying to process what his senses were experiencing. His cheeks flushed and his eyes were wide with surprise, betraying his normally composed facade. For a moment, he reached for his pocket watch, fingering the chain as though to settle his nerves.

Charlotte's gaze locked onto the aristocrat, and her voice faltered. Time seemed to slow as she reached up, drew back the scarf, and brushed aside her hair, revealing the ghastly scar on her neck – a permanent reminder of the watch chain that had once been wrapped tightly around it. The orchestra stumbled to a halt, and the audience erupted in hushed whispers.

Taking advantage of the sudden silence, Charlotte's voice filled the room once more, this time unaccompanied. It was a song about a murdered lover, the eerie melody floating through the air like a ghostly lament, her eyes never leaving the nobleman's box. Panic flickered across his face, the implications of her song unmistakable. The Nightingale's voice echoed through the theatre, the audience sat spellbound, their expressions a mix of shock and awe. Some glanced nervously at Lord Kempton, whose panic-stricken face suggested some unrevealed guilt. Sweat beaded on his brow, and he clenched the railing of the theatre box so tightly his knuckles turned white.

Perry felt a growing sense of dread in the pit of his stomach. He couldn't tear his eyes away from the spectacle unfolding before him. Charlotte's performance was both captivating and horrifying, sending a chill down his spine. It was a performance only one who had been beyond the grave could muster.

Kempton appeared as though he might collapse at any moment, his face pallid and twisted with fear. His eyes darted around the theatre, searching for an escape from the damning accusations that seemed to hang in the air. The audience shifted uncomfortably, exchanging uncertain glances, sensing the undercurrents of accusation and fear.

He blanched, scrambling to his feet as the dreadful and spectacular rendition ended on a broken, mournful note.

The audience erupted into stunned and sporadic applause. Charlotte bowed low, a grim smile on her lips. She clutched at her neck, stumbling, but she threw out a hand and shook her head as Perry rushed forward.

'Now's your chance,' she cried hoarsely above the wave of noise, stumbling back towards the opposite side of the stage. 'I must prepare myself for my... encore – I can feel my neck... constricting. It's happening...the sun is going down – hurry!'

Perry rushed to the front of the stage, blinded by the intensity of the lights. He blinked and vaulted towards the blackness of the front row, narrowly missing an alarmed society woman trussed up in her peacock finest, and raced towards the doors to the circle level. Unsure if this was part of some bizarre final act, the audience drummed their feet and clapped in unison for the encore as the curtain fell.

Kempton's entourage blocked his way, their confusion at his request to be let past at odds with their duty to prevent any unscheduled appointments with their master.

Perry's jaw clenched as anger coursed through him. He pulled out his revolver, the cold metal a reassuring weight in his hand. With a swift motion, he shoved past the entourage and reached the theatre box floor. To his dismay, he found it empty, the stage curtain having been lowered during his confrontation below. A thick drift of flowers, flung to the stage, piled high against the velvet drapes.

Applause erupted around him, echoing off the walls – an encore was no longer expected, it was demanded. The theatre swelled with anticipation, but Perry's thoughts were consumed by fear. Sunset was underway, and Charlotte would die, but now the fear was that Kempton would get there ahead of the unstoppable dusk. Was she already gone?

His heart raced, adrenaline sharpening his senses. Perhaps Kempton had escaped, out into the night, or had he gone backstage to finish what he'd started. Perry's eyes narrowed as he realised he could only explore one possibility, determination burning within him like a furnace.

Suddenly, a blood-curdling scream pierced the air, freezing the auditorium in its tracks. Faces drained of colour and hands flew to mouths in shock. Perry's heart skipped a beat, terror clawing at him as he realised the scream had come from the direction of the dressing rooms.

The wail cut through the auditorium like nails on a chalkboard, tearing through the very soul of anyone who heard it. Gasps and murmurs rippled through the crowd, their faces twisted in shock and horror.

Perry froze in his tracks, his heart hammering against his chest so violently that it threatened to break free. The scream had come from the direction of the backstage area – the very place where he feared Charlotte, and now Kempton, might be.

His eyes widened with terror, emotions threatening to spill over as he fought to keep his composure. There was no time to waste, no room for hesitation. He needed to find her now.

Dead or alive.

The dimly lit backstage area seemed to swallow Perry whole as he stumbled through the labyrinth of props and costumes, his ears still ringing from the blood-curdling scream. The air was thick with tension, and a sickly-sweet scent – the combined fragrance of greasepaint and fear – clung to his nostrils. His heart hammered relentlessly against his ribcage, every beat screaming at him to find Charlotte before it was too late.

'Where are you?' he muttered under his breath, his voice strained and urgent. His eyes darted left and right, scanning every shadowy corner for any sign of Charlotte or Kempton.

'Charlotte!' he called out again, louder this time, his desperation growing with each passing second. 'Kempton!'

In response, all he heard was the distant echo of the scream, still bouncing off the walls like a malevolent banshee. It gnawed at his nerves, fuelling his anxiety until every muscle in his body quivered with anticipation.

He crept towards the dressing rooms, revolver at the ready. Gas lamps flickered overhead, casting dancing shadows over the walls. Each shape seemed to twist and turn into a lurking figure. Perry blinked hard, trying to clear the illusion. Panic would only lead to mistakes.

'Inspector,' came a hushed voice, barely audible amid the chaos. Perry whipped around, his eyes locking onto a trembling stagehand who had appeared from the shadows. 'I—I saw him go that way,' the young man stammered, pointing towards a rapidly filling corridor. Perry pushed his way through, rattling the handle of the locked door. Throwing his shoulder at the obstinate oak, a surge of stagehands and runner boys helped breach the portal and Perry staggered forward into the small and dimly lit, elaborate room, revolver raised.

But the darkness offered no answers, and as Perry stood there, thronged by onlookers. The sight that befell him raised only more questions.

CHAPTER TEN

He was too late.

Dreadful gasps and murmurs echoed along the corridor as onlookers peered into the dressing room. They huddled together like frightened birds, their eyes wide with shock and disbelief.

The actress' sanctuary was cast in an orange glow from the setting sun filtering through the west-facing window. Perry's eyes adjusted to the dimly lit interior and darted towards Lord Kempton's lifeless body, lying face down with his watch chain, glittering in the lamps surrounding a large table-mounted makeup mirror, tightly wrapped around his neck. Even from the doorway, Perry saw the same starry emblem on the back of the watch case and he knew it belonged to the dead man.

Kempton's starched collar was flecked with blood from the bite of the golden garrote; the marks matching those he had inflicted upon his female victims. His middle ring finger bore a bandage, further evidence of his guilt. Perry felt certain it hid the teeth marks from the actress who had struggled to escape his grasp less than a day before. The trap had been sprung, and he had walked straight into it at great cost. But it was the sight of Charlotte beside him that twisted Perry's insides like a vice. She lay limp and pale, her chest neither rising nor falling. Her unmarked face was serene, as if she were only sleeping.

'It's a crime of passion,' someone whispered behind him, but Perry barely registered the sound. Instead, he approached the window and noticed it was locked from the inside, eliminating any possibility of another person's involvement. He glanced back at Charlotte and the silver umbrella resting atop a Gladstone bag near the window. She hadn't had time to retrieve the hidden blade, let alone use it. Yet she had found the strength to strangle him with his own weapon, even as her own life slipped away. Had she somehow disarmed him? Charlotte must have acted in self-defence; she had died fighting. The thought brought a bitter taste to his mouth, and he swallowed hard, feeling the weight of his guilt pressing down upon him.

He took a sharp breath and stumbled back against the wall, sliding down until he sat on the floor. They were both dead. Gone.

'Everyone out!' The theatre manager appeared, and his voice cut through the clamour like a knife. 'We're closing the theatre. There will be no encore!'

The crowd dispersed, leaving Perry alone in the room with the dead. His heart raced, and he muttered an apology to the lifeless actress. 'I should've revealed the secret, Charlotte. I'm sorry.' He sat frozen, torn between anguish and satisfaction. Justice had been served, but at too high a cost. Kempton would never again stalk the streets of London, preying on innocent women. But neither would he face justice for his crimes, and neither would the clever and captivating Charlotte Bloom grace the stage or his life.

He put away his gun and stepped out of the room, taking deep breaths to steady himself. Sweat clung to his forehead as he leaned against the wall, haunted by the knowledge that he could've saved Charlotte. If only he had found the courage to confess his deception, she might still be alive. In the corridor, the manager's panicked shouts to clear and close the theatre rattled the walls.

'Thomas?' Samuel Rook's voice sounded like a lifeline, and Perry looked up to see his colleague's concerned expression. 'Are you alright?'

'Rook... I should've told her. She might still be alive if I'd just—' Perry shook his head, unable to finish the sentence.

'Kempton?' Rook asked gently, placing a hand on the inspector's shoulder. Despite his emotional turmoil, Perry appreciated the gesture of support.

'They're both dead; it seems Charlotte subdued him before she—'

Rook's hard hand gripped his shoulder, startling him from his reverie. 'I'm sorry, old friend. I should not have encouraged you in this – there is always a price to pay. At least the Strangler is gone, and Charlotte died knowing she had defeated him.'

So the villain had finally met his end, not by the hangman's noose as Perry had envisioned, but by the woman he had condemned to die by his principles.

Another breath, slower this time. He needed to think clearly, logically. Dwelling in regret and self-recrimination would not undo the damage wrought. He had to do better, be better. Learn from his mistakes instead of repeating them.

Re-entering the dressing room, they were met with another unexpected sight: Charlotte's body was gone, along with the umbrella and Gladstone bag. The window stood open, curtains fluttering in the breeze. The key that had been missing from the lock earlier now rested on the windowsill. Perry blinked, pulse racing as he swept the room again.

Rook's gaze landed first on Kempton's body, pale and motionless against the floorboards. 'Dear God,' Rook whispered, his throat tightening as he took in the grisly scene. He searched for the body of the actress. 'You said she was...' Rook's voice trailed off, his eyes wide in disbelief.

'Dead?' Perry finished for him, his shock mingling with a new sense of mystery and intrigue. 'Yes. Or so it seemed.'

The two men exchanged glances, knowing that what lay before them was far more complex than they could've ever imagined. As Perry stared at the key, he couldn't help but wonder about the secrets that remained hidden, waiting to be unlocked, and those being forged in that very room.

'Well,' Rook said after a moment, 'this is... unexpected.'

The scent of Charlotte's perfume still lingered in the room, reinvigorated by the cool breeze from the open window, a haunting reminder of her presence. Perry could only stare at the empty room, thoughts spinning out of control. Charlotte was gone. But how? And where?

The questions tumbled through his mind as a cold, impossible truth took root. Death's shadow had not taken her from this place, or this world.

Perry lingered in the doorway of Charlotte's dressing room, assaulted by the coppery tang of blood and a profound sense of failure.

His gaze drifted over the disordered room, settling on Kempton's lifeless body sprawled on the floor, maroon beads clotting from the garrote mark on his throat. Perry's stomach churned, bile rising in his throat. He swallowed hard, steadying himself against the doorframe as his vision swam.

After a moment, he stepped into the room. His boots crunched on shattered glass and he glanced down, noticing the remnants of a broken perfume bottle hitherto unmarked by his earlier entrance.

He approached Kempton and crouched down with a quiet groan, joints protesting. Up close, the ugliness of violent death assaulted his senses. Perry grimaced, reaching out a gloved hand to tilt Kempton's head to the side. A bruised smudge pooled on his temple, a wet, perfumed patch taking the place of blood that was already congealing beneath the skin, and a smear of lipstick imprinted on his chalky-pale lips.

Perry blinked hard, trying to dispel the image of Kempton's lifeless eyes staring into oblivion. He rubbed his temples, a headache forming behind his eyes, and rocked back on his heels, realisation dawning. His heart thudded as the pieces fell into place. Of course. He should have seen it sooner. Charlotte wasn't dead. She had escaped, slipping out amidst the chaos following the grisly discovery of the bodies.

A spark of hope and wonder kindled in his chest, chasing away the gloom that had settled there. She lived. Against all odds, the songbird yet sang.

'The greatest actress of our time...risen like an act three Shakespearean heroine...'

He glanced around the room again with fresh eyes, noticing her missing purse and personal items she had insisted on collecting from her apartment earlier in the day. The locked door. The open window. Yes, it was all quite clear now. Charlotte had outwitted him, planning her escape even as she played the part of the victim. He couldn't help the smile that tugged at his lips, despite the circumstances.

Clever girl.

Rook closed the door behind them. 'She's gone then,' he said flatly. It wasn't a question.

Perry studied him. The undertaker's inscrutable mask had cracked, revealing a glimpse of emotion. Guilt? Or something else? He narrowed his eyes. 'She knew about *The Breath*; you knew she planned to escape after luring him here.'

Rook's mouth twisted. 'I did not know the particulars of her scheme if that's what you mean.'

'But you were aware of what she meant to do. To disappear after...'

'Forgive me,' Rook entreated, eyes gleaming gold in the dim light. 'I did not wish to deceive you, but I could not abandon her. 'Earlier today when she returned with news and your request, she probed me for the truth, seeing that I survived past my own sunset. She suspected much, and I only confirmed her suspicions. I had to warn her, to give her a chance.' He glanced at the shattered perfume bottle. 'It seems she was ready for him.'

Perry understood, as much as it galled him to admit it. Were their positions reversed, he would have done the same to save Charlotte.

He turned from the window, scanning the room once more. His gaze landed on a vase of lilies, their creamy petals curled and browning at the edges. He plucked a petal, rubbing it between his fingers. So soft. So fragile. Much like the woman who had captivated him, body and soul.

With a smile, he pinched the bridge of his nose. What a fool he had been. Charlotte possessed a guile and cunning to match his own. She had played him masterfully, evading any chance of arrest for her vengeance. Perhaps this was a fitting payback for his own deception?

Rather than anger, he felt a surge of pride and reluctant admiration. Charlotte had bested him, but she had also trusted him enough to reveal the truth through her little deceptions.

Let the world mourn the tragic death of the Nightingale. Word would soon circulate, but the Nightingale had earned her freedom, her life, and he would guard it with his life.

Perry straightened, smoothing the lapels of his coat. The time for sentiment had passed. He grasped Rook's arm, clinging to the only friend left who knew the truth. 'You did what you had to do. As did she. the problem we now face is that we have only one body.'

With a heavy sigh, Rook turned to Perry. 'I'll be bound by your decision and be honest with any investigation into the surroundings of the past twelve hours, but until then, hear me out. Charlotte is still close by and if we reveal that she still lives, then she may be caught as the prime suspect. She would hang if her story was not considered worthy of the asylum, and we would have to testify against her. I don't think I could look her in the eye and do that.'

'What are you proposing?'

'I will arrange for two coffins, one of which we can weight with items from the room and I will leave up to you the length of head start we give her. The coroner may still be hesitant to return to my premises after his encounter with Colm Flynn's body and that might buy her, and us, time. Gregory has used me on post-mortems before, in a pinch; he might decide that my swift and independent findings will give him swift answers to probing questions about the inadequacy of providing Charlotte Bloom with a police presence after his finest detective suggested she may be in danger. After that, I place myself in your hands.'

Perry considered it. Having an empty coffin would buy Charlotte time, but how would he explain it? Would a new coroner be found in time, or would Gregory insist on a rapid conclusion to avoid any scrutiny or incompetence in a force that wouldn't trust one of its own? The rabbit hole tunnelled on and on with no obvious way out except escape. He shook his head; it was not his way. Perry pondered the logistics, weighing his duty as a detective against his desire to ensure Charlotte's safety. The idea of fabricating her post-mortem in a coroner's absence and burying an empty coffin went against everything he stood for, but the thought of Charlotte alive and free filled him with a sense of joy he could not ignore.

'Very well,' Perry finally agreed, his gaze unwavering. 'We'll do it. For her. The world isn't ready for the knowledge of the talent you bear — arrange for two coffins, and I'll try to figure this out once I've slept. Just promise me one thing...'

Rook frowned. 'Of course.'

'If I ever fall victim to misadventure or the King's justice,' he said. 'Don't ever bring me back.'

Rook's eyes gleamed knowingly. 'As you wish.'

Perry retreated to the theatre office and placed a call to the local police station, informing them of the circumstances. He hung up the telephone and gazed out the window at the dark, rain-slicked street below. Somewhere out there, Charlotte was alone and on the run, forced to abandon everything she knew.

He sighed, a bittersweet ache in his chest. The dead could bury the dead, while the living moved on.

CHAPTER ELEVEN

The cold London air clung to Perry's coat as he turned the key in the lock, his breath fogging the glass of the door. His walk had done little to dispel the turmoil swirling within him, the weight of his recent actions and choices bearing down on him like a leaden weight.

He pushed open the door, stepping into the dark lounge, his hand instinctively reaching for the matches on the side table. But as the moonlight spilt through the window, casting eerie silver shadows across the room, the faint scent of tobacco hit him, like an icy finger tracing down his spine. He tensed, his heart pounding in his ears as he searched for the source.

A figure sat in the darkness, the outline of their form barely discernible among the gloom. Perry's heart stuttered, his pulse quickening as his eyes adjusted to the dim light. Moonlight seeped through the window, painting a silver trace across the room and revealing Flynn, seated within the shadows. Algernon, Perry's cat, was nestled contentedly on the gangster's lap.

Perry swallowed hard, forcing steadiness into his tone. 'How did you get in here?'

'I have my ways.' Flynn's lips twisted in a bitter smile. 'I hear you're a loner, Detective. You can't have been expecting someone else?' Flynn asked, his voice cold and calculated. 'Being a solitary man has its advantages and disadvantages.'

Perry swallowed hard, making his way against the wall to the cabinet housing his revolver. 'What do you want, Flynn?'

'Answers.' Flynn leaned forward, the moonlight catching the grief etched onto his face. 'My son died in my arms yesterday at sunset. I'd say I had very little from my end of the bargain while you gained everything.'

'You broke into Kempton's estate and took away priceless objects – I'd say you came out on top and I never said how long your son would live after his injuries. A wave of guilt crashed over Perry, but he held firm. 'I warned you not to agree to this.'

Even as he reached the cabinet, fumbling behind in the drawer, he heard the click of the drawn revolver pointing in his direction.

'Can it be done again?' Flynn demanded, his voice taut with barely restrained fury. 'The resurrection?'

'No,' Perry replied firmly. 'It's a one-time deal.' Desperation clawed at his insides, clamouring to be set free, but he fought to keep it contained. 'Even if it were possible, Colm would continue to die repeatedly from his injuries.'

'Your words are of little comfort,' Flynn snarled, the threat in his voice unmistakable.

Perry's mind raced, searching for a way to appeal to Flynn's humanity. 'You wouldn't want that for your son, would you? To die over and over again?' He knew he was treading dangerous ground, but it was all he could do to defuse the situation.

For a moment, they locked gazes, each man assessing the other, weighing their strengths and weaknesses. Perry knew the scales were tipped in Flynn's favour – the gangster could end his life with a pull of a trigger. He held his ground, determined to face the consequences of his actions, whatever they may be.

Flynn studied Perry, his eyes narrowing. 'I think you owe me an explanation, Inspector. My son did not die a second time from his wounds, dreadful though they were – he was lucid and almost...human in the few brief hours after his return. He simply expired like the ending of a seaside amusement automaton. Whatever she did to him was only temporary, and you both knew that.'

'Where is he now?' said Perry trying to deflect the rising temper in his adversary. He moved over to the window. If he was going to be shot, then at least it would shatter the glass behind him and possibly bring aid. Flynn and the armchair fell into shadow.

The silence pressed in, broken only by the ticking of the mantlepiece clock.

'In God's sweet earth minus the crude imitation of a face your undertaker friend fashioned for him. What did you lose, I wonder - your soul or your sense of right and wrong? Is that why you've been out wandering the streets these past nights trying to reconcile the light and the shadows? Can you even tell one from another after what you've done?'

'I don't know what you mean,' Perry lied, his voice cracking slightly. 'I lost Charlotte Bloom – she also died at sunset as well you know.'

'Ah! Charlotte Bloom,' whispered Flynn towards the cat. It purred, oblivious to the danger. 'Let me tell you what another little bird told me the night of her last performance.' He flicked the revolver towards a high-backed desk chair indicating for Perry to sit.

'What little bird?'

Flynn lowered the gun, placing it on the arm of the chair and rose, ejecting the cat who stretched languidly before licking its hind leg with indignation.

'A very loyal but lecherous bird prone to hanging around the windows of dressing rooms late at night to fulfil its voyeuristic fantasies.'

Perry screwed his face in disgust.

'We share something in common, Inspector – a loathing for the sexually depraved.'

'Charlotte's dead too,' Perry lied, feeling the weight of his deception like a stone in his gut. The dim glow of moonlight streaming through the windows cast eerie shadows on the walls, adding to the oppressive atmosphere.

'Is she now?' Flynn questioned, his gaze sharp and searching. 'Funny, my little pervert says someone fitting her exact description and carrying your heirloom of an umbrella and a travelling bag left rather hurriedly via the dressing room window; perhaps she wanted to avoid her audience's incessant adoration?'

Perry stiffened, his heart pounding against his ribcage. Flynn couldn't know about that unless he was telling the truth.

'Seems my informant has quite the eye for the ladies,' Flynn continued, smirking at Perry's visible discomfort. 'Likes to watch them when they think they're alone, but he's also curious, so he followed her. Would you like to know where she went?'

A surge of disgust washed over Perry as he realised the implications. Some twisted pervert had been spying on Charlotte, and now her safety was compromised.

'He is mistaken,' said Perry, calculating the time and distance to snatch the revolver opposite. 'We carried out the post-mortem on her the morning before last. She's already been embalmed—'

'Perhaps,' Flynn mused, studying Perry intently. 'But whoever it was made it to the river ferry well after sundown before my informant's urges drew him back to the centre of town for easier, lower-hanging fruit.'

Flynn moved to the chessboard, examining the state of play. 'Either he, or you are lying. What I know is that there is at least one other capable of bringing the dead back to life, as Charlotte Bloom herself was revived. Who might the other person be, I wonder?'

Perry's blood ran cold at Flynn's words, his mind racing through the possibilities. Could the gangster somehow know that he was involved in Charlotte's resurrection? He had to tread carefully, lest his secret be exposed.

'Your guess is as good as mine,' Perry replied cautiously, hoping to steer the conversation away from dangerous territory. 'I'm just a detective, after all.'

'True,' Flynn conceded, still eyeing Perry with suspicion. 'But one must wonder if this mystery person is local – perhaps even closer than we realise.' His gaze bored into Perry's as if trying to pry open his very soul.

Perry's pulse thundered in his ears, the weight of his lies and deceptions threatening to crush him. He knew that if Flynn discovered the truth, it would mean an uncertain future for the undertaker. Would Flynn kill him, or torture him until he agreed to any future demands?

'Like I said,' he repeated, striving for nonchalance, 'I'm just a detective. My concern is catching criminals, not playing God, but I do not know the secret and I tell you it died with Charlotte Bloom.'

'Very well, Detective,' Flynn finally relented, his tone clarifying that the matter was far from settled. 'But remember – I have eyes and ears everywhere. And I won't rest until I find out if this ungodly power to return the dead to us exists in others. If I find out you knowingly held back information that could have prolonged my son's life—'

Perry sprang for the gun, swiftly flipping the revolver

towards Flynn's dark silhouette. The cat sprang into the adjoining room in alarm.

Perry's breath hitched, caught between fear and surprise as the gangster pushed forward his fist into the shaft of moonlight and opened his hand to reveal the glitter of six bullets. Perry struggled to maintain composure, feeling the weight of Flynn's gaze dissecting his very soul. He lowered the gun.

The moonlight cast sharp shadows upon the board, emphasising its stark black and white squares. In a deliberate motion, Flynn reached out his free hand and plucked a black rook from its position, rolling it between his fingers thoughtfully.

'An interesting game, chess,' he mused, his voice like gravel. 'A battle of wits and strategy – much like our current situation, wouldn't you say?'

Perry swallowed hard, feeling the cold sweat dampening his collar. He could not allow Flynn to uncover any further truths. 'What do you mean?'

'Each player must make sacrifices for the greater good of their cause.' Flynn toyed with the rook, his eyes boring into Perry's. 'But sometimes, those sacrifices can lead to betrayal.'

'Betrayal?' Perry echoed, his throat dry.

'Perhaps withholding information that could save my son, if only to secure your own interests,' Flynn accused, his voice low and dangerous.

Flynn held up the chess piece, his eyes never leaving Perry's. 'I'm going to find the truth, Detective.'

'Is that a threat?' Perry clenched his fists, his knuckles turning white.

'Consider it... a warning,' Flynn replied, pocketing the rook. 'I feel like killing you for not giving me my due and keeping my son alive past sunset. At least he had vengeance before he died.'

'What do you mean by that?' asked Perry.

'You'll find out,' Flynn added, turning toward the door. He hesitated in the doorway. 'I think if we ever meet again... it will be your last.'

The door shut with a soft click as Perry's apartment was once again engulfed in darkness, lit only by the silvery moonlight that crept through the window. Perry stood stock-still, his heart pounding like a metronome set to an impossibly frantic tempo. He listened for any other sound – the faint creak of floorboards, the rustle of fabric – but there was only silence. It appeared Flynn had truly departed, leaving behind only the palpable tension that coiled in the air like a malevolent serpent.

Perry was left with the ghost of their conversation, the echo of a deal gone sour haunting him. He stared at the empty square on the chessboard where the rook once stood, wondering if Flynn's choice was mere coincidence.

With that ominous warning hanging heavy in the air, Perry sprang to the window to see Flynn depart into the silent street. From every vantage point and shadow, hooded and cloaked figures joined his entourage, the cumbersome figure of Crooked Jack leading the vanguard.

A plaintive meow jerked him from his reverie. Algernon butted against his leg, eyes luminous in the shadows. The cat had always sensed his moods, providing comfort when Perry needed it most. He lifted the fluffy lump and stroked the Persian's soft fur, drawing strength from the familiar warmth and weight of the animal in his arms.

His resolve hardened, determination etching lines in his face. The clock chimed one o'clock, the sound startling in the silence.

'I think we are outnumbered,' he whispered to the cat and the shadows, glancing across at the chess board. 'But hopefully not outplayed.'

CHAPTER TWELVE

The office of Superintendent Gregory was as dark as his mood. The narrow windows, half-shrouded by tattered curtains, allowed only meagre rays to penetrate the gloom and cast weak shadows across the worn floorboards. Perry stood rigidly before Gregory's desk, the air between them thick with the weight of unspoken thoughts.

Gregory unfolded a piece of paper on his desk, revealing a detailed sketch of a hidden room found within Kempton's apartment. 'This room, Perry... It's where he kept morbid trophies from his past victims. We have our man, thanks to Flynn's information.'

Perry stared at the drawing, his stomach churning as he took in the grotesque details; the shelves lined with jars containing locks of hair and teeth, small bloodstained trinkets arranged with macabre precision. He could almost smell the metallic tang of blood lingering in the air, the putrid stench of decay.

'The place was raided before we arrived, and it's no coincidence that Flynn has moved his centre of operations,' Gregory said, his voice heavy with resignation. 'The Wapping warehouse is empty. We have no leads on where he'll set up next.' Gregory sighed, pinching the bridge of his nose as if to ward off an impending headache. 'I should've trusted you, Perry,' he admitted, his voice barely audible above the creaking of the old oak floor beneath their feet. 'I am grateful for your discretion on my failings to pursue Kempton and provide the poor dead woman with a guard. You were right.'

'Maybe we both were, sir,' Perry replied humbly, surprised at the vulnerability he heard in his superior's confession. 'The world isn't black and white. It never was.'

'There's something you aren't telling me about this case,' said Gregory. 'That Charlotte Bloom died from a seizure or fit following her act of self-defence seems improbable.'

Perry held the Superintendent's gaze. 'But not impossible, sir. I'm sure Mr Rook would be more than happy to allow the second opinion of a coroner to—'

'No, no,' interrupted Gregory with a raise of his hand. 'I trust him almost as much as I should be trusting you. Let there be an end to it. I hear the grand funeral arrangements are being made for her and that they rival those of the old queen herself. No good interfering with further investigations or sparking off further gossip about what went on last week. It's a shame the Nightingale of Knightsbridge won't be around to see it.'

Perry hesitated before nodding. 'Indeed. But perhaps Charlie Flynn will lie low for a while, which might be the only positive out of this whole affair.'

As they stood in the dim light, the spectres of past failures seemed to gather around them, whispering reminders of the lives they couldn't save. Perry's gaze drifted to the corner of the room, where rainwater dripped through a crack in the ceiling and pooled on the floor. A shiver ran down his spine, and he wrapped his arms around himself as if trying to hold on to something solid amidst the uncertainty.

'Speaking of which,' Gregory continued, his voice wavering slightly. 'The officer who chased Colm Flynn into the path of the tram, Sergeant Higgins... he's been found dead, Perry.'

'Dead?' the word escaped Perry's lips before he could swallow it back down. The cold reality of it struck him like a physical blow, leaving him breathless.

'Of a heart attack, in a police box,' Gregory explained, his tone heavy with unspoken questions. 'He was clutching a morbid wax mask in his hands as if clawing at its face when he died. I believe the poor fellow must've been suffering some sort of breakdown to create such a horrible and disturbing totem. I understand you worked with him on several of your earlier cases?'

'Yes...' Perry whispered. He felt the world shift beneath his feet, tilting and swaying like a ship caught in a storm. The policeman's death had brought the cost of their bargain into sharp focus; Charlotte and Flynn had been resurrected, but now another life had been taken in payment. Perry briefly thought of the dark and enclosed space, a place of sanctuary for any policeman. The thought of being pursued or trapped within by the resurrected and disfigured revenant was too awful to consider.

'The dead always seek vengeance...' he whispered, steadying himself against the back of a chair.

'What?' Gregory asked softly.

'Nothing... Nothing, sir,' Perry lied, feeling the weight of his guilt settle around his shoulders like a leaden shroud. 'It's just... a tragedy.'

'Indeed,' Gregory agreed, his eyes clouded with sorrow. 'I need you to visit the officer's sister and only surviving next of kin. Break the news to her; she deserves to know.'

Perry nodded stiffly, his throat constricted by the words he couldn't bring himself to say. How could he face the man's sister, knowing that he was partly responsible for her brother's death? The thought sent a fresh wave of grief crashing over him, threatening to drown him in remorse.

'I'll do it,' he choked out, gripping the chair tightly enough to turn his knuckles white and recalling Rook's words:

There's always a price to pay...

'Thank you, Perry,' Gregory murmured, his gaze lingering on the detective for a moment longer before he turned away.

As Perry left the office, he felt the shadows of doubt and

sorrow clinging to him like a funeral cloth. The world outside seemed cold and unforgiving, a place where justice and retribution were locked in an eternal dance, balancing death and resurrection on a knife's edge. As he walked through the rain-slicked street towards the train station, his heart heavy with the burden of truth, he couldn't help but wonder if fate had extracted its toll.

Perry walked down the dimly lit cobblestone streets of the suburb, his polished shoes crunching on gravel and soot. A thick fog clung to the ground, muffling the usual clamour of carriages and costermongers hawking their wares.

His mind churned as swiftly as the Thames, replaying his conversation with Gregory on a loop. He had been wrong to agree to bring back anyone, let alone Colm Flynn. So wrong. And now an innocent man was dead.

Justice. The word left a foul taste in his mouth. His duty was to uphold the law, not seek to redefine it. And yet with Kempton, the line between justice and vengeance had blurred beyond all recognition.

Perry sighed and ran a hand over his face, feeling the scrape of stubble against his palm. His head pounded in time with his footsteps as he walked on through the veil of fog. Somewhere in the distance, Big Ben tolled the hour with a mournful peal of bells.

The ramshackle house loomed before him, shrouded in shadows. Perry steeled himself and strode up the front steps, his hand closing around the brass door knocker. It was time to face the consequences of his actions. The price had to be paid.

The door opened to a kindly-faced woman with golden, grey hair pulled back into a neat bun. A row of pins lined the tip of her temples. She peered up and blinked in surprise through thick glasses that magnified her brown eyes.

'Miss Higgins?' he said heavily. 'My name is Detective Inspector Perry. It's about your brother – may I come inside?'

CHAPTER THIRTEEN

Perry's breath hung in the air as he stood on the Victoria Embankment, his gaze fixed on the murky waters of the Thames. The winter sun was a weak, pale disc that did little to warm him, but the crisp air held a certain clarity that seemed to cut through the fog of recent events. A smattering of well-dressed Londoners strolled along the promenade, their faces flushed from the cold.

'Even in my wildest dreams,' Rook's voice broke the silence between them, 'I never never thought my... abilities would bring about such chaos.' He cleared his throat. 'I'm sorry for what transpired with Sergeant Higgins; he was a good man.'

Perry winced, swallowing against the tightness in his throat. The hollow ache in his chest flared, as the image of Mrs. Higgins' tears and anguished sobs flashed in his mind. He stared across the river, blinking hard. 'Yes, well. It was...it is a tragedy, and I'll bear that scar for the rest of my days.'

Silence stretched between them, broken only by the cries of gulls wheeling overhead. Perry fished the silver flask from his pocket and took a long swig, relishing the burn of absinthe down his throat.

Rook shifted beside him and reached into his coat pocket. 'This came for you today,' he said, handing Perry a neatly folded letter.

'From whom?' Perry asked, his curiosity piqued. The envelope bore no return address, only his name written in elegant script and the address of the undertaker's premises.

Perry's heart clenched as he unfolded the letter, his hands suddenly trembling. The notepaper was from a hotel in Cairo, and amidst the neat handwriting lay an impression of a lipstick kiss. Within the crimson mark, a tiny drawing of a nightingale's silhouette perched. A quote from Homer graced the bottom of the page:

Behold, on wrong swift vengeance waits; and art subdues the strong.

'Well?' Rook prompted. 'What does it say?'

Perry glanced at his friend, unable to contain a smile. 'It seems the reports of Miss Nightingale's death were exaggerated, despite her lavish funeral this afternoon. Let us hope that this information remains so.'

He read the note again, tracing the faint impression of her lips at the bottom of the page. Foremost was a profound sense of relief.

'So she *is* alive,' Rook repeated, as much to himself as to Perry. 'But why has she only just now chosen to contact us?'

'I cannot say.' Perry shredded the letter and cast it into the Thames. 'Though I suspect she has her reasons. Whatever they may be, it seems she is safe, for now.'

Rook frowned at the letter. 'For now. You sound as if you expect her safety to be impermanent.'

'She may be clever,' Perry said, 'but she is not infallible. No one can disappear completely, not even Charlotte Bloom. There will be a trail, however faint, but I don't intend to pursue her. She should be more concerned with what Flynn might do if he catches up with her.'

As they stood side by side, the opening chimes of St Paul's Cathedral filled the air, marking the passage of time. Perry and Rook exchanged a look, their resolve solidifying, bound by their shared experiences and the weight of the secrets they carried.

Rook sighed, breath pluming in the chilly air. 'I am aware

of the consequences my ability carries. With every life restored, the scales of fate are thrown out of balance in ways none of us can predict.' His brow furrowed further. 'Each breath invites its own form of vengeance, be it swift or slow. But for now, let us take comfort in this minor victory; The Shadow Strangler is no more.'

Perry nodded, turning his gaze back to the river. The sunlight seemed brighter, the colours of the world more vivid. He looked up at the winter sun glinting off the river, a myriad of emotions churning within him. Joy and sorrow. Hope and fear. Love and longing.

Rook stood silently beside him, giving him the space to process it all. Perry did not know what the future held, what new horrors or wonders it might contain, but he took comfort knowing Rook would stand with him.

A weight had been lifted from Perry's shoulders, even as an additional burden took its place. Charlotte was out there somewhere, her life intertwined with his own, their fates as much in the hands of destiny as their own choices.

He drew in a deep breath, clasping the letter close to his chest. The last chimes of St Paul's Cathedral rang out from the cold, distant haze, resonant and strong. Perry listened to their song, finding solace in their familiar rhythm. He turned to Rook with a smile, offering the hipflask to the undertaker. 'It seems we have been given a second chance, all of us, to find our purpose and fulfil our destinies. That is something worth fighting for.'

Rook's eyes glinted with understanding. He grasped Perry's shoulder, squeezing it. 'Indeed it is, Inspector – I'll drink to that.'

The End

THE CRESSET SQUARE

Brother Eadric shuddered against the biting wind as he emerged from the chapel into the courtyard. The cold air stung his face and crept through his once-white, threadbare robes. He pulled his cowl tighter and hurried across the exposed hilltop, the frozen ground crunching beneath his sandaled feet.

The monastery loomed above him, all hard stone and sharp angles, a stark contrast to the sweeping moors and dense forest surrounding it. Built to withstand the harsh northern winters and even hardier invaders, its walls were thick, its windows narrow. An imposing edifice, yet also a sanctuary from the wilds. Norman lords now ruled England where centuries before, their ancestors had come in boats to raid the treasure houses of the one true God.

Eadric descended the winding stair to the scriptorium in the undercroft. By the guttering light of a single tallow candle, he could make out his fellow scribe hunched over his desk, pen scratching faintly.

The monk glanced up, dark circles under his eyes. 'This

cold is hard on my fingers today,' he complained. 'I can barely grip the quill.'

Eadric nodded sympathetically. 'I feel it in my bones, Oswin, from matins to vespers.'

Their thin robes and the unheated room offered little respite. He sat at his desk, setting out ink and pigments ground from local plants and minerals – blues from woad, reds and yellows from ochre-rich clay. With these simple tools, they brought the illuminated manuscripts to life.

In the dimly lit scriptorium, they toiled over their parchment sheets, faces illuminated by the flickering light of a single candle, casting eerie shadows on the stone walls around them. Their ink-stained fingers danced across the pages with painstaking precision, as they carefully traced intricate patterns and embellished the text with vibrant colours.

'I have finished this demanding page, Brother,' said Oswin, his voice tinged with satisfaction as he held up a completed manuscript page. The young scribe's work was truly a sight to behold – the gilded letters seemed to dance upon the page, surrounded by delicate tendrils of ivy and intricately woven patterns that shimmered in the candlelight. Each detail was rendered with such loving care that it seemed to breathe life into the sacred words.

'Your work never ceases to inspire me,' said Eadric, admiration clear in his deep-set eyes. He glanced down at his own efforts – an illuminated capital letter adorned with a vivid scene of angels and demons locked in eternal combat. Though he knew his work paled in comparison, there was a quiet satisfaction in knowing that together, they were preserving their faith through these glorious works of art.

As Eadric began sketching delicate vines along the border of a page, his mind wandered, thinking of long summer days, honeyed mead, and rumours of better, former times from the mouths of the oldest monks who themselves were passing on hearsay and remembrances from an earlier age. The monastery had not always been so impoverished, and the old brothers fondly recalled Abbot Cuthbert with a reverence bordering on beatification, if not canonisation.

The Crusader knight-turned-monk had returned from the Holy Land and embraced a hermetic lifestyle. Cuthbert had improved the destitute monastery with his insight and leadership, which he had sharpened on the battlefield. Legend spoke of divine blessing and single-minded adherence to the word of God, illustrated by his devotion to carrying a large book or bible at all times, even while he slept. Tales of famine and failed harvests were miraculously provided for, plague and disease subdued swiftly, and legendary feasts left generations of monks that followed weak in the knees and stomachs. Cuthbert had lived to a great age, his tomb memorialised in the stone wall of the chapter house where Mass was held annually on the anniversary of his death. Strangest of all though, was the four-by-four stoned cresset square that sat empty all year round except for that day – a relic thought to be plundered from some Byzantine church during Cuthbert's reckless early days.

'Do you think there is any truth to the rumours about Abbot Cuthbert?' Eadric asked, surprised he had said out loud what had been on his mind.

Oswin shrugged. 'You mean about his miracles or his methods?'

'Both,' said Eadric, tickling his nose with the end of the goose feather. 'What I wouldn't give for a glance at that book – Brother Matthew says it came from—'

'The library of Alexandria,' mused Oswin. 'There must have been stylistic arrangements within that have been lost to us over the centuries. I wonder what happened to it after the Abbot's death? I heard tell it contained many wonderful but unusual illuminations.'

Eadric laid aside his quill and blew into his hands for warmth. 'It never left his side, so I assume it still lies somewhere within the monastery, if not within our own abbot's lodging.'

'Then one of us must promise the other, that should one of us attain that high office, he shares the knowledge of what it contains with the other.'

'Agreed,' said Eadric, his stomach grumbling from hunger. 'Though doubling the carp pool's size is my priority if elected.'

Oswin looked mournfully around the damp room at the meagre bookshelves. 'And I will insist we double the size of the library to house the greatest works we can afford to reproduce. I'd rather go hungry in body and have more books.'

At the ringing of the bell for vespers, Eadric set down his quill. As he and Oswin climbed the stairs to the chapel, a low rumble sounded from deep within the earth. The ground began to shake, dust raining down from the rafters as the tremor intensified, and the monks staggered to their feet, exchanging uncertain glances. Fearful whispers echoed through the chapel, only silencing as the trembling subsided.

Eadric's heart pounded as he took his place. Several conflicted, and anxious faces were soothed for the present as the service began. He stood beside his fellow scribe, his eyes downcast and his hands clasped tightly together while his heart beat a rapid staccato against his ribs.

A waft of incense permeated the chapel, its smoky tendrils coiling about the heads of the assembled monks like a ghostly serpent. The rich aroma of myrrh and frankincense filled the air, mingling with the damp mustiness that clung to their robes and the cold stone walls. The oppressive cold and settling dust weighed heavily on their spirits, but the divine presence summoned by their prayers offered a fragile bulwark against the encroaching gloom. As they raised their voices in song, it appeared even the very stones themselves might tremble before their faith.

And then, without warning, the ground beneath them began to shudder once more. At first, the trembling was barely perceptible, a mere whisper of unease that seemed to echo the disquiet that had settled over the monastery. But with each passing moment, the tremors grew stronger, until the very air itself seemed to quiver with dread. Unease crept through the assembled monks, a palpable sense of dread that mirrored the disturbance below.

As the tremors continued to escalate, the very foundations of the monastery seemed to fracture beneath them, and the monks clung to the only certainty they had left – their unwavering belief in the divine.

The ground shook violently beneath Eadric's feet, sending a tremor up his spine. He gripped the stone walls as the cracks spidered across the floor, the ceiling crumbling in clouds of dust and mortar.

'God's wrath!' someone shrieked.

The monastery's ancient stone walls had withstood the test of time for centuries, but even they were not impervious to the forces that now shook the very ground beneath them. The monks scrambled away from the falling debris, their sandals slapping against the stones. Eadric's heart pounded as he ran, dodging the shards of pottery and glass shattering around him. Statues of saints and angels, which had stood serenely in prayerful repose, toppled as if bowing before an unseen force.

'Run! To safety!' cried the Prior, his heart pounding in his chest like a drumbeat. The monks stumbled through the haze, their lungs burning with each laboured breath.

'Quickly, this way!' urged Eadric, his eyes streaming with tears from the dust that filled the air. The monks ran for their lives, their robes billowing behind them like dark spectres as they fled the wrath of an unseen foe.

A tremendous crash thundered through the cloisters as a far corner of the chapter house collapsed in on itself. Eadric collided with his fellow scribe and fell to the floor, gaping at the ruinous gap. Broken stones were strewn about, the air thick with grit that stung his eyes and coated his tongue.

Through the haze, he glimpsed the wall-recessed tomb, cracked with much of the side panel missing. His chest tightened at the sight of the mouldy wrappings and lolling right arm, skeletal but bound still by small vestiges of skin and sinew binding the bones of the former crusader abbot, Cuthbert. The man's eternal rest has been disturbed, one whose labours in life had brought mythical prosperity and stability to the monastery. Something glittered on the floor beside the tomb's breach, sparkling among the few remaining candles in a nearby cresset. The ground grew still, silent, and spent as Oswin wound over and around obstacles to retrieve the object.

In the eerie silence that followed the calamity, the dust-cloaked figure of Prior Anselm emerged cautiously from behind the remnants of a shattered pillar. His eyes scanned the devastated chapter house, seeking his charges amidst the rubble and debris.

'The danger is passed! Everyone, remain calm.'

The monks huddled together, clutching their robes and murmuring prayers as the Prior surveyed the damage wrought upon the chapter house. The air was thick with a funereal silence, punctuated only by the occasional distant groan of shifting stone or whispered reassurance from one of the other monks. Their once-cherished sanctuary now lay in shambles, as though a vengeful tempest had torn through it, leaving behind only chaos and ruin.

'Oswin!' called the Prior, his voice hoarse and strained. 'Where are you?'

'Over there,' said Eadric, pointing with trembling fingers towards the far corner of the damaged chamber. There, half-buried in the rubble, lay the broken tomb of Abbot Cuthbert. Once an imposing testament to the monastery's bygone glory, it now resembled the ruins of a forgotten temple, its once-immaculately carved panel obscured by dust and debris.

Oswin emerged from the dust like a shadow-given form and held up a mighty leather book studded with semi-precious stones.

The monks stepped closer to the tomb, their eyes drawn irresistibly to the body of the highly regarded abbot. The familiar cresset square, used to commemorate the venerable corpse, sat undamaged on top of the nearby pillar. Made from an exotic stone – dark, smooth, and seemingly impervious to the ravages of time – the four-rowed cresset, each with four columns, contrasted with the pale sepulchre.

'Such intricate craftsmanship,' Oswin murmured, his fingers tracing the grooves of the cover and the dark, polished stones embedded within the thick leather cover. 'It's only likeness is the cresset square.'

'They are of the same period and origin,' agreed Eadric, his gaze locked upon the embossed leather book. He turned it over in his hands, examining the stones and comparing it to that of the cresset square on the top of the tomb.

'God's wounds,' breathed the Prior, crossing himself as he approached the broken sepulchre. 'What has become of our sanctuary and our blessed father's rest?'

'An earthquake, Prior,' Eadric explained, struggling to contain the thrill in his voice. 'It has shaken loose secrets from the very foundations of the monastery.'

'Indeed,' Anselm murmured, his eyes narrowing as they fell upon the ancient book nestled in Eadric's grasp. He reached out, his fingers brushing the cold stone of the tomb and inhaling the musty scent of age that clung to it like a second skin. 'And what secrets would those be?'

'Could it be the blessed abbot's book – perhaps a record of his miracles?' Oswin wondered aloud, his pulse quickening as the weight of the book seemed to press down upon him. 'It was lying at the side of his tomb, as though it had been dislodged from his eternal grasp. Perhaps it was delivered to us to help us—'

'Curious,' Anselm muttered, taking the book and carefully leafing through its pages. The parchment crackled under his touch, each turn revealing more cryptic designs and tantalising illustrations. He tapped in the uppermost corner of the page. 'What are these marks?'

The scribes peered down to see a series of neatly arranged dots and crosses on each page. Their arrangement formed a box, four by four square, but subsequent pages revealed a different arrangement of the two symbols.

'An ancient page numbering, perhaps?' said Eadric.

Oswin shook his head. 'If it is, then I have never seen the like.'

A shiver of excitement and awe coursed through Brother Oswin's spine as Prior Anselm, his hands trembling, flipped through the pages of the ancient tome. The air in the dim chamber felt heavy with the weight of centuries past, hanging like a suffocating fog around them. Oswin could feel the oppressive force of history bearing down upon him as his eyes took in the illuminated manuscripts before him, which seemed to be from an age long gone.

'Look at this...these images...' Anselm whispered, his voice barely audible. Each page flicked by revealing new mysteries and horrors, strange text intertwined with images of fine food, feasts, and gifts so vividly depicted that it seemed as if they could reach out and partake in the bounty.

There were fantastical creatures whose forms twisted and writhed on the parchment, their grotesque features blurring the line between imagination and reality.

Oswin's heart raced as he caught sight of naked dancers moving lithely around a curious flat exotic stone marked with sixteen holes, their limbs contorted in unnatural positions. The colours used in these illustrations were unlike any he had ever laid eyes on; they seemed otherworldly, a different palette altogether from the hues available in the monastery's workshop.

As Anselm continued to turn the pages, an image of an Old Testament angel brandishing a bright sword appeared, its many eyes gazing piercingly at those who dared to look upon it. The divine figure was then replaced by a demonic one, a creature of flame and darkness whose sinister form appeared almost too lifelike in its rendering to suggest it was taken from one who had used only imagination to render such terror. Oswin could not suppress a gasp at the horrifying accuracy with which such evil had been captured in ink. Above lay scrawled the names of once embattled and captured foreign cities, some of which were still in existence – Antioch, Tyre, and Ma'arrat al-Numan remembered even to that day as a brutal siege, known for its atrocities committed by crusaders against the city's Muslim and Jewish inhabitants.

'Prior Anselm,' Oswin hesitated, his voice quivering with trepidation and excitement, 'perhaps we should transcribe this...for study?'

'Absolutely not!' Anselm hissed, slamming the book shut with a resounding thud. 'This...abomination must be re-interred as soon as the repairs to the tomb and chapter house can be arranged.' The prior's eyes narrowed as he contemplated the implications of their discovery, his brow knitted in concern. 'Until then, it will be kept safe in the reliquary or until our blessed abbot returns from the conclave in York and determines the nature and importance of this tome – take it to the reliquary and see that none disturb its blasphemy.'

Eadric lay in the dark of the communal dormitory, staring blankly at his rough and blistered hands. His physical exertions had failed to bring on any sleep. He had spent hours with the other monks making the habitable areas of the monastery safe by removing rubble and assessing damages, which were thankfully minimal except for the chapter house. Through the rough hemp curtain that separated their beds, Oswin's voice could be heard as he whispered restlessly. The other monks in the dormitory snored and mumbled in their sleep.

'I can't get the wondrous images out of my mind,' Oswin breathed, a mix of frustration and curiosity clear in his tone. 'Did you ever see the like?'

'No,' Eadric whispered, his breath caught in his throat. 'And we will not see it again, so do not tempt me with the memory of its wondrous pages.' He was painfully aware of the hard stone floors beneath him and the chill of the monastery walls that seemed to wrap around them like a shroud. He thought of the old book, its secrets out of grasp. His dark eyes were thoughtful as he considered a question that had been growing in his mind: Could this book be a record of Abbot Cuthbert's journeys or a testament to his minor miracles?

A veil of darkness enveloped the monastery, pierced only by the faint glimmer of moonlight that filtered through the narrow window in the dormitory's narrow windows. The shadows seemed to dance upon the walls as the wind whispered its mournful lament through the gaps in the ancient stones.

'Brother,' Oswin breathed, his voice barely audible through the crevice that connected their cells. 'I have it with me here and I will repent for my transgression, but I need your help to place it back in the reliquary.'

Eadric sat up and pressed his face against the curtain, whispering. 'Have you forgotten your vow of obedience? Why didn't you place the book back as Prior Anselm told you to?'

Oswin sighed. 'I intended to, but Brother Eadric was nowhere to be found to unlock the door, so with all the commotion from the movements in the earth I concealed it beneath my bunk for safekeeping.'

'Meaning you could continue studying it,' Eadric commented, the accusation clear in his tone.

'Well, yes,' said Oswin, 'but not for any other reason than to witness the fine work of a scribe long dead, one last time. His work should be appreciated and understood before being lost to us again, and surely, there is much to learn from such an artefact. What harm would there be if we were to examine it before it is re-interred?'

'It must be placed in the reliquary at the first opportunity however curious we both are,' said Eadric. 'I will pray that your punishment is not severe—'

'I can return it to the reliquary now with your help,' said Oswin, 'after a last glance at its marvels.'

'How will you do that without a key?'

Oswin clutched at the curtain, his trembling hands shaking the coarse cloth. 'The movements of the earth caused the frame to twist and part from the stout oak door; it could be lifted gently to raise the bolt out of its lock where the gap is at its greatest, but it would require two of us to ensure success.'

'You are asking me to become complicit,' said Eadric.

'I'm asking you to help me put it back and take a quick look at the pages so that we may benefit in our endeavours for God's glory—that is all.'

Eadric's fingers traced the cold, rough edges of the wall behind, his thoughts racing like a tempest. He could almost sense Oswin's own curiosity seeping through the material, mingling with his own insatiable desire for knowledge.

'Imagine everything we could learn,' Oswin murmured almost inaudibly. 'Perhaps it's an account of Abbot Cuthbert's military feats during the crusade or an undiscovered version of a bible or apocrypha from faraway lands. I promised that if I got my hands on the Abbot's book I would share it with you.'

'Yes, but only as Abbot, not as a scribe,' Eadric replied. 'One look is sure to only heighten our yearning for what we can't have.'

A silence hung heavy between them, thick with unspoken questions and the weight of their shared curiosity. Even as Oswin hesitated, Eadric knew he harboured the same burning desire to explore the enigma that lay within those ancient pages.

'Matins is in two hours,' Oswin reminded Eadric. 'Will you not help me?'

'I might,' Eadric finally replied, a hint of longing in his voice. 'But we must consider that this isn't meant for us to see – you noticed the symbols of light and shadow, the terror and wickedness in some pages; it looks like an ungodly text in an antiquated form of Aramaic.'

'There were marvellous things also before I was forced to quit my brief study.' Oswin said. 'You saw some of the other serene pages – feasts, weird plants with healing powers; those women dancing—'

'Yes, yes,' Eadric interrupted, trying to avoid any thoughts that could challenge his chasteness. 'Let's not overlook that harvests come and go and information about plants passes and then reappears. That doesn't prove that this is the book said to have been saved from the fire at Alexandria.'

'It is not translated into Greek,' Oswin said encouragingly. 'So it must be old, perhaps one of a kind.'

'I agree the book is ancient, and I also know you saw the names of those cities written above the demon's head,' said Eadric, quickly glancing over as the monk on his other side shuffled and turned over in his sleep. 'You know their significance as well I as do, having transcribed many a land deed granted from the plunder of those places. What happened in those cities still haunts people a century after the events.'

'Yes,' Oswin interjected, reciting from memory what he had learned from old records. 'And it came before us, bidden and driven by a desire for fire and blood, and our enemies knew that death was nigh and God had abandoned them – I wonder if their capture was solely down to the valour and religious fervour of men at arms.'

'There is enough of Satan's corruption in the hearts of men without resorting to the conjuration of whatever it is you speak of,' said Eadric. 'Likely it was some modern machine of war, perhaps even Greek fire itself—'

'Well, we won't know for sure unless we see for ourselves.' said Oswin. 'If Abbot Cuthbert was its custodian then it can't be wholly evil, even if his early years were questionable in the eyes of God.'

'Yet he insisted he be buried with it or was interred with it to avoid the light of day,' said Eadric.

'You saw the cherubim with the flaming sword,' said Oswin. 'Its source has to be an early bible or at least one with knowledge of the older testaments.' Oswin pressed closer to the curtain. 'You saw the curious dots and crosses on each corner. You thought they were page numbers, but you are wrong; there is purpose behind them.'

'And what purpose would that be?'

'Something to do with the cresset that sits by the Abbot's tomb,' said Oswin. 'Do you know what I think?'

Eadric gave a resigned sigh and turned his back on the curtain. 'I'm sure you're going to tell me anyway.'

'I only caught a glance at each page, but each series of dots corresponded to a different square of only four by four distinct marks; just like the cresset square that sits by Abbot Cuthbert's tomb.'

'You are certain of this?' said Eadric sitting up and approaching the wall.

'Certain enough to know that each page has a unique pattern of crosses and dots. Prior Anselm agreed with us that the book's semi-precious stones are matched to the cresset square. However these things were acquired, it is plain they are connected.'

Eadric's heart quickened, a shiver of anticipation coursing through his veins. The thought had crossed his mind. What insight might be contained within that mysterious volume? And why would someone bury such a book rather than pass on the knowledge?

'True,' Eadric whispered, his breath fogging in the chill air. 'It was buried with Abbot Cuthbert for a reason, and we may never know that reason if we simply return it to the earth.'

'So what harm could come from merely reading its pages or examining its illustrations alongside the placement of candles within the cresset?' Oswin persisted. 'We will require light for our study. What if it was a codex – a grimoire – enabling what was drawn to manifest?' said Oswin. 'Would the great abbot not have availed himself of the bounties within for the benefit of his charges? Perhaps during times of strife and want he used what he had found in the Holy Land—'

'Do not speak so,' said Eadric. 'That would be blasphemy.'

'And how are we to judge that without knowing its origin? Will you not let me make a trial of my plan? Perhaps the Prior could be made to understand its significance if we succeed, not only providing for the community at large but enabling further study of the artistry and mechanism of its pages. Help me replace the book, Eadric,' Oswin pleaded, his words alight with excitement. 'The door is heavy and will make a noise without the two of us working together.' He paused, the conflict in his eyes apparent. 'But before we do that... I must examine it one last time. Let us do so by the light of the candles in the chapter house cresset and put my theory to the test.'

Eadric hesitated, torn between his duty to obey Prior Anselm and his desire to unravel the tantalising mysteries that lay before them. The conflict gnawed at him as he weighed the consequences of their actions. He glanced around the sleeping forms of the other monks, a gnawing unease settling in his stomach. But the allure of the unknown was too powerful to resist. He swallowed hard, his mouth dry as parchment.

'Very well,' Eadric agreed, his voice strained with uncertainty. 'We shall look, but only briefly, and only to ensure you learn humility when your theory fails. At least I will get some sleep on my return with the book finally in its place.'

The moon cast its pale, ghostly light upon the ruined chapter house, a wide octagonal room now desolate and broken. Shadows flickered in the uneasy glow of the candles that burned low in their sconces, illuminating the cracked walls and the rubble that lay strewn about the floor. In one far corner, part of the roof had collapsed outwards from the force of the earthquake, allowing unsupported vines to creep into the once-sacred space. The arched stone entrance, where the heavy wooden door once stood proud, now framed a scene of the wild forested moor, bathed eerily in the moonlight beyond, like a portal to some otherworldly realm.

'By the saints, look at this place,' Brother Eadric muttered, his voice wavering. He could feel the weight of dread settling upon his shoulders like a heavy cloak as he gazed around the dim chamber, struggling to reconcile its current state with the memories of solemn gatherings held until recently.

'Indeed,' replied Oswin, his tone betraying both fascination and unease.

As they stood before Abbot Cuthbert's partially ruined tomb, surrounded by the remnants of the shattered roof and debris from the quake, Eadric couldn't help but question their decision to come here. Whether it was his curiosity about the book or his loyalty to Oswin, who was driven by an insatiable obsession, he remained rooted to the spot.

'Oswin, remember our vows. We are monks and we must follow the Prior's instructions and replace the book in the reliquary, not to satisfy our curiosity.'

'Curiosity?' Oswin scoffed, flipping through the pages of the book with an almost feverish intensity. 'This is about more than simple curiosity, Eadric. This is about knowledge – something that could change everything we know about the world.'

As Oswin collected several cresset candles from nearby stands, Eadric couldn't help but be drawn in by his fervour, despite the gnawing fear that chewed at the edges of his mind. He glanced back at the entrance, where the moonlit moor beckoned like a siren's song, and knew that he was irrevocably trapped, caught in the tangled web woven by his own conflicting desires.

From the sleeve of his robe, Oswin retrieved and carefully struck the flint and steel, creating sparks that danced in the gloom of the ruined chapter house. One by one, the candles on the makeshift table – a large block of stone fallen from the roof – came to life, their flickering flames casting eerie shadows across the ancient walls.

'Listen,' Oswin whispered, pausing for a moment to look up at Eadric, a mischievous glint in his eyes. 'I can hear your stomach rumbling from here, my friend. What say we make trial of my plan and summon a feast to quell the earthquake within you?'

Eadric felt a blush creep up his neck as he realised it was indeed his hunger echoing through the desolate chamber. He pressed a hand to his belly, hoping to silence the traitorous sound, but it was no use. The emptiness gnawed at him with a relentless persistence that mirrored the unease coiling within his chest.

Oswin turned to the middle of the book to rediscover the page beautifully illustrated with a table laden with all manner of earthly delights. He ran a finger over the page, tracing the intricate symbols that adorned its aged surface. 'It appears to be a simple arrangement of candles – see here, these crosses and dots must represent their positions. If I'm not mistaken, the dots indicate where the candles should be placed.'

With painstaking care, Oswin began to arrange the candles according to the pattern he had deciphered. 'Three and the first row, one on the second, two on the fourth, just so...' Oswin muttered under his breath, placing the last candle with a satisfied nod.

As the last candle found its place, a shiver ran down Eadric's spine as if some unseen presence had brushed against his soul. He glanced around nervously, searching for any sign of movement in the moonlit shadows that stretched across the chamber like grasping fingers. No sooner had Oswin completed the pattern, than a gentle, fragrant breeze swept through the chamber, causing the candles to flicker and dance. Eadric stepped back in fear as the wind seemed to coalesce before them, weaving itself into a shimmering tapestry that hung in the air, ghostly at first but manifest nonetheless.

Before their astonished gaze, the tapestry wavered and solidified, taking on the form of a large wooden table covered in a pristine white tablecloth. The shadows retreated from its warm glow as if banished by the mere presence of such a spectacle. And upon the table lay a feast fit for kings: steaming dishes of roasted meat, glistening with succulent juices; mounds of buttery vegetables, their vibrant, glistening hues contrasting with the crisp, golden crusts of freshly baked bread.

'By all that is holy,' Oswin breathed, his eyes wide with wonder. He reached out tentatively as if fearing the vision would vanish at his touch, but his fingers met the solid wood of the conjured table. 'It worked, Eadric! It truly worked!'

Eadric could not deny the evidence before him, but a sense of unease tugged at his heart, making it beat faster within his chest. 'What have we done?' he asked, trying to suppress the shiver that ran down his spine. 'Have we not broken the law of nature?' His stomach growled despite himself. Oswin let out an exhilarated laugh, breaking off a chunk of bread and dipping it into the gravy of a meaty stew.

'Silence your doubts, my friend,' Oswin replied, his voice filled with excitement. He slowly savoured the soaking bread, closing his eyes in ecstasy. 'This is a miracle – a gift granted to us by our curiosity and perseverance. It has been sent by God to help us in our hour of need.'

Eadric's stomach growled hungrily at the sight of the

roasted meats, the fragrant steam from the vegetables awakening an insatiable desire to taste their flavours. He swallowed hard, struggling to resist the temptation that beckoned him.

'See?' Oswin grinned, his eyes shining with triumph. 'There is no cause for fear, only joy in our discovery. Abbot Cuthbert's miracles have returned to us.' He held out a luscious, pomegranate from a bowl of exotic fruits. 'I have only ever drawn such a fruit from a copy and have never seen one in the flesh.'

'Don't!' Eadric lurched forward, batting the fruit away. It bounced across the floor, landing atop a pile of debris. 'This is not right. We should return the book immediately.' Eadric set his jaw. 'The Prior commanded you to—'

The ground shuddered, an aftershock throwing him off balance. Candles toppled from their positions, rolling across the floor, spluttering briefly before recovering their flickering vigour. The scent of food vanished, as did the table before them.

Oswin's face darkened. 'Return it? When we've barely scratched the surface of its contents? With this knowledge, we could transform the world. Do you want people to go hungry needlessly?' He turned the page, pointing to an elaborate illustration of a vast library filled with towering shelves of books. 'I can make out the ancient word for Alexandria – it's the secrets of the ancient world made available again by this single book. Think of the knowledge that awaits us within these volumes! If we can summon them, just as we did the table, there will be no end to what we could learn.'

Eadric hesitated, feeling a pit of unease forming in his stomach. 'The movements of the earth are a warning – the Prior commanded us to return the book to the reliquary. We have already strayed from that path.' His voice wavered, betraying his growing fear.

'True,' Oswin admitted, his eyes still fixed on the image of the library, 'but he only said we must return this book. These books,' – he gestured at the illustration – 'are different. Surely they are meant for us to study, to learn from.' The scribe collected the candles from the floor and began to place them into the exotic stone cresset according to the placement of dots and crosses on the page.

Eadric, unable to bear it any longer, reached out to pull the book away from his fellow scribe, hoping to halt the conjuration. Yet Oswin's grip was firm, and a mild scuffle ensued, each monk grasping at the ancient tome. As their hands grappled, Eadric saw the fervour in Oswin's eyes, the unyielding obsession with the book's hidden knowledge. His hands slipped, and he was flung back, dislodging a candle from the cresset.

Oswin replaced the fallen candle, fumbling to find a slot and keeping his gaze fixed on his wavering friend. 'It's only books, Eadric. That's all I truly want.'

But what appeared moments later was not the lost treasures from the Great Library of Alexandria, but something else.

A sickening darkness began to seep from the ruined arch, tendrils of blackness reaching out into the moonlit chamber like the groping fingers of some unseen spectre. The air grew thick with the stench of decay and horror, suffocating any semblance of peace that may have lingered within the ancient walls.

Something moved in the darkness of the archway. A presence, ancient and malevolent. Eadric's mouth went dry, a scream building in his throat.

'What is happening?' Oswin cried, his voice barely audible above the howling wind that now tore through the room, sending the pages of the abbot's book into a frenzied dance.

'Something's wrong,' Eadric muttered, his eyes wide with

terror as he stared at the all-consuming darkness that continued to pour from the archway.

Eadric, despite the fear that clutched at his heart, drew nearer to the book, his gaze fixated on the dancing pages. With trembling fingers, he reached out to still them, desperate for answers. As he pinned the page down, the horrifying truth struck him like a bolt of lightning.

'Oswin, you placed the candle incorrectly!' he shouted, the words heavy with dread.

'Impossible! I followed the illustration precisely!' Oswin looked over Eadric's shoulder at the open page, his face paled, drained of all colour.

Before them, the page did not depict the promised library shelves laden with precious tomes, but a monstrous figure that seemed to leer from the parchment, its burning eyes boring into the monks' very souls. It was the visage of a demon, and their misguided summoning had called forth this abomination instead of the knowledge they so craved.

The darkness continued to billow forth as if fed by the monks' growing horror. Eadric could feel the icy tendrils of fear wrapping around his chest, constricting his breath as the oppressive heat and blackness drew ever nearer.

'God help us,' he whispered, his voice trembling with the weight of his terror. 'What have we done? Quickly, extinguish the candles; we must undo our mistake before it is too late!'

'Forgive us, Lord,' Oswin prayed silently, his hands shaking as he extinguished the last candle. 'Deliver us from this abomination and grant us the strength to resist the temptations that led us here.'

The demon advanced, fully three times the height of a man, crushing the smaller fallen stone blocks beneath its scaly feet. Half jumping and running like a great ape, it surged forward reaching out its claw towards them.

'It's still here!' cried Oswin from behind one of the remaining pillars supporting part of the remaining roof.

'It is the fiend from Acra and the other cities!' said Eadric. 'The old records were true – it will not return until it is sated!' As if in accord, the smouldering smoke of the candles twirled and ignited into a shower of sparks falling upon the wicks of the cresset square and setting the candles alight with a ferocity that brightened what remained of the chapter house into an incandescence that blinded the two monks. With his eyes of little use, Eadric rolled beside one of the remaining pillars and heard the demon bellow, bringing down pieces of the roof. His heart thundered within his chest, his body slick with sweat as he clung to the cold stone for support. Far away, the distant shrieks and shouts of the woken monks provided little comfort.

Blinded by the sudden resurgence of light, Oswin stumbled forward, his arms flailing wildly to regain his balance. He staggered unwittingly into the path of the waiting demon, whose claws were raised high in anticipation of its prey. With a malevolent swipe, the demon's razor-sharp talons slashed across his chest, tearing through flesh and fabric alike. Scarlet ribbons of blood blossomed from the wounds, marring their sanctity with a vivid display of violence.

Eadric blinked, his eyes adjusting to the dreadful scene from beyond the pathetic safety of cover. 'Oswin!' he screamed, his words choked by the bile that rose in his throat. His gaze remained fixed on the gruesome tableau before him, unable to tear himself away.

But the demon was not yet finished. Its cruel, fiery eyes locked onto the dying monk, and with a guttural growl, it lunged forward once more. Grasping Oswin's broken form in its vice-like grip, the creature brandished him like a rag doll, slamming him against the unforgiving walls of the chapter house. A sickening crunch echoed through the air as bones shattered under the force of each blow. Oswin's blood sprayed in slick rivulets across the stones, a red rain that heralded a coming storm. Eadric's heart thundered in his chest as he watched the demon toss the lifeless form before it like a macabre plaything. From beyond the far entranceway, the other monks arrived like a collapsing train of baggage carts and stopped in their tracks, their faces twisted with terror and disbelief, unable to fathom the nightmare that had befallen their sanctuary.

'Stand fast, brothers!' Prior Anselm roared, his voice cutting through the night like a blade. Grasping shards of broken wood from the rubble, the stout monk charged towards the creature, brandishing his makeshift weapon like a crucifix. 'Exorcizamus te, omnis immundus spiritus!'. The demon recoiled, the air around it crackling with malevolent energy, yet it did not retreat. Instead, it lunged at the defiant prior, teeth bared and claws slashing through the flickering shadows.

Several of the stout-hearted monks formed a vanguard around their leader, distracting the beast with tossed stones and taunting its fell hide with makeshift spears and clubs from splintered pews. 'Have we no recourse against this terror that has awoken from the bowels of the shifting earth?' said Prior Anselm retreating, his eyes wide and vacant with despair. 'Is this truly the end of our order?'

Eadric clenched his fists, his nails biting into his palms as he wrestled with the crushing weight of guilt. He knew that to give in, to abandon all hope, was to condemn not only himself but also his brethren to a grisly fate. And yet, what could he do in the face of such overwhelming darkness? What power did he possess that could banish this infernal beast back to the abyss whence it came? Curiosity and disobedience had caused this, and he knew that more than faith would be needed to banish the foul creature, even if it cost him all he held dear.

'Lord, grant me strength,' he prayed, his voice barely audible amidst the chaos. 'Whatever price must be paid to cure me of my folly and this fiend, I swear I will endure it!' At that moment, a spark ignited within him, a fierce determination that burned away the shadows of doubt and fear. He caught sight of the book and knew what to do.

'Lord, guide my hand,' he said, his thoughts a chaotic whirlwind of fear and determination. The demon's shadow loomed over him, ignoring the inconsequential blows from the stinging white-robed gnats about its feet trying to penetrate its scaly hide. Eadric's fingers seemed to move of their own accord, guided by some unseen force. His heart clenched with a mixture of fear and burgeoning hope as he landed on the page he sought, even as the darkness belched forward, threatening to swallow him whole.

In that heartrending moment, Brother Eadric's gaze fell upon the image he had been seeking – the sword-wielding angel, resplendent in its divine radiance. The intricate lines of the illustration seemed to shimmer and dance on the parchment, as though imbued with a life force of their own, defying the filth that spewed forth beside him. A valiant and concerted strike by the monks, aimed at the creature's heel momentarily distracted the beast, and it turned to swipe the air scattering the brothers in a cloud of billowing robes.

With trembling hands, Eadric began to rearrange the candles in the cresset square, his eyes darting back and forth between the sacred image and the flickering flames. He could feel the sweat beading on his brow as he moved each candle with painstaking precision, the weight of their collective fate resting heavily upon his shoulders.

'Dear Lord, guide my hands,' he said, the words slipping from his lips like a fervent prayer. As the last candle settled into place within the cresset, the pattern was complete, and the darkness seemed to recede ever so slightly, the oppressive gloom giving way to a faint glimmer of hope.

No sooner had the last candle settled into place than the demon, sensing the threat of its celestial counterpart, lunged towards Eadric with a guttural snarl. The searing heat of the creature's approach was palpable, like the breath of an infernal forge. As it closed in, the smell of burning parchment filled the air, the ancient pages of the tome curling and blackening in its wake. The pain in his hands was unbearable, like hot iron branding his flesh, yet he stubbornly refused to relinquish the book, clutching the tome closely to his chest and falling to his knees in agony.

'Please, Lord,' he whispered, his thoughts a mixture of hope and despair. 'Let this be enough.'

As if in answer to his plea, a blinding light suddenly burst forth from the ruined archway, cutting through the darkness like a divine blade. The demon, surprised, turned its attention towards the new threat, momentarily forgetting about Eadric and the other monks.

The blinding light intensified, casting an ethereal glow upon the crumbling walls of the chapter house. Brother Eadric, still sprawled on the floor, felt a divine warmth wash over him, momentarily easing the pain of his scorched hands and smouldering robes. He dared not look directly at the source of the radiance, but he knew in his heart that their salvation had come.

'Stand back!' a monk cried out, pulling Eadric further away as they all stared, wide-eyed, at the ruined archway. 'Mercy! – the lord has sent us a champion.'

And indeed it was. A towering figure emerged slowly, its form terrible to behold, yet awe-inspiring in its magnificence. The angel's eyes, too many to count, burned like the very fires of heaven, while its wings, vast and multi-layered, shimmered with an iridescence that seemed to defy the very laws of nature. In its right hand, the celestial being clutched a flaming sword, the weapon's edge gleaming like the dawn itself.

The demon snarled, its eyes narrowing into burning slits as it appraised its new opponent. With an enraged roar, it lunged at the angel, claws slashing through the air like razors, only to be met by the swift arc of the heavenly blade. As the two titanic forces collided, the very foundations of the monastery seemed to tremble under the weight of their struggle. Sparks flew as sword met claw, and the air crackled with an energy that sent shivers down Eadric's spine.

'Down on your knees, brothers!' the Prior urged his fellow monks. 'Our prayers will strengthen the angel's resolve!'

With every passing moment, the battle between angel and demon grew more intense, their movements a blur of light and shadow as they danced a deadly ballet within the confines of the ruined chamber. The angel's flaming sword cleaved the darkness, while the demon's claws raked against stone and air alike, seeking to tear its divine adversary asunder.

Eadric shivered with pain, and the monks' prayers rose around him like a chorus, their voices united in a desperate plea for salvation.

'O Lord, grant us deliverance from this evil!' they cried, as the demon snarled and lashed out with renewed fury, sensing the tide of battle turning against it.

The angel rose into the air like a rising sun, its sword blazing as it struck again and again at the monstrous form of the demon. With each blow that landed, the demon seemed to shrink, its dark essence disintegrating under the relentless onslaught. It turned, seeking escape from the fury of its adversary's holiness, but found only a shield wall of kneeling, unbreakable faith before it.

And with that, the angel raised its sword high above its

head, the blade gleaming with a light that seemed to pierce the heart of the darkness itself. As it plunged the weapon down, the demon let out a final, guttural cry – and then, in a burst of acrid smoke and flame, it was gone.

A stillness descended as the first light of dawn began to filter through the broken windows, casting the chapter house in a pale, ghostly glow that mingled with the iridescent halo surrounding the angelic being. It stood, bathed in its radiance, shifting as though searching for someone or something.

Eadric, his heart pounding in his chest, rolled to his knees as well, clutching the ancient book with hands that shook from both relief and exhaustion. 'Lord,' he whispered, his voice barely audible amid the murmured prayers of his brethren. He glanced over the corpse of his friend and bowed his head in shame and grief. 'I thank you for your mercy and protection.'

As the angel advanced towards him, Eadric felt a strange mix of awe and fear. There was something about its presence that made him feel small and insignificant – a testament to the power of the divine. The angel's radiance dimmed, allowing Eadric to see clearly for the first time. Its form was both benign and holy, yet terrible in its majesty; an Old Testament seraphim with six wings, myriad eyes, and a countenance too much for mortal eyes to withstand.

From within the divine being, Eadric heard his earlier words clearly relayed:

'Whatever price must be paid to cure me of my folly...'

'I will endure it...' Eadric choked out as the angel reached out to retrieve the book from his grasp. The pages fluttered as though moved by an unseen breeze, and his gaze was drawn downward to the page upon which lay a vision of heaven, so clearly and beautifully depicted that it seemed almost real. The image seared itself into his mind, becoming the last thing he would ever see, for in that moment, his eyes became opaque and sightless, the whites inked with a tattoo of such richness and complexity as to conjure the memory of some great illuminated work.

All who saw them in later days, marvelled at the sight, buoyed by the tale of the miracle and the banishing of evil from the chapterhouse, restored and renewed by offerings from the pilgrims who came to see the blind brother who had seen a vision of heaven and looked into the face of a servant of the almighty.

In quieter moments and later years, old Brother Eadric would hold vigil next to the repaired tomb of the abbot, and the simple plain stone floor slab of the grave to a scribe whose curiosity and folly had restored a monastery, strengthened a faith, and humbled a man whose first and last bittersweet remembrance each day was of heaven, until the day he died.

SLEEP NOW, ADELARD

The Scillonian II lurched over another swell, spraying salt water against my face. I clutched the ferry's railing with white knuckles, the cold metal biting into my palms. I stared out at the turbulent waves and felt a strange sense of relief to have left Penzance behind, heading towards the furthest point in England and away from the past six months. This time last year we were all together: Robert, Sarah, and I, and now I felt sick for even thinking about taking a break from my grief. The air was thick with May's promise of summer, and in brief interludes, like the occasional calm lulls in the swell before me, it was a welcome change from the oppressive weight of memories that haunted me back in Oxford... But the guilt still clawed inside my chest, sharper than the Celtic sea wind whipping my auburn hair, threatening to dislodge my crocheted beret.

I blinked back tears, Sarah's face flashing before me. My little girl, so full of joy and mischief, until the meningitis took her before she'd seen her tenth birthday. I should have noticed sooner, should have realised how ill she was. If only I'd been a better mother, perhaps she'd still be here.

And Robert. My husband who'd held me as I wept, telling me it wasn't my fault. Six months later, gone in a test flight accident. I'd pushed him away in my grief, barely speaking or looking at him those last few weeks. If I'd been stronger, would he have been distracted that day? Would he be here now, holding my hand on this ferry instead of lying at rest beside our daughter?

'It was an accident, Jane...they both were...' How often could family and friends repeat it until I had to escape across the sea to avoid hearing it one more time, and seeing the pity in their eyes as I looked away refusing to accept it.

I dug my nails into my palms, relishing the pain. I didn't deserve solace or closure. But I had to keep going, had to find a way to live with the gaping holes they'd left behind. The ferry sailed on, carrying me towards whatever awaited on the distant Isles of Scilly. Towards a new chapter, or maybe just more heartache. I didn't know anymore. All I could do was place one foot in front of the other and keep breathing through the storm.

'Are you all right, miss?' A concerned crew member approached, eyeing my pale complexion and trembling hands.

I forced a small smile, nodding as I wiped away unbidden tears. 'Yes, thank you. Just a bit seasick, I suppose.'

He nodded, seemingly accepting the explanation, and offered me some words of comfort before continuing on his rounds. I sighed, turning my gaze back to the roiling sea. I caught sight of St Mary's on the horizon, the largest inhabited island in the sub-tropical archipelago twenty-eight miles off Land's End – perhaps this journey would be the beginning of something new, a chance to heal and find closure. The ship heaved and rocked beneath me, the churning waves mirroring the chaotic storm within my heart, and as I watched the waves crash against the hull, I made a silent promise to myself, just for the three or four days I had planned to stay. No-one here would judge me, or feel sorry for me.

The best I could do was try to do the same.

As we rounded Peninnis Head, the entrance to the largest island settlement, Hugh Town, came into view. I couldn't help but marvel at the vibrant sight, ripped from a picture-perfect postcard and into reality – an array of brightly coloured boats bobbing in the harbour, their reflections dancing on the water's surface like a kaleidoscope of hope. Beyond them, rows of quaint houses with whitewashed walls and painted doors stood proudly, a testament to the resilience of island life against the unforgiving elements. For a few short days, I could pretend I was just a tourist on holiday, not a woman hollowed out by tragedy.

The ferry pulled alongside the granite quay, its ancient stones worn smooth by countless footsteps and the passage of time. As I disembarked, my legs wobbled slightly, unsteady from the turbulent crossing. I took a deep breath, inhaled the salty sea air, and felt a small sense of accomplishment in having made it this far.

'Welcome to St Mary's,' said a voice, pulling me from my thoughts. I turned towards the harbour office, where a woman with a warm smile and friendly eyes greeted me. She was middle-aged, her red hair streaked with grey and drawn back into a neat bun. Her practical clothing and salt-tanned hands hinted at a pragmatic nature, while her mannerisms were kind and approachable of the type far removed from the stresses and strains of urban, mainland life.

'Thank you,' I replied, trying to match her warmth with a wavering smile. 'I'm Jane French. I have a reservation at the Star Castle Hotel.'

'Ah, yes,' she said, her face clouding over with regret. 'I'm afraid there's been some issue at the hotel, and they're closed for emergency repairs. I'm so sorry for the inconvenience.'

She paused, considering her options before continuing, 'The island is quite busy at the moment because of the gig rowing championships, but I'll do my best to find you alternative accommodation. Even the locals are pitching in to take up the extra people – we're fit to bursting in Hugh Town.'

The woman clucked sympathetically as she rifled through her files. 'Let's see what we can find for you.'

I nodded numbly, too weary to muster any genuine reaction. At this point, all I wanted was a horizontal surface to collapse upon. She nodded and disappeared into the small office, leaving me alone with my thoughts. As I gazed out across the harbour, the picturesque scene seemed almost surreal, as if it belonged to a world that existed separate from my pain. Joy seemed tangible and free. Even the gulls chuckled as they hovered effortlessly and expectantly above a bench full of chip-eating sightseers.

'I only have one option, though it's a bit...unconventional,' the woman said slowly, returning and holding up a card. 'It's isolated, but the views are breathtaking.'

She hesitated, seeming unsure. My curiosity stirred faintly.

'The old widow who owns it is a touch eccentric – it's available for the three nights you are here, but...' She pointed to a faded, laminated map on the counter. The cottage sat on Garrison Head, overlooking the cheerful town, but set further back from other houses around it. Solitude again. Perhaps that was for the best.

The woman hesitated, her eyes darting away from mine. 'I'm not sure,' she admitted, pulling back the card with a slight frown. 'I don't usually recommend it to visitors.' She bit her lip, obviously torn between offering me the details and keeping quiet.

'Please,' I urged her, desperation creeping into my tone. 'I'll take anything at this point.'

She sighed, handing me the card with a look of uncertainty. 'It's called Hellweathers Cottage. It's... well, it's a bit noisy.'

'Noisy?' I echoed, raising an eyebrow. My curiosity was piqued despite my exhaustion and disappointment. 'What does the old lady get up to?'

She looked up from her paperwork, eyebrows knitting together as she chewed on her lip for a moment. 'Well,' she said slowly, seeming to choose her words carefully, 'I suppose 'noisy' isn't quite the right word. 'Unquiet' might be more fitting. The host, Mary Pender, is a lovely old sort, but the place has something of an unusual reputation.'

'Unusual?' The word sent a shiver down my spine, but my determination remained steadfast. I needed a place to stay, and if this was my only option, I would take it.

The woman held up her hand. 'Nothing unwholesome—'

'I'll take it,' I said firmly. The woman nodded, relief flashing across her face. She'd done her duty; another desperate, roofless widow was no longer her problem.

I squared my shoulders as I walked out. The sea mist hung heavy, obscuring whatever awaited me on that lonely cliff-side. But I would keep putting one foot in front of the other. For Sarah. For Robert. Until I found absolution, or until the sea swallowed me whole.

The sun lowered into late afternoon easiness as I approached the pretty, paint-peeling gate of Hellweathers Cottage, casting a warm glow over the idyllic sub-tropical, postage stamp-sized front garden. I marvelled at the vibrant riot of colours in such a small space; lush ferns and stumpy palm nestled alongside vivid blue agapanthus and fragrant honeysuckle. Mossy stone walls encircled the granite cottage like an embrace, creating a cosy and inviting atmosphere that seemed to wrap itself around me. The air buzzed with life as bees and insects flitted among the blossoms. I followed the stone path to the front door, brushing past fragrant jasmine vines.

I raised my hand to knock just as the door swung open. Before me stood a petite, white-haired woman, her kind eyes crinkling at the corners as she offered me a warm, wide, whiskered smile.

'You must be Jane! I'm Mary, come in dear, I've just put the kettle on.' Her voice was warm and comforting.

I stepped inside the cosy living room and put down my case as she busied herself in the kitchen.

'It's not often we get visitors out here. Milk and sugar?'

'Just milk, thanks.' I settled onto the sofa.

Mary returned with two steaming mugs. 'We don't get many tourists, they all prefer to stay in town. But we like the peace and quiet out here, don't we?'

'There was a problem with the hotel,' I said, careful not to suggest that my only alternative to sleeping beneath the stars was at Hellweathers. 'But I'm so glad you could accommodate me.'

'Please, make yourself at home. We want you to be comfortable here,' she continued, her voice warm and gentle. I couldn't help but notice the odd way she used 'we' when talking or answering questions, but I brushed it aside for now. A widow was entitled to guests or family members staying after all. I stopped the train of thought in its tracks. My eyes were drawn to a series of children's drawings framed on the wall. They appeared to be done in crayon, depicting crudely drawn ships with stick figure passengers. Some stood on the decks, while others seemed to be swimming in the blue scribbled sea surrounding the vessels.

I stood up and leaned in for a closer look. The hand was

that of a child, no older than eight or nine. Yet the paper ranged from crisp white printer paper to aged, yellowing sheets. One was even on an old letterhead, the watermark barely legible.

'Did you do these?' I asked.

Mary chuckled. 'Oh no, those have been up for many years now. We find them charming in a strange sort of way, don't we?'

'One of your grandchildren perhaps?' I inquired, curiosity piqued by her continued use of 'we.'

Mary paused, her hand extending me a plate of custard creams. She looked thoughtful for a moment before replying, 'You flatter me – I'm eighty-two. Well, it's just me, dear, but we've had many guests over the years. They leave a bit of themselves behind, you see.'

'Like these drawings?' I asked, gesturing towards the wall.

'Exactly,' she replied, her eyes twinkling with a hint of mystery.

I smiled, realising it was genuine and not forced for the benefit of others. It felt freeing and fresh, as though it was the first time I had ever done so.

Mary patted my hand. 'You must be tired from your journey, let me show you to your room.'

I nodded, unsure of what to make of her words, and turned my attention instead to unpacking my case and settling in.

A short hallway led to two adjoining rooms and Mary brushed past to open the door to the farthest. I stepped into the bedroom, taking in the whitewashed walls and small blue window frames that looked out onto the harbour below. Climbing roses framed the view, peeping in to see the new occupant. It was a quaint, comfortable room, just what I needed for several peaceful nights' rest.

My gaze fell upon the old wooden school desk tucked

against the far wall. Foxed papers and broken crayons littered its surface, bearing the scratches and scribbles of many small hands over countless years.

I ran my fingers over the carved initials and dates etched into the desk's surface, some dating back to the mid-1800s. A flood of memories washed over me as I pictured my daughter sitting at such a desk, her hand furiously scribbling some indecipherable story or careful drawing.

The pain of losing her felt as raw as the day she'd been taken from me. But here, in this quiet room with only the cry of gulls outside, the ache felt less acute, dulled by the thick stone shielding of the granite walls.

'We hope you like the room?'

I took a deep breath and turned to Mary. 'Thank you, this is perfect. Will your...other relation be in the room next door then?'

Mary paused, confusion clouding her warm eyes. 'Other relation, dear?'

'Yes, the one you keep referring to as 'we.' I just assumed...'

The way she used 'we' once again caught my attention. There was more to the story, but Mary didn't seem keen to share it just yet. I let the matter rest and instead focused on the idea of another occupant in the cottage – perhaps a child, given the drawings.

Mary smoothed down her pinafore and scratched at the back of her liver-spotted hand. 'That'll be Adelard's room, but don't worry – he won't bother you.'

I nodded, trying to convince myself that the woman at the harbour office wasn't going to be right about the cottage being noisy if there was a child in the house. I wasn't wholly sure if I was ready to engage with someone who might be of Sarah's age.

She smiled and squeezed my shoulder. 'I'll leave you to

settle in. I recommend the Mermaid down by the quay if you want an evening meal though you might like to watch the woman's gig race tonight - they usually set off around seven.'

The door closed behind her with a soft click, leaving me alone with my thoughts in the cosy room. I unpacked and stood, soaking in the sea view when the tin of crayons suddenly tipped over and spilled across the floor, rolling beneath the bed. I kneeled to retrieve and replace the waxed miscreants to their tin realising a gust of wind could not have unsettled the artist's materials as the window was shut. Selecting a sun-yellow crayon from the desk, I began doodling on the uppermost piece of paper, sketching a simple sun with lines radiating out in all directions. Without thinking, I added two dots for eyes and a slight frown. Even my absent-minded drawings reflected the sadness that clung to me.

I needed to get out, breathe some fresh air, clear my head. I had come to the Isles of Scilly seeking solace and healing, and perhaps in the quiet corners of this idyllic haven, I would find just that, but not imprisoned in a gilded cage with a beautiful view.

'Mary, I'm going into town to explore a bit. I'll be back later.'

'Of course, dear, enjoy yourself!'

I stepped outside into the warm afternoon sun. From the rear, a cobblestone path wound downhill hill, and I followed it eagerly, breathing in the scent of scented herbs, emerging bracken, and good Atlantic air. I emerged ten minutes later onto a narrow street lined with quaint shops and cafes. Tourists milled about, popping in and out of the various narrow doorways of gift shops. I wandered, simply taking in the sights and sounds.

In the newsagents on the corner of a wide thoroughfare, I purchased a postcard featuring a striking granite brown lighthouse, its tall form rising from a single outcrop of rock amidst crashing waves.

'That's Bishop Rock,' said the shopkeeper. 'Finest lighthouse in the south west and as far as you can go in England; next stop is New York. You can take boat trips out to see it up close, and you might even spot some puffins along the way.'

I tucked the postcard into my bag. Perhaps I would do just that. For now, I was content to lose myself in the charming streets. The ache inside me had eased ever so slightly, and I breathed deeply of the island air, grateful for this moment of peace.

After several lazy hours of exploring the town and wading barefoot on Porthcressa beach, I made my way back to the quay. The sun was dipping towards the horizon, casting a golden glow over the water as locals and tourists alike gathered to watch the women gig rowers set off for the nearby island of St Agnes.

'Excuse me,' I said to a man standing nearby, his eyes scanning the boats. 'Which ones are the gig boats?'

'Ah, you're in luck!' He replied enthusiastically, pointing at the many coloured boats being carried by the lithe and tanned arms of the woman rowers. 'Look for the long, slim boats just leaving the boathouse. There's Bonnet, Slippen, and Golden Eagle, coming out now – they are brightly coloured to stand out when they are far from shore.'

'Thank you,' I murmured, my gaze following his outstretched finger to where other boats from the off-islands were lining up in a rough line out in the bay. Their vivid colours danced on the water's surface, their reflections shimmering like jewels.

The late arriving boats jostled and spun with their counterparts ready for the signal like the start line of a great steeplechase, manoeuvring for position, aiming for the faster waters and currents that only generations of Scillonians could know and master. The marshal boat tooted its horn, signalling the start of the race. Oars rippled through the waves, slicing into the water with precision as the cox's loud commands rang out across the bay, keeping the rhythm steady. My heart swelled with the energy of the moment, the excitement contagious as I joined the spectators in cheering on the rowers. Oars dipped and pulled as one, cutting swiftly through the bay water's glassy surface. The boats glided past in a blur of motion and sound, determination etched on the rowers' faces.

I found myself transfixed, drawn into the power and grace of their synchronised movements. The ache inside receded further as I lost myself in the dance of oars and boats, living in the triumphant present, if only for a moment.

'Come on, Bonnet!' A woman next to me yelled, her hands cupped around her mouth to amplify her voice. Her enthusiasm was infectious, and I couldn't help but join in, letting the cathartic release of my own shouts carry away some of the heaviness that had settled in my chest.

'Go, Slippen! You can do it, Golden Eagle!'

As I shouted and clapped alongside the other onlookers, I felt something inside me begin to shift. For the first time since Sarah's death, I was allowing myself to be swept up in the present moment, to let go of my grief and guilt, if only for a short while. It was as if the rowers' determination and strength were acting as an anchor, grounding me in this foreign yet welcoming landscape.

'Who are you rooting for?' The woman next to me asked, her eyes sparkling with excitement.

The boats raced onward, churning up white caps as they rounded the headland and disappeared from view. All except one – a trailing red boat called Czar, with a rower in the prow clearly struggling to match the others' timing.

'Czar,' I replied without hesitation, surprising even myself with my newfound certainty and the use of the present tense. 'Red is my daughter's favourite colour.'

'Well, they've got youth on their side but it's a scratch crew – they've got quite the catching up ahead of them!' She exclaimed, gesturing to the other boats racing past the struggling gig I had chosen, slicing through the water like arrows.

As the swells buffeted their scarlet gig, the woman rower's uncertainty was plain, her oar strokes tentative against the power of her teammates. My heart went out to her at that moment, recognising the fear of not being enough. She was out of sync, her movements hesitant and unsure.

'Come on,' I whispered to myself, feeling an inexplicable bond with this stranger. 'You can do this – there's nothing you can't do right now!'

It was as if my silent encouragement reached her across the waves, for she suddenly seemed to find her footing. Her eyes locked onto those of her teammates, and soon her oar was slicing through the water in perfect synchrony with theirs. The boat began to surge forward, gaining on its competitors.

'Go, Czar!' I shouted, clapping my hands together. 'Keep going!'

My heart raced as I watched them fight against the waves, the rower's newfound determination and inner strength propelling her boat ever closer to the leading gigs. It was as if she embodied a resilience I had been searching for within myself, a symbol of what it meant to face adversity head-on and triumph.

'You can do it!' I whispered, my hands gripping the rough stone of the quay wall as if I could will her onward through sheer force.

Around me, the crowd buzzed with anticipation, their voices blending into a chorus of encouragement and awe. The boats raced around Garrison Head, disappearing one by one into the horizon like colourful specks on a vast canvas. My heart thudded in my chest, the thrill of the race coursing through my veins. I waited, listening to the excited chatter and babble of the expectant crowd, straining to hear who might have won.

'It's close!' someone shouted, and we all strained our ears for the distant sound of a horn. Moments later, it came – a triumphant blare echoing from the distant inhabited island of St Agnes, signalling the end of the contest.

'Who won?' I couldn't help but ask, my breath hitching in my throat.

A man raced down the Garrison path and into the crowd, reaching for the lid of the wooden box next to a short flag pole. His hands rummaged within and I caught glimpses between the tightly packed wall of onlookers of what I thought at first to be colourful bunting. A moment later he was tying something to the cord at the base of the pole, hoisting the vivid red pennant high into the air. It snapped into shape and flew with pride.

'Czar made quite the comeback,' the man replied, out of breath. 'They say she went from trailing to leading in the final stretch. A healthy dose of beginner's luck! It's a lesson for us all – there's no force greater than determination and hope.'

'Or the promise of free beer at The Turk's Head over there on St Agnes!' one replied, much to the amusement of the locals.

My heart swelled with emotion, the impact of my unseen support on Czar's performance washing over me like a tidal wave. I had witnessed a transformation, a testament to the power of the human spirit and the unbreakable bond between people working together. And although the woman in the red boat would never know it, her journey had deeply touched my own.

I realised life was a series of waves, some gentle and others fierce, but always presenting an opportunity to rise or sink. I wondered whether I was still rowing, or drowning as I made my way back to Hellweathers Cottage, my footsteps crunching softly on the gravel headland path. Once inside the cottage, I closed the door behind me and leaned against it, allowing myself to fully absorb the events of the day.

I found my room just as I'd left it, save for several minor details. The postcard of Bishop's Rock rested atop the worn desk, not where I had left it, its edges curling slightly. I picked it up, running my fingers over the glossy image of the lighthouse standing tall amidst the crashing waves. Like a beacon, guiding lost souls home. I set the postcard aside, planning to write and post it the following morning. That's when I saw what lay on the paper beneath.

The crude sun from earlier still radiated on the blank page, but a smile, heavily drawn to hide my down-turned expression, now lay upon its face. Someone had been in the room.

With the first stars of night beginning to twinkle outside my window, I prepared for a restful night. As I slipped off my shoes and reached down to smooth the quilt, a flash of orange caught my eye. A single crayon lay on the floor beside the bed, its vibrant hue a stark contrast to the muted tones of the room.

Had it been there before? I was certain I had collected all the spilt crayons earlier. I glanced at the door, pondering the mystery briefly before shrugging it off and placing the crayon on the desk beside the postcard. Despite the trespass, whoever Adelard was, I felt oddly comforted now imagining a child's presence in the room next door.

As I settled into the comfortable bed, the gentle sounds of a distant sea bell drifted through the open window, lulling me into a restful sleep. The world seemed to hold its breath, waiting for me to find my way back to the surface – and perhaps, with each stroke forward, I was beginning to do just that.

A waking dream wrenched me into sudden darkness, unexpected and unfamiliar – the hum of a child, accompanied by what seemed to be the soft scratching of crayon on paper.

I jolted awake, my body tense, my breath stolen by the surprise. The melody was sweet and innocent, some old nursery rhyme I half-remembered, yet it sent shivers down my spine. It couldn't be possible. Sarah was gone, and I was alone in this strange house, far from the memories that haunted me.

'Who's there?' I demanded, my voice trembling as much as my hands, but the only response was the continuation of the humming and drawing. I sat up, the blankets falling away from me, my eyes searching the dimly lit room for the source of the sound. I needed to know if this was real or just another cruel trick my subconscious was playing on me in its twisted attempt to soothe my broken heart.

As I scanned the room, my gaze flitted between the dresser, the school desk, and the rough, plastered craters on the white-washed wall, ever seeking the elusive figure making the noise. The sensation of being watched was undeniable. Even so, no one appeared.

'Sarah?' I uttered her name hesitantly, knowing deep down that she was gone – that she would never return to me, no matter how much I longed for her presence. The humming and drawing continued, and I felt my heart race in my chest. I was at a loss, unsure of whether to cling to the hope that somehow, somewhere, my daughter had found her way back to me or to accept that perhaps I was truly losing myself to the darkness within.

My breath caught in my throat. 'Hello?' I whispered. 'Is someone there?'

The humming stopped abruptly. In the silence, a soft chuckle echoed through the room. It was unmistakably the sound of a small boy. With a surge of adrenaline, I bolted upright and reached for the lamp on my bedside table. Light flooded the room, blinding me momentarily.

Blinking rapidly to dispel the sudden spots dancing in my vision, I scanned the room again. Still empty. Just the mismatched furniture and me.

The silence that followed felt oppressive, wrapping around me like a heavy shroud. My thoughts churned, and I could feel my heart pounding against my ribcage, each beat a stark reminder of my loneliness, my isolation, my stupidity at waking from a dream, and my mind playing tricks on me.

The only response was the creaking of the old floorboards beneath my feet, as though the house itself was groaning under the weight of its hidden secrets. I stood rooted to the spot, waiting and listening, but the stillness remained unbroken.

And then, just as the last vestiges of sudden brightness began to recede from my vision, something caught my eye. A red crayon rolled across the floor, stopping at the side of the bedpost, its vibrant hue a stark contrast to the surrounding purity of the walls. I reached down and picked it up, its smooth wax surface warm in my trembling hand.

With a renewed sense of urgency, I hastily threw on my robe and opened the door, stepping out into the dimly lit corridor. The air was colder here, causing goosebumps to rise on my skin. My heart raced, fuelled by both fear and hope that I might find someone – anyone – to talk to.

Nothing. No sign of the intruder. Just the ticking of the old grandfather clock counting the early morning hours.

'Hello?' I called out tentatively, my voice echoing through the hallway. 'Is anyone there?'

The silence was deafening, and I felt an odd mixture of relief and disappointment wash over me. Desperate for any hint of sound or movement, I pressed my ear against the door of the room next to mine. My pulse thrummed in my ears as I strained, listening for the faintest whisper or footstep. A sudden creak from the floor behind me caught me off guard. I pivoted on my bare heel, colliding with something solid, and let out an involuntary gasp.

'Mary!' I exclaimed, my hand flying to my chest as my pulse quickened.

'Jane, dear,' Mary whispered, her wide eyes filled with concern. 'You're trembling. What's the matter? I heard you call out.'

I tried to slow my ragged breathing, to calm the tremor in my hands. 'I'm sorry, I – I thought I heard something. Someone in my room – a child—'

Understanding dawned in Mary's eyes. She laid a gentle hand on my shoulder. 'I'm sorry, the dear boy does so love to draw. I suppose he heard you stirring and thought you might like some company.'

'At this hour?'

'There now, no need to fret. Curious, that's all.' She raised her voice slightly, addressing the empty hall. 'Sleep now, Adelard.'

I listened intently, but no sound came from the adjoining room.

'He won't bother you again tonight. Adelard's a good boy, always does what he's told, except that one time...' Mary drifted off into a murmur.

'He gave me quite a shock,' I said.

Mary turned back to me with an apologetic smile. 'I'm afraid he's drawn to those who are...sad. He likely sensed you were troubled.'

I dropped my gaze. 'I just...miss my family, that's all.' The half-truth tasted bitter on my tongue.

'I know, dear. We understand better than most what you mean.' Mary's eyes clouded with memories I could not fathom. Then she blinked, and the look was gone.

'Fancy a nightcap?' she said with a smile returning on her face. 'Help you get back to sleep it will.'

I nodded, following Mary down to the living room. My hands still trembled slightly as I accepted the brandy she offered. The alcohol burned pleasantly as it slid down my throat, warming me.

'Please, sit,' Mary urged, guiding me towards an overstuffed armchair by the fireplace. The flickering glow of the woken fire cast shadows across the room, imbuing the space with a warm, albeit haunting, ambience.

'Mary,' I began, my voice barely a whisper as I struggled to find the right words. 'Why did you say he's drawn to unhappy people? Is it that obvious?'

'Islanders have always been sensitive to emotions, and he's no different,' Mary replied, her gaze soft and understanding. 'We can feel when someone is carrying a heavy burden; comes from being part of a small community.'

'It's hard to be apart from my family,' I lied, disguising the true depth of my sorrow behind a more socially acceptable reason. The grief I carried was like an anchor, pulling me down into an abyss from which I feared I would never emerge.

'Ah, yes,' Mary nodded, her eyes filled with sympathy. 'Being far from home can be difficult, and some places are harder to get back to than others.'

'What do you mean?'

'Just me talking about the past,' said Mary staring into the fire. 'You can never go back, even though every part of you would swap an entire year for a day to be with those we loved once upon a time.' She turned, and I saw her lined face filled with sadness. 'I know I would.'

'Mary,' I said, my voice barely more than a whisper. 'Thank you for not pressing, even if I've been less than forthcoming about my reasons for being here alone. I know it's unusual, even in 1971.'

She reached out and squeezed my hand, her touch warm and comforting. 'You don't have to say anything, dear,' she assured me. 'We all carry burdens, and sometimes it takes time to lighten the load. Just know that being alone and being lonely don't have to be the same thing.'

'Perhaps the child was lonely,' I suggested, trying to make sense of the situation. 'Or maybe he was sleepwalking? I didn't hear my door open or close.'

'Adelard used to have your room before I had help converting it into a guest room. It has a better view of the sea, you know.'

'Here you are,' Mary said, refilling my glass despite my meek protestation. The warmth of the brandy seemed to radiate through the crystal, and I wrapped my fingers around it gratefully. 'Night medicine we call it.'

'Thank you,' I murmured, taking a tentative sip. The liquid burned its way down my throat, igniting a warmth in my chest that slowly spread throughout my body. It felt as though the brandy was chasing away the chill that had settled in my bones, and for a moment, I allowed myself the luxury of basking in its comforting embrace.

As I raised my eyes from the glass, I found myself drawn to the crayon artwork that adorned the walls of the living room. The fire sent flickers of shadow that created the illusion of movement in the boats depicted. There were dozens of them, each with boats and ships in various states of motion, their sails billowing in the wind like wings about to take flight. Some had names, presumably ships that had visited the islands, and there were several small, brightly coloured gigs whose names were unfamiliar. There was an innocence to the artwork that resonated within me, stirring memories of days spent with Sarah, colouring our dreams onto blank sheets of paper.

'Adelard?' I asked softly, gesturing towards the drawings.

Mary nodded, a wistful smile gracing her lips. 'Yes, he was always taken with the sea; always drawing boats and ships, dreaming of adventures on the open water no doubt.'

'There's a lot of them.'

'Too many,' she said with a long sigh. 'But it's important to keep up traditions and the lad's drawings of boats are no different.'

I shook my head. 'I don't understand.'

'It's very important that, before the morning tide, the head of the Boatmen's Association learns of any new drawings made by Adelard that show a boat. Very important.'

'Why is that tradition so important?'

Mary sucked at her lips as though reticent to elaborate. After a moment's thought, she went on, clasping her hands together, eyes fixed upon the largest of the drawings: a huge multi-rigged sailing ship that covered the paper. 'Traditions are powerful. They bind us together but also give us courage when we dare to embrace them, even if they at first seem like folly.'

I traced the lines of one particularly intricate drawing with my gaze, feeling a familiar ache settle heavily in my chest. 'Sarah and I used to draw together,' I confessed, my voice barely more than a whisper. 'We loved to create imaginary worlds and fill them with the most fantastical creatures.'

'Sounds like she had quite the imagination,' Mary said, her eyes filled with warmth and understanding.

I nodded, swallowing the lump that had formed in my throat. 'She did. We would spend hours lost in our drawings, creating stories that only we knew. It was our way of escaping the world, if only for a little while.'

As I spoke, it felt as though the weight of my grief was slowly being chiselled away, replaced by something lighter and more manageable, yet it left a feeling of vulnerability and rawness as its counterpart. And as I looked into Mary's eyes, I saw not only empathy but also a quiet strength that seemed to say, '*You are not alone.*'

My heart clenched as I realised I had spoken of Sarah in the past tense, and the word 'we' echoed in my ears. The pain returned full force, threatening to swallow me whole. I took a deep breath, trying to steady myself.

'It's difficult to talk about it,' I replied softly, struggling to keep the emotion from my voice. 'She was such a bright, creative soul.'

Mary studied me for a moment, her expression gentle but perceptive. 'We understand loss better than most here, don't we? Sometimes it's good to talk with strangers – we like to listen and ask even fewer questions – am I right?'

For a moment, I felt less alone in the world. I looked into her eyes, surprised by the depth of empathy I saw there. She didn't ask for details or pry into my grief – she merely offered her silent support, her presence an anchor in the storm of emotions churning within me.

'Thank you, Mary,' I whispered, my throat tight with unshed tears. I emptied my glass and stood up, readying myself to leave and embrace sleep's forgetfulness. 'And yes, you're right.'

The morning sun cast a golden glow on the bustling harbour, its warmth a gentle kiss on my skin. Fishermen and boatmen touted their services to tourists, their voices mingling with the cries of seagulls overhead. The old granite quay stretched out from Hugh Town, connecting the small outcrop of Rat Island upon which the ferry terminal stood. I took in the scene before me, finding solace in the vibrancy of life that surrounded me, the fresh air clearing any remnants and memory of broken sleep.

My gaze fell upon the various chalkboards advertising trips to the off-islands – Tresco Abbey and Gardens, St Martins, and The Eastern Isles. A pang of disappointment struck me as I noticed the trip to Bishop's Rock was cancelled because of high tide. Approaching a nearby boatman mooring his tender, I asked if there might be a trip tomorrow.

'Can't say for certain, ma'am,' he replied, wiping his brow with a weathered hand. 'Weather looks to be improving, but it's ultimately down to Frazier Jenkins, head of the St Mary's Boatmen Association.' He nodded towards a small granite cubicle at the beginning of the quay where a stocky, elderly man with a salt-and-pepper beard was selling tickets to a line of tourists. 'Frazier decides on the trips for the day and where we all go.'

'Thank you,' I murmured, joining the queue. As I waited, I studied Frazier from a distance. His gruff, weathered demeanour reminded me of my father – kind, but no-nonsense. This boatman's leader seemed to command the same quiet authority over the quay, given the orderly queue for tickets.

When my turn arrived, I stepped forward. Frazier's eyes crinkled in a smile beneath his bushy brows.

'Where to today, missus?' His voice was gravelly, but warm.

'I was hoping for the lighthouse and the seabirds today – is there any chance the trip to Bishop's Rock will be on tomorrow?' I asked, my voice barely above a whisper. Frazier glanced skyward, assessing the cirrus clouds above.

'Possibly, but not today,' he answered, his voice firm yet kind. 'The sea is too rough near the rock shelf out near Hellweathers on account of the gales we had a few nights ago. High tide covers the rocks and we don't want you spending a day out there with nothing but the Atlantic for company; not even gulls perch out there. Sea's still angry that far out, and the puffins will be tucked up in their burrows if they have any sense.'

'Ah, I see,' I mumbled, a pang of disappointment settling in my chest. 'A coincidence, as I'm staying at the cottage named after the rocks you mentioned.'

Frazier's eyes widened in surprise. 'Hellweathers? You're staying with Mary?'

'Yes,' I replied, my fingers unconsciously twisting the strap of my bag. 'I needed a place to stay unexpectedly, and she kindly offered me a room.'

'Good old Mary,' Frazier murmured, his expression softening. 'It's been a while since she's had company at the cottage. Not many choose to stay there.'

'I'm not surprised,' I asked, curiosity piquing. 'The lady at the harbour office seemed reticent to recommend it, even as a last resort.'

He chuckled. 'Mary's a character and no mistake. Ain't nothing in that cottage to fear.' He leaned in conspiratorially, tapping the side of his nose with a rope-calloused finger. 'Safety lives there, as every boatman knows, or should know.'

'I don't fancy any of the other trips – what would you recommend I do today?'

Frazier stroked his beard thoughtfully. 'Hmm, since you're staying at Hellweathers, which is single-handedly responsible for a good many sunken ships, maybe you'd like to visit the maritime museum in town. We've got quite the collection of artefacts from shipwrecks around these parts. Might interest you to learn some local history.'

I nodded, intrigued by his suggestion. 'That sounds interesting, thank you.'

Frazier tipped his cap. 'My pleasure, missus. You enjoy your time on St. Mary's now, and I might see you tomorrow for the lighthouse if the weather behaves itself.'

I paused before turning, still puzzled by his words. Safety lives there? If that were true, why had the harbour woman tried to steer me away from the cottage?

The sun warmed my skin as I made my way past the bulging, open-windowed guesthouses towards the maritime museum, the scent of saltwater and sizzling sausages filling my nostrils. The lively bustle of the quay slowly faded behind me, replaced by the quieter atmosphere of Hugh Town. As I passed through the narrow streets lined with stone cottages, their window boxes overflowing with brightly coloured flowers, I couldn't help but feel a sense of comfort. There was something timeless about this place as if the weight of my troubles could be suspended, even for just a while.

The cobblestone path beneath my feet felt cool through the thin soles of my shoes as I walked towards the museum. The sun filtered through the lush leaves of trees that lined the streets, casting dappled light on the ground before me, and the gentle whispering of the wind carried the distant laughter of children playing at the beach, their joy a bittersweet reminder of Sarah's absence.

Entering the museum, I was greeted by a soft-spoken woman behind a wooden counter, who handed me an illustrated guide to the exhibits. The air inside was cool and musty, holding onto centuries' worth of secrets and stories.

I wandered past glass cases filled with relics from shipwrecks, each item a small piece of a larger puzzle, a snapshot in time. The weathered faces of sailors stared back at me from black-and-white photographs lining the walls; their gazes were distant as if they knew something I didn't.

And then, as I rounded the corner of the final exhibit, I stood before a wall of photos depicting the many ships that had met their end in these treacherous waters. One particular schooner caught my eye – 'Sarah' – wrecked in 1853, the same name as my beloved child. My heart thudded in my chest, the revelation coiling within like the rope of an anchor waiting to be released.

The emotional impact of seeing her name etched into the photograph hit me hard, like a wave crashing against the shore. I grasped at my chest, my breath coming in shallow gasps as I fought to keep my emotions in check. But despite the turmoil within me, I couldn't help but feel a growing sense of connection between the names of the ships that had foundered, and the drawings on the wall at Hellweathers. My curiosity piqued, I scanned the sepia photographs, putting to memory the names of the great vessels that had travelled the world to end on the bitter shoals about the islands.

I left the museum pondering the tragedies of the past, long gone but not entirely forgotten, and I stopped by a small bakery on the way back to the cottage, picking up a sandwich for lunch. The afternoon's walk to Porth Hellick's secluded beach would require a full stomach and a change of shoes.

The moment I stepped foot back into the cottage, a sense of unease washed over me. The air seemed heavy, as if it carried the weight of a thousand whispered secrets, and I suddenly felt the need for company, and for safety.

'Mary?' I called out, my voice wavering. There was no

response, not even the faintest sound of footsteps or the rustle of clothing. I walked further into the kitchen, feeling the cool tiles beneath my sandalled feet, trying to shake off the inexplicable anxiety that clung to me like a second skin. I waited for the kettle to boil and scooped out some leaf tea into a chipped china teapot.

A note lay on the worn table. Mary's looping handwriting explained she had been called away suddenly.

'Dear Jane,' it read, 'I'm needed in Bryher to help a sick friend in need. I trust you'll be alright on your own. Warm regards, Mary.'

'Friend in need' – such an odd phrase, so vague. It only heightened my sense of isolation. As I set the note down, I glanced through to the spare room door.

'Hello?' I called out. 'Is anyone home?'

Silence greeted me once again. I frowned, contemplating the possibilities. Perhaps the child had gone with Mary, or maybe he was at school. Regardless, I couldn't shake the feeling that something was amiss, tense, waiting to happen.

I turned from the living room, my eyes searching for something to distract the growing sense of being watched. The postcard of Bishop's Rock I had left on my bedside table – where was it now?

I sifted through my room like forensics at a crime scene, peering into every drawer, item of clothing, and crannies that I could have inadvertently placed it for safe-keeping, without success.

I shook off the annoyance and reached for my sturdiest walking boots – their leather cracked and worn but still reliable – and laced them up securely. A long walk would help clear my thoughts, I reasoned.

Returning to the kitchen to pour my tea, my gaze wandered to the living room wall adorned with the child's maritime-inspired artwork. Childish scrawl appeared in each of the bottom left corners and I had assumed them to be nonsensical scribbles, but as I studied them now, one jumped out – a crude ship, smashed upon jagged rocks. In the corner below its broken hull was written 'Sarah'. My heart skipped a beat.

Glancing across, I made out the names of the other ships and slammed down my cup onto a side table, spilling its contents.

Calliope, Eagle, Endurance. Each one sent a spike of recognition through me. They all depicted similar scenes: stick figure people flailing in the water amidst the shattered timbers of their sinking ships. In each, the sad face of the sun looked down, radiant and impotent.

My first casual glances the evening before had led me to believe the figures were swimming or larking about in the water. But on closer inspection, the truth dawned on me slowly, then all at once, like a penny dropping onto a hard, tiled floor.

They weren't swimming.

They were drowning.

Dozens of them, mouths open in silent screams, arms grasping at nothing as they sank beneath the waves.

A chill swept over me, raising the hairs on my arms. What dark fascination did this child have with death at sea? A creeping sense of dread trickled down my spine like the icy water out towards the rocks of Hellweathers.

'It's just island history, Jane,' I whispered to myself, shaking off the unsettling thoughts. It was just a coincidence, nothing more. The child might have picked up on some local history during a museum visit or school lesson and found inspiration for his drawings.

I backed away from the wall, a swell of unease rising within me. My skin prickled with the sense of being watched, though I knew I was alone. I hurried to shut the living room door, closing off the disturbing images.

A walk. I needed a walk to clear my head of my overthinking, and the trip to Porth Hellick Bay seemed like the perfect solution. Picking up my bag, I stepped outside into the midday sun, feeling the warmth on my face as I left the shadows of the cottage behind.

The birds sang sweetly above me, their melodies filling the air with a sense of peace and tranquillity. Only the occasional bus or cyclist disturbed the serene atmosphere of the dry stone wall lanes, their receding presence rippling like a mirage rising from the sun-soaked tarmac heat haze.

I reached the horseshoe bay and the beach of Porth Hellick. The sight before me took my breath away – the vast expanse of golden sand, the endless cirrus smudged. cerulean sky, and the small, distant lighthouse, a sentinel standing resolute against the horizon. At that moment, it felt as if I were gazing out at the edge of the world, all my sorrow and heartache about to be washed away by the gentle lapping of the waves.

I raised my hand to shield my eyes from the sun's glare as I gazed out at the distant Bishop's Rock, the most southwesterly point of the British Isles. Beside it, the jagged teeth of Hellweathers rocks jutted menacingly from the sea, a stark contrast to the otherwise idyllic scene. Gulls circled and cried overhead. The only other living soul in view was a lone fisherman checking his crab pots along the rocky shore.

I closed my eyes and breathed deeply, filling my lungs with the briny scent of the sea. The anxiety brought on by the feeling in the cottage, and those disturbing drawings faded entirely, were washed away by the enhancement of my other senses. I had come here to find peace, and for the rest of that afternoon, I did.

The soft light of a waning moon filtered through the curtains, casting a gentle glow over the room as I slept peacefully in the unfamiliar bed at Hellweathers Cottage. My dreams were a swirling mix of memories and shadows, but for the first time in months, they didn't torment me with visions of Sarah or my husband. A sense of calm enveloped me, like a warm embrace from a long-lost friend. The sense of being watched lingered on the margins as did the feeling of accompanying urgency, like that of an insistent child, ever circling, drawing closer like spiralling water being swallowed by a plug hole.

My serenity and uncertainty were shattered by the sudden but now familiar sound of a child humming, accompanied by the unmistakable scratching of a crayon on paper. The noise jolted me awake, my heart pounding in my chest as confusion washed over me. Was this a vivid memory of the previous night? I sat up in bed, straining to hear the source of the sound.

'Who's there?' I whispered into the darkness, my voice barely audible even to myself. The humming ceased, but the sensation of being observed intensified. My mind still foggy with sleep, I echoed Mary's words from the previous night. 'Sleep now, Adelard,' my voice barely audible even to my own ears. The humming and scratching ceased as suddenly as it had begun, leaving only a heavy silence in its wake. For a moment, I allowed myself to be lulled by the quiet, but then my brain began to stir, questioning why I had even uttered those words as no one, it appeared was in the house.

My body tensed, every muscle poised for action as I listened intently. The room remained shrouded in darkness, making me feel vulnerable and exposed. Yet I felt frustrated, both at the lack of sleep, and the odd, desperate feelings that came in waves.

'What is it?' I whispered as though expecting an answer from the empty room.

I swung my legs over the side of the bed, planting my feet firmly on the floor and rubbed my eyes clear of sleep. Whatever had caused the noise, it seemed I was alone once more in the moonlit room.

Perhaps I had imagined it—a waking dream conjured by grief and exhaustion. My mind playing tricks, hearing what I wanted to hear. The scratching, the humming. It had all seemed so real in the moment.

The hushed whispers of the wind outside did little to assuage my growing confusion and frustration. The house, which had seemed so welcoming earlier in the day, now held an air of disorientation and disbelief. I checked each room, my bare feet padding softly on the cold wooden floor. Adelard's room was firmly locked.

'Hello?' I called out, my voice wavering slightly. 'If there's someone there, please...please just talk to me; I'm not cross but it's very late...' Yet there was no reply, only the distant creaking of the timbers above me as if they, too, were shifting uncomfortably in their sleep.

'Please,' I whispered one last time, my fingers curling around the doorknob. 'Just tell me what you want.'

And then, without warning, the sensation washed over me – a sudden but benign presence that seemed to seep into my very soul. It was as if something was trying to communicate a message of the utmost importance, its meaning hovering just beyond the edge of my conscious mind.

The silence bore down upon me like a crushing weight, suffocating me with unanswered questions and unsettled emotions. For a moment, I hesitated in the doorway of my bedroom, staring into the shadows as they seemed to dance and flicker beneath the soft glow of the moonlight.

Wondering whether I was going mad, I stepped back into

the room and closed the door behind me. This time I locked it. The sense of watchfulness eased, but the feeling I was missing something terribly important remained, preying on my mind. My thoughts wandered to the lady in the harbour.

'Unquiet might be more fitting...'

I crawled back into bed, and as the first glimmer of morning crept slowly across the sky, I fell once more into a doze, the fading shadows held at bay by the fragile barrier of the approach of nautical dawn.

It was the chattering noise of a long group of people making their way down to the harbour that finally woke me into blinking, glorious sunshine. I glanced at my watch, ripping off the sheets and hurriedly jumping into fresh underwear, one hand grasping for the toothbrush.

8.36 am

My first thoughts were of the boat trip, the chance of visiting the lighthouse fading with every hop of my feet into socks and shoes. I fell sideways into the school desk, upsetting the crayons once again, but it was the drawing on top that caused the sharp words to die on my lips. The darkness of my unscheduled waking had failed to highlight the recent work of art.

It was a boat, yellow and white with its name scrawled in blue in its accustomed place in the bottom corner. A pencil-thin lighthouse sat in the distance with simple 'm' like birds swirling around its top-heavy and tilted lantern. The radiant sun's smile had been obliterated, for this was indeed the same piece of paper from the previous day. In its place a dreadful and unmistakable open mouth, as though capturing a scream, was highlighted and ringed as though to emphasise the powerful emotion. Small blue droplets, that at first I took for cloudless rain, fell from its face and I realised they were tears.

I returned to the boat; its full form interrupted but showing the jagged rocks of Hellweathers granite teeth nearby. Stick figures floundered, falling, sinking, drowning. I folded the sketch into my pocket and raced for the door, tugging on my shoelaces to tighten and tie them as I flew out of the cottage, the boat's name still on my lips.

Golden Spray.

I barely processed my thoughts as I raced to the quay, late, with only Mary's insistence that any drawing made should be shown before high tide to the head of the Boatmen's Association.

Frazier...

I caught sight of him, tying the mooring rope of a long, golden yellow tourist boat, high prowed and already filling with passengers.

I called out, and he waved, not realising my designs.

'Best get in line! We are going to be full today for Bishop's Rock – looks like you'll see the lighthouse after all if you don't mind standing.'

My anxiety rose as the boat filled, wondering if I might be turned away, and pressed close to almost force my way onboard until I was face to face, still out of breath.

'Whoaa!' he said, grabbing my forearm in a boatman's grasp. 'Hellweathers got the better of you?'

I unravelled the drawing, still on the lowest, tide-rising step of the quay. 'Mary told me of the tradition—'

Frazier stared in disbelief. 'Adelard?'

'Yes,' I said wondering when I would be pulled aboard and over the gap between boat and shore. 'He drew this yesterday —last night—this morning...I don't know, but I think it's important.'

Several boatmen called from above. 'Are we going out or not, Frazier? We'll miss the tide if you don't get the Golden Spray underway.'

Frazier breathed deeply and stared so intently into my eyes that I thought they would swallow me whole. 'Everybody off, ladies and gents, if you please. Trip's been cancelled.'

He broke away, almost pushing me back against the wall of the quay steps, and I could see his hands shaking as he helped offload the disgruntled passengers. They glared at me as they passed, shaking their heads with scorn and disappointment. I barely heard his reassuring and apologetic words.

'No need to worry, ask for your money back at the kiosk... yes, missus...maybe tomorrow, but not today...bad news I'm afraid...yes I'm as sorry as you are but there we go...boat to Tresco leaving in twenty minutes—beautiful gardens to explore...lighthouse will still be there in the morning...'

When the last person brushed passed me, Frazier untied the rope and backed the Golden Spray away from the quay, heading for the closest mooring buoy, eighty yards away. He killed the engine, calling and answering the shouts of the boatmen with stern and final words.

'Not today! You do as you are all told and stick to the sound — no one is to go further than Annet, do you understand? Stick to Tresco and Bryher only and don't argue!'

With a look of resignation, the boatmen turned to make ready muttering about superstitions and old men. The sea was calm, the harbour full of eager tourists with money burning holes in their pockets. The trip to Bishop's Rock was a lucrative one, and the collective share of the proceeds would be lessened at the end of the day's tally.

Frazier jumped into a small rowing boat and headed for the harbour beach, and I raced up the steps and along the harbour wall, meeting him as he dragged the fibreglass craft beyond the high tide mark. I still clutched the fluttering drawing. He struggled at first to look me fully in the face, but I could see he was at once anxious and relieved at the same time.

'What have I done?' I said.

'The right thing, at the wrong time, or maybe the other way around.'

Motioning for me to follow him, we made our way to a quiet place out of view of the string of visitors and the commotion at the kiosk.

'You tell Mary that the warning's been heeded. Going to be a stink with the lads, but what's been passed down to me will be passed down to one of them in time. What they do with it is up to them when I'm long gone.'

'I don't understand,' I said. 'Why does the child draw pictures of old boats wrecking or sinking that would make you nervous about going about your daily work?'

'No boat ever drawn by that child ever came back. I told you safety lives over at Hellweathers, and I'm not one to test the tradition and go out after I've been warned.'

'But the boy has drawn lots of wrecks—'

'They weren't wrecks when he drew them,' said Frazier fixing me with purpose. 'All of them were afloat.'

'But most of them go back before he was born, some as far back as the last century.'

Frazier nodded. 'I don't have the answers, and it's better to be safe than sorry. You'll find him over at the church in Old Town, beyond that, I've been told little else, and you wouldn't believe an old fool even if I tried. If Mary won't tell you, then it's best you go on thinking we are all superstitious old fools; it's better than being dead ones.'

I frowned, and he turned to make his way up the slippery ladder of the quay to avoid any further questions. At the top, he gave me a quick nod, the smiling face and rough, authoritative demeanour returning as he raised his hands to deal with a sea of problems. 'One at a time...One at a time, if you please...'

I called out, asking why the child would be at church,

early on a Friday morning, but either he did not hear or chose not to.

I turned, wondering whether to toss the sketch into the sea, such was my confusion and disappointment, but found I had already folded and stored it within my bag. Golden Spray rocked in the harbour, bobbing and tugging at her line as though desperate to sail against her master's wishes, and I wondered what I had done. Desperate to avoid any of the passengers milling around the quay, I walked along the narrow sand and climbed the low harbour wall, my feet unknowingly taking me to Old Town, and the church.

I trudged, alone, over the rise from Hugh Town to the smaller settlement of Old Town, my steps and thoughts heavy as my own feelings of poor self-worth and guilt returned. As the glittering sea sparkled below me upon this new and enchanting vista, I knew that even here, the ache had found me.

As I descended into Old Town, the feeling subsided, and the quaint, living postcard hamlet began to wrap around me like a warm embrace. Scattered cottages overlooked the serene waters of Old Town Bay, their chimneys crowned with seagull nests like comical hats. I couldn't help but think how different this place was from the bustling streets of Oxford, and what it might be like to escape here permanently.

This former capital was a place of solitude now, the cries of gulls echoing across the all-but-empty sands of the bay. A lone boy flew a trio of brightly coloured kites, their tails looping and curling, leaving colourful, fleeting marks against the blue as if drawn by an invisible hand. My thoughts returned to the drawing in my bag, but this youth was too old to be responsible for such childish art. Their tails drew patterns in the air like crayons against a sketchbook of blue, evoking memories of when Sarah used to draw with her own set. A bittersweet smile crept onto my face as I watched the kites dance gracefully, their movements echoing the ebb and flow of my emotions.

'Beautiful, aren't they?' a gentle voice said beside me.

I turned to find an elderly woman watching the kites with a nostalgic gaze. 'Yes,' I replied softly, 'they truly are.'

'Sometimes, it's the simplest things that bring us the most joy,' she mused.

'Do you know him?' I asked. 'Is his name Adelard, by any chance?'

She shook her head. 'He's a mainlander, staying over by Carn Vean; not from round here. Adelard's up there if you're wanting to see him.' She pointed at the space between the kite's tails and the grassy slopes beyond. A tiny church hiding behind wind-bent pines. I was about to thank her but she had already departed, listing side to side like an old galleon on her way into Hugh Town.

My steps quickened, the church drawing me like a magnet. The quaint, tiny structure seemed to huddle against the elements, its exposed belfry cradling a single bell that lay silent and still.

I followed the winding path towards it, the grass crunching underfoot. The closer I got, the more diminutive it seemed, as if it might vanish or crumble to dust at any moment. As I neared, the weatherworn wooden doors creaked in protest as I pushed them open, revealing the dimly lit, cool interior within. Cobwebs clung to the white-washed walls like aged lace, giving the space a sense of now-rarely-used timelessness.

'Hello?' I called out softly, my voice echoing throughout the empty sanctuary. There was no response, only the whispering of the wind through the cracks in the walls and the distant cries of seagulls filtering through the silence. Stepping further inside, I took in the sparse furnishings and austere beauty of the church. The air was thick with the scent of damp stone and aged wood, mingling with the faintest hint of salt carried in from the sea. I stayed there for a few moments longer, basking in the quiet. And then, with a deep breath, I rose to my feet and turned towards the door. The outside world rushed back in, the sounds and smells overwhelming after the hush of the church.

As I left the sanctuary behind, I ventured further into the graveyard, where ancient headstones stood sentinel over the resting places of long-forgotten souls, many of whom had died out at sea. The old stones bore the marks of time and the elements, worn and weathered by countless seasons. Many were covered in lichen and moss, their inscriptions almost illegible, whispering secrets of lives long past.

'Adelard,' I murmured, my breath catching as I scanned the headstones, searching for any trace of the mysterious child artist who had somehow found his way into my life. Frazier had said that he might be here, somewhere, though he hadn't been more specific than that.

As I wandered deeper into the graveyard, I noticed a group of headstones bearing names of ships that were strangely familiar. Vessels that had foundered, drawn by a small boy before they had dashed themselves to pieces at the edge of the Old World.

An unassuming, moss-covered headstone caught my eye, nestled between two larger monuments. It seemed to radiate a quiet sadness, the dampness of the stone a mute testament to the passage of time. As I drew closer, I noticed a curious array of items scattered around its base – colourful shards of crayon and chalk, their vibrant hues a jarring contrast against the sombre grey of the stone. Several sweets, their wrappers faded and worn, lay among the makeshift tokens.

I crouched down and gently brushed the moss away. The name carved into the weathered surface was unmistakable. My breath caught in my throat. I had finally found him.

. . .

Adelard Hicks
1848-1857

Leaving the churchyard behind, I felt the weight of revelation heavy upon my shoulders as I made my way back towards Hellweathers Cottage. The sun shone brightly overhead, casting a warm glow on the coastal path beneath my feet. What had happened to Adelard? Why had Mary kept his room as some kind of shrine? I quickened my pace, suddenly desperate for answers. The winding lane rose and fell with the contours of the land, and I could see the cottage in the distance, perched upon the headland.

Hope fluttered within me as I approached the cottage, my heart pounding in anticipation. Perhaps Mary would be there, and she could help me make sense of the tangled web that the drawing, the noises in the night, Frazier's riddles, and Adelard's grave had spun around me.

'Mary?' I called out tentatively as I stepped inside, my voice echoing through the empty space. Disappointment washed over me like an icy wave, leaving me shivering despite the warmth of the cottage. I hurried to the kitchen, rifling through drawers until I found the key to Adelard's room. With trembling fingers, I unlocked the door and pushed it open. My breath left me in a rush—the room was completely bare. No furniture, no sign a child had ever slept here. Just a single, dusty window illuminating the once whitewashed walls, covered in layer upon layer of drawings. Ships, lighthouses, the sea in all her moods; barely an inch was not covered with pencil or wax. I found myself drawn to the overlapping scenes trying to unravel the multitude of objects, people, and island life, my eyes tracing the lines that had been etched by an unseen, child's hand. In many places 'Adelard' was scrawled, its evolution from a crude and misspelt signature into a more confident and practised hand.

The maritime scenes were both intricate and chaotic, a flurry of activity that captured the essence of life on these remote islands. Sailing vessels cut through frothy waves, seagulls swooped down to pluck fish from the sea, and children played on sandy beaches, their laughter almost audible in the strokes of colour. It was as if Adelard had poured his love for this place onto the walls, filling the emptiness with memories of days long past.

As I stood there, lost in thought, the sound of the front door opening and closing snapped me back to reality. Mary had returned, her bag in tow, just as I was about to step out of the room.

'Jane, dear, what are you doing in here?' she asked, her voice soft but tinged with concern.

I hesitated, unsure how to respond. My cheeks flushed with embarrassment, and I looked down at my feet, the floorboards suddenly fascinating. 'I... I wanted to see Adelard's room,' I confessed, my voice barely above a whisper.

Mary studied me for a moment, her eyes searching my face for something – understanding, perhaps, or forgiveness. Then, with a sigh, she stepped into the room, her gaze sweeping over the walls and their colourful array of drawings.

My heart raced as I held out the drawing, my voice trembling. 'Someone drew this last night – I showed it to Frazier, and he heeded the warning by cancelling the trip. But why... why the pretence of there being a child in this room?' My gaze fell to the floor, my thoughts swirling with confusion. 'I've seen Adelard's grave.'

Mary's eyes widened, and she hesitated before crossing the threshold into the empty room. The sunlight streaming through the window cast her frail frame in a warm glow, illuminating the lines etched on her face by time and sorrow.

'If I don't leave the paper out for him, he'll draw on every wall, and it's a bother to paint over,' she began, her voice soft and tired. As she spoke, I could see her shoulders sagging under the weight of her unspoken secrets.

'Adelard... he's not like other children,' Mary continued, her gaze fixed on the drawings that adorned the walls. 'He's been in this place for so long, yet he's a good boy.'

'Adelard's not real?'

Mary smiled sadly, taking the drawing. 'He's real enough to me, and you, by the look of things.'

'The woman at the harbour—'

Mary nodded. 'What was it she said this time – noisy, eccentric, haunted?'

'Unquiet,' I said.

My chest tightened with a mix of pity and curiosity.

'Adelard has been here for a very long time,' she began, her voice soft and wistful. 'He had a talent for drawing boats that never came back and folk began to think it queer. Forced to stay at home with nothing but pencils and chalk to play with, he continued in silence, until his father, the then leader of the Boatmen's Association took notice and began to notice the coincidence.'

'What happened to Adelard?'

'I told you he never disobeyed a command from his elders, except once.' Mary wandered over to the window, shoving at the stiff frame to let in the afternoon air. 'There was an urgent need to send a pilot boat out to the lighthouse, and he tried to stop his father from going out with words when his drawings could not.'

'The pilot boat was wrecked?'

Mary nodded. 'But not before the young rascal escaped through this here window, stole a boat of his own, and followed behind. When the pilot boat struck Hellweathers, the eight on board had been in the sea for an hour before they caught sight of the small craft. The sea was dreadful, and the poor lad was thrown overboard and lost as he tried to heave the men to safety. Only three ever came back; his father was one of them.' Her voice quietened to a whisper. 'Cruel thing guilt, but we know what it's like to lose them on dry land, too, don't we?'

She gently ran her fingers over a drawing of a tall ship, sails billowing.

Whether I nodded inadvertently or not, I don't recall, but she went on.

'He started leaving me and those that lived here well before, brief sketches, warning of wrecks to come. At first, I didn't understand, but in time I learned that if I passed them along, ships would change course or not go out at all, and lives would be spared.'

Mary turned to me, her eyes glistening. 'He's just a lonely soul who wants to prevent others from suffering his fate. That's why he drew for you.'

I nodded, a lump rising in my throat. This spirit had reached out to save my life and those of others.

'You can feel him, can't you?' Mary asked softly. 'His presence is woven into the very walls of this cottage.'

'Yes,' I whispered. 'I feel him.'

'I know it's hard to believe,' she said. 'But Adelard has helped so many over the years. Those who come here grieving or lost somehow feel his presence, and it comforts them. It's why I stayed so long after...' She trailed off and clutched at a locket around her neck.

I glanced around the room, taking in the multitude of drawings. Scenes of sailors hauling nets, women hanging laundry, children playing. All of it brought to life by the hand of a lonely boy who still loved these islands more than a century after his death.

'Why didn't you tell me about him before?' I asked.

Mary sighed. 'Most find it easier once they've felt his spirit for themselves. I didn't want to frighten you away.'

'You've been keeping him from being lonely all this time,' I said. 'Leaving out paper and pencils, passing along his drawings to Frazier.'

She smiled. 'He knows, just as you and I do. We call it tradition and that works just fine.'

'Frazier said safety lives here, and now I know what he meant.'

Mary patted my hand. 'Maybe that's why he drew while you were here,' she said gently. 'Because he knew you'd understand.' She withdrew the locket from around her neck, clicking open the silver, oval lozenge to reveal the picture of a middle-aged man with a young girl.

'I lost both mine over fifty years ago,' she said. 'And it's a comfort to be here, knowing what I know about the place — does that make any sense?'

I gazed at the faded photographs, and up to her glistening eyes, wet with the first welling of tears. In that moment, I felt the first stirring of peace in my ravaged heart.

I took a deep breath. 'There's something I need to tell you. The real reason I came here.'

I shared my tragic story — losing Sarah, blaming myself, my strained marriage, and my husband's tragic death. The words tumbled out in a rush, my voice thick with emotion.

Mary listened quietly, her eyes brimming with empathy. When I finally finished, she enfolded me in her thin but surprisingly strong arms.

'I loved them,' I sobbed into her shoulder.

'I know,' she said squeezing me gently. 'But never describe

love in the past tense. If we didn't still love them, we wouldn't be in such a mess, would we?'

I nodded.

'Oh my dear, we've all suffered,' she murmured. 'But you mustn't blame yourself. What happened wasn't your fault.'

I choked back a sob, clinging to her. After a moment, she gently released me and looked into my eyes. Behind her on the wall, the smiling face of a stick-figure child, hand raised caught my blurry attention. And for the first time, in the presence of a stranger, I knew she spoke the truth. In that dusty room covered with a lonely, kind-hearted spirit's drawings, I felt the heavy weight I'd carried for so long easing from my shoulders. I finally believed in those words.

I stepped onto the ferry, leaving behind St Mary's. The warm afternoon sun cast a golden glow on the waves below as they lapped against the hull of the Scillonian II. A light breeze brushed my cheeks as I waved my farewells to Mary and Hugh Town. The air was filled with the briny scent of the sea, mingling with the faint aroma of diesel fuel from the boat's engines.

As I stood at the railing, I reflected upon the hours spent in her company and the peaceful feelings of that most unquiet cottage. Together, we had shared our grief, finding solace in each other's pain, and discovering that death was not always the end. Our combined journey through sorrow had led us to Adelard, the ghostly child who had brought us an unexpected sense of closure. My heart swelled with gratitude for the moments we had shared, and I whispered a silent prayer of thanks for this newfound serenity.

My eyes searched the harbour for the Golden Spray; the

vessel that had been absent for days now during my extended stay. The sight of its yellow prow slicing through the water would have brought me comfort, but I knew deep down that it wasn't necessary. For I felt a renewed confidence in the power of Adelard's drawings—those simple lines on paper that had saved countless lives over the years. I had faith the tradition would continue. Adelard would keep warning seafarers of danger, just as he had for over a century. Lives would still be saved.

'Goodbye,' I murmured, gazing at the receding quay. 'Watch over them, Adelard.'

As the boat pulled away from the island, I took one last glance at Hellweathers cottage, perched on the headland like a sentinel guarding the unaware tourists and boatmen. The afternoon sun painted it in hues of gold and orange, making it look more ethereal than ever. It was there that I made a silent vow, promising myself that I would move on from the losses and guilt that haunted me, and embrace the second chance I had been given.

The open sea beckoned, sunlight dancing on the placid stillness, the waves barely foaming as the ferry took me home. I closed my eyes and felt the ocean breeze on my cheeks, breathing deeply. For the first time in years, I felt ready to be happy again.

A week had passed since I had returned home, and life seemed to move forward with a newfound ease. The sun shone brighter, and my days were filled with a quiet hopefulness that had been absent for too long. People began to notice, not through words or looks but by the gentle care they took not to ask me if I was 'alright'. I was never sure whether they were concerned about the change before them, or whether they feared asking, lest it remind me and return me to my former, fragile emotional state.

One afternoon, as I returned from running errands around town, I noticed a padded letter in the mail with a Cornish postmark. My heart quickened with anticipation, curiosity piqued by the unexpected correspondence.

I took the mail inside and settled into my favourite armchair, the sunlight streaming through the window casting a warm glow on the room. Carefully, I opened the package to find a postcard of the Bishop Rock lighthouse — the postcard that had gone missing, and a letter written in familiar handwriting.

My fingers traced the contours of the lighthouse, feeling its glossy texture, and I sighed, wondering if I would ever see it in person. It was a reminder of the strength we all possessed to weather our own storms, no matter how fierce they may be.

Eager to confirm who had sent the postcard, I unfolded the gracefully handwritten letter, my heart pounding in anticipation. The words blurred together as I read, my mind racing to piece together the puzzle before me.

'Dear Jane,' the message began, and I knew at once that it was from Mary. 'Frazier came by with some news that I thought you should know,' Mary's words continued. 'After you showed him Adelard's drawing of the Golden Spray, he took it upon himself to inspect the boat in the dry dock before he trusted himself to take it out again. He discovered a broken fuel line, and a crack in the rudder which could have caused a loss of power and steering, if not a terrible accident; God forbid it had happened out towards the lighthouse.'

I set the letter down on my lap, breathing deeply for a moment, trying to smother the sudden urge to imagine the lifeless tourist boat packed with people, without power or control, drifting towards the rocks. Mary's words grounded me.

'I can scarcely believe the events of the last few days. Never did I imagine our meeting would unveil such revelations. I've stopped locking the door to his room but still put out the paper, and you'll be glad to hear that there has been no need to draw boats since you left, which is a comfort to all of us. He drew something else though and your postcard turned up, posted back through my letterbox – now what do you make of that? My daughter used to have a ribbon like that. Write soon, Mary.'

I frowned, flipping over the postcard.

My breath caught as I glimpsed the crayon drawing decorating the other side. A vibrant, smiling sun beamed down on a pair of stick figures standing on the opposite headland of Penninis, their colours bright against the rough texture of the card.

There was a boy, his hand raised in a cheerful wave, and beside him stood a girl with a red ribbon in her hair, her smile unmistakable even in such a simple rendering. My heart clenched painfully at the sight of her face, and her characteristic headband for it was Sarah, I was certain.

I blinked back tears, my vision blurring as I studied a third figure: a man seated in what appeared to be a crudely drawn jet plane, complete with a fiery exhaust that intermingled with the beaming sun. The artist had never seen a plane before, of that I was certain; yet the details were uncanny, from the dangling feet of the undercarriage to the coloured red, white and blue of the Royal Air Force roundel, plastered on the leading wing.

And there, beneath the horseshoe-drawn helmet, was a moustache and a wink that sent my eyes into floods, for it was precisely how my husband used to look at me from the earthbound cockpit of his Land Rover before leaving to fly those damned, experimental machines.

'Richard,' I breathed, my throat tight with emotion. How could the ghostly child who had died in 1858 have known these intimate details of my life? And yet, here they were, captured in bold strokes of crayon that seemed to pulse with energy, as if to assure me that my loved ones were still present in some form, watching over me from beyond the veil.

Folding the postcard to my chest, I wept – for those I had lost, for the peace I had found. The sun streamed through the window, warming me like an embrace. And whether it was my emotional state playing tricks on me, I suddenly caught the tang of saltwater and sea air. 'Thank you,' I whispered to the light. 'I feel better now.'

Seven years had passed since I first stood before Hellweathers cottage, and yet each year it felt like coming home. The paintwork on the door had weathered, its once vibrant hue faded to a muted whisper of the past. The overgrown garden was wild with untamed beauty; ivy crept up walls that had once been pristine, embracing the bricks in a lover's hold. Despite the slightly dilapidated exterior, warmth filled my heart as memories of previous visits washed over me, each peel of paint revealing a different and earlier moment in time, much like the layers of memory we accumulate.

'Mrs French?' A voice interrupted my thoughts.

'Jane, please,' I replied, turning to face the housing agent who approached with a key in hand.

'Did you have a pleasant sailing?' he asked, raising an eyebrow.

'Yes, I came over on the new Scillonian III,' I answered,

recalling the gentle sway of the boat as it carried me across the water.

'Ah, a vast improvement on the old ferry, I understand. Things endure here in the Scillies, though salt and sea erode even the toughest of man's creations.'

'Indeed,' I murmured, extending my hand to take the key. I felt its cool metal weight in my hand. This small object held so much power – the power to unlock not just the door, but a new chapter in my life. I turned the key and nuzzled open the stiff, creaking door.

'Here are the documents you'll need,' said the estate agent, handing me a folder filled with papers. 'The family were very grateful you agreed to take the house furnished. The offer that was accepted at auction was above even my expectations – no doubt inflated by those seeking to turn the old place into a self-catering or holiday home. Not that it matters to the family, as they are moving back to the mainland.'

'It was important that I bought the place, and that it remains a home,' I explained, my voice wavering with emotion. 'I knew Mary well. She put me up on my formative visit to the islands many years ago, and every year after. The isles—the cottage left a profound mark on me.'

'A positive one, it seems?' he inquired.

'Yes. I became a grief counsellor because of my own experiences until I took a sabbatical to write more self-help books on the subject. When I learned of Mary's death and saw Hellweathers for sale, I just knew I had to come back—the place has never really left me.'

'Many people have the same feelings about the islands,' he said with a smile, opening the door wider for me. 'You'll find all the items inventoried, plus the house deeds and documents. But let me know if any things are awry. I'll leave you to get reacquainted.'

'Thank you,' I whispered again, watching him retreat down the garden path before turning my attention back to my newly-acquired sanctuary. The memories swirled around me like eddies in the tide, and I half expected to see my old friend coming out with a tray of biscuits to welcome me.

Stepping inside, I took a moment to appreciate the familiar surroundings, the scent of dried flowers and lavender grounding me in this place that had become such an integral part of my soul. It was here that I had finally found the path to closure, acceptance, and peace, as well as a successful pathway on my own.

I peeked and poked into those rooms once occupied by Mary still bearing her faint remembrance. I opened the window to let out a painted lady butterfly, and it bobbed and weaved with joy with its newfound freedom. Faded pictures, of little importance to those who are oblivious to their significance, stood stacked against the bed and I leafed through several cobwebbed portraits.

One damp-rippled, glossy print, foxed and spotted, showed a younger version of my friend, possibly taken in the fifties from the dress and pinafore she was wearing. Beside her, the tanned and muscular frame of the younger Frazier Jenkins squeezed her affectionately, captured for all time, at the quay on a fine day long ago. There was nothing in their cheery demeanour to suggest anything but friendship, but perhaps a unique, tethering closeness that only Adelard could have mastered. Behind them, boats lay at gentle rest moored to buoys in the harbour.

I lifted the picture placing it back on its matching square spot on the wall, brighter and less faded than the rest of its surroundings; a testament to two people long gone, but the memory of them now restored. I thought of my new obligations, willing as I was, and the recently invested leader of the St Mary's Boatmen's Association now that Frazier had retired.

I was glad he had forewarned him, that previous summer, to save me from having to explain the tradition. The new incumbent had taken the odd superstition with grace and relative ease and luckily had yet to see or act upon any prophetic warnings in wax.

'It's up to me now,' I murmured.

I glanced around the kitchen, stalling for time as my anticipation or anxiety—I couldn't tell which—rose within me. Unable to wait any longer, I walked down the short hallway and opened the door of the room that had changed everything.

I was unaware my eyes were closed, but the feeling of nervousness subsided as my other senses steeped in the sounds of the seagulls and the smell of a cursory polish to clean the vacant cottage. When I opened my eyes, I was instantly transported back to that long weekend so long ago when I had arrived a wreck, like those dashed against the rocks around the isles, but left emboldened, raised from my personal deep to find a calm sea had replaced a tempest.

As I looked around the small room, everything was as it had been, minus a few personal items. The small school table lay in its place against the far wall, stained and scratched as it had been. I moved my fingers over the names of children, noticing for the first time the scratch of a new name, more recent and rough, freshly scratched with perhaps the end of a compass instrument or ink nib.

Mary

'I'm here,' I said rather foolishly at first, getting out a large pencil case from my bag. I slipped in my hand and retrieved a handful of brightly coloured crayons, placing them on the desk and watching them roll to a colourful standstill in the channelled recess at its bottom edge. I placed a sheaf of drawing paper beside the darkly stained inkwell before an overwhelming sense of calm descended and I left the room for the place I yearned most of all to see.

The headland at Penninis blustered and blew, the gulls whirling and alighting on the automated lighthouse as though the touch of its rusted metal trusses were scolding to the touch. I knew the spot instinctively, even from the rudimentary but powerful image that had stayed with me all those years. Rounding the final outcrop I gazed out at the distant tanker and trawlers, sea trains riding the track of the horizon on their way to Bristol from the Americas. This was the spot. The place Adelard had drawn on the postcard, and to which I always returned, no longer to cling to an old life without them, but to acknowledge they were still part of me, somewhere deep and safe.

'Never use love in the past tense,' I murmured, remembering Mary's wise words from so long ago. I picked up a fallen pine twig and drew a child-like sun in the coarse quartz sand, a broad smile mimicking how I felt. The ocean breeze lifted my hair, whispering of adventures yet to come, and I caught the distant horn of the departing ferry, leaving me behind, stranded for a future I was ready for.

BRIC-A-BRAC

The sun crept higher in the sky and Sarah pulled the lace, net curtains across the tea room window, setting filigree shadows dancing off the recently whitewashed far wall. She closed her eyes and listened to the children playing on the nearby Green, the customers murmuring over their scones and Battenberg, and the thrumming of a motorcar rumbling across the cobblestones outside.

It was a successful start to her first day of business—Spring holidays had brought many tourists back to Wiltshire, modern-day adventurers interested in exploring Salisbury Plain's ancient monuments while they refreshed themselves at her spartan but cosy tea room. The air was filled with sweet aromas of freshly baked goods and fragrant tea, as well as blooming narcissus from Sarah's recent explorations to the woods that surrounded the otherwise sleepy village.

She pushed back memories of London and her former life as she surveyed her new domain: a small five-tabled lobby, an upstairs cluster of tiny rooms, a kitchen/bakery overlooking a postage stamp garden with its well, and countertops full of cakes, muffins, and brightly patterned but chipped crockery.

She smiled when she saw a child playing with a toy locomotive under one of the mismatched tables; his parents were completely unaware that he was attempting to industrialise this part of the tea room—something that seemed so far removed from 1923 in this part of the country as to be altogether futuristic.

A gentleman tucked away his newspaper and stood, stretching from the aftermath of a slice of Dundee cake, ready to pay. Sarah approached the counter and pulled out a wooden, under-cupboard tray to return his three shillings and sixpence change; there was no prospect of a cash register here, not yet. He graciously tipped his hat as she offered him the door, then took off with his bicycle positioned against the glass window, leaving behind a trail of dust.

'Been here long?' asked a lady in a tweed overcoat as Sarah refilled her china cup from the teapot. 'I don't remember seeing this tea room last time I was here - just the junk shop across the way.'

'I've only been here a short while,' Sarah said, topping up the woman's cup with tea from an old, brown-glazed teapot. 'It used to be a milliner.' She had heard about the opportunity from a friend who was travelling through the region on one of the newly popular tourist trails to Stonehenge. Motorcars had been a rarity to the village, according to the previous owner, but now they passed, rumbling and tooting their way towards the megaliths, occasionally stopping for refreshments or to visit the unusual shop opposite. 'We—or I should say I—just opened today.'

'Oh, that is pleasant,' said the lady stealing a glance at the ringless left hand of her host. 'A proper thoroughfare this is during the summer and on Sundays. You ought to do well here, just like the old lady across the way – proper Aladdin's Cave it is.'

Sarah nodded and glanced at the dark, sunless window

opposite, which had an array of strange items and antiques hanging or stacked up inside. Even with the faded 'Bric-a-Brac' sign above the door, it seemed difficult to determine what kind of business was behind it.

At that moment, the old shopkeeper stepped out of the store and onto the doorstep to take in some fresh air. She shaded her eyes with her hands as the sun shone through the windows and glinted off her silver hair. Sarah waved a hand in greeting, and the proprietor smiled, then shuffled over to peer through the glass at what treats were available.

'Hello,' said Sarah, holding the door open for a departing customer. 'I've just made a fresh pot of tea if you'd care to come in – no charge.'

'Ivy,' she grinned. 'No thank you, I need to stay here and keep an eye on my wares.' She peered at the Victoria sponge sitting atop its glass pedestal. 'But do feel free to pop by later if you want some company—I'm open till the sun or the tourists go to their beds, whichever is latest.'

The busy opening day ended and Sarah wiped her forehead with a handkerchief, running her fingers through her hair to untangle the locks that had come undone. Her hands were sore from all the hard work, but she knew they would heal just like the memories of another life in a distant city. She stole a glance in the mirror on the wall and noticed the rosy tint of her cheeks, which had developed after so much fresh air and activity. 'You're going to blend right in with the locals,' Sarah said to her reflection, even if it wasn't sure whether she was being serious or sarcastic. With everything tidy, she cast her gaze over the shop window sparkling in the twilight across the street. Then, looking down, she spotted a lonely wedge of sponge cake imprisoned within the glass cloche on the counter.

Carrying a plate with her, Sarah ventured into the bric-a-brac shop and carefully put down the cake on a shelf. She was amazed by the different treasures from around the world that took up every corner of Ivy's store. Amongst the polished and heavy Jacobean furniture were wooden boxes engraved with Indian riverscapes, elaborate silk scarves with Chinese characters, mismatched French porcelain, cuckoo clocks, and chandeliers. As she stood there gawking at the items in awe, the old woman beamed at her from behind a glass counter filled with trinkets and jewellery.

Sarah introduced herself, thanking Ivy for letting her have a look around, and asked about some of the pieces. Ivy shared stories of where each item had come from along with her grandfather and father's tales of the mysterious East. Then she noticed the jam-filled sponge Sarah had brought.

'That for me?' said Ivy, pointing to the cake.

'Yes,' said Sarah, presenting it to the woman. 'The customers seem to like my baking.'

'Fair's fair,' said Ivy as she unlocked the counter from her dress pocket. She carefully chose a velvet-covered pad bejewelled with all manner of glittering, wearable treasures and placed it under a bright Tiffany lamp nearby. 'Pick one, if you like.'

'Oh no,' said Sarah, rubbing at her fingers. 'I can't afford anything just at the moment. I've spent everything on the tea shop—'

'Pretty girl like you should have something nice, go on. If that cake is as good as it looks, you can pop over with more till you feel it's paid for.'

'I really couldn't,' said Sarah lightly brushing a fine silver brooch. A smooth, glassy green stone glittered within its ornate finding. 'That's beautiful.'

'Take it,' said Ivy, lifting the jewel reverently and turning it over for a moment as though recalling some long-forgotten memory.

Despite her protestations, Sarah accepted the gift and

pinned it to her blouse.

'Don't worry – it's only paste. Consider it a token of friendship. It looks far better on you than it did on me.'

'Thank you,' said Sarah, 'but please consider it on the slate – I'll pay for it good and proper when I can.'

Ivy shrugged and replaced the velvet pad on the glass shelf below. 'You on your own — not married then?'

Sarah glanced about the shop searching for the right words. 'Not any more, but it wasn't my decision.'

Ivy took her hand gently. 'We have something in common and you don't need to explain anything further. In my day, divorce was different, but we don't have to be ashamed anymore.'

'In London, it's still regarded as the woman's fault, one way or another,' said Sarah. 'It's why I came out to Westercombe – to start again away from the gossip and whispers.'

'Men,' said Ivy rolling her eyes. 'You can't live with them, and you can't live with them.'

Sarah chuckled at the new and honest interpretation of the well-known saying. It felt good to share a moment with a friendly stranger without fear of judgment. She glanced at the stunning silver and brass cash register on the counter nearby, admiring its beauty as it sparkled in the lamplight. Ivy explained that her grandfather had been given it when he was an antiquities trader in Arabia about a hundred years prior. A thief had offered it in exchange for his life, saying that it would bring him a tremendous fortune if he used it wisely, but would also strip him of luck if he ever sold it. Her grandfather took pity on the man and bribed the judge enough to change his sentence from death by hanging to four years of hard labour. Sarah sensed Ivy's deep affection for her grandfather and felt sad along with her as she talked about his passing and her father's, twenty years later.

'One day I'd like to have a till myself,' Sarah said wistfully, gazing at the beautiful item. 'Though of course not nearly as grand or as lovely as yours.'

'Your taste is impeccable,' Ivy replied with a wink and adjusted her shawl. 'It's the most valuable item in the store.'

'I suppose it would be, keeping all that money safe and sound.'

Ivy smiled as she furrowed her brow. 'Something like that.'

A couple then walked into the shop and after a gentle amble, purchased an elegant black walking cane topped with a silver, Anubis-shaped headpiece, as well as a lady's parasol, both of which Ivy claimed were from nineteenth-century Egypt. Ivy opened the register to a charming singing chime and dropped the guineas into its ebony wood counting tray. Just for a moment, Sarah thought she caught the scent of sandalwood and jasmine, the fragrance conjuring up images of an exotic bazaar that she had never experienced before. Ivy slammed the drawer shut, and the daydream faded, replaced by the doorbell as the customers departed, happy with their purchases.

The two women exchanged pleasant farewells, and Sarah went home. When she looked closely at the brooch in the soft light from her Bakelite bedside lamp, Sarah had an unmistakable feeling of something special. If this was to be the start of a friendship, it certainly seemed encouraging.

The day dawned chill and foggy as if the cloud had taken hold of the valley and was refusing to let go. Apart from an eager, wax-coated motorcyclist who dripped and steamed alongside his coffee and walnut cake earlier, the morning was sombre and quiet, the tea room empty.

Sarah glanced across at the bric-a-brac shop, where Ivy was standing looking up into the sky wrapping her shawl around herself tightly. They shared a mutual sigh of resignation over their lack of customers. The bakes would likely go to waste if the tourists remained in their hotels and guesthouses.

Wrapping a large and misshapen iced bun that had been bothering her since its emergence from the oven during the earlier hours of the morning, Sarah entered the shop across the street just as it began to rain.

'Sun won't show her face today,' said Ivy, licking her fingers from the sticky sugar coating of the bun. 'They'll be back in greater numbers tomorrow, you mark my words, Sarah; always a rush after Mother Nature washes the stones.'

Sarah nodded hopefully, then, spying the familiar ebony cane and parasol from yesterday still in place, she noted, 'Why, you have an identical set unless the customers came back. I've only seen the postman this morning and didn't catch the gentleman and his wife from yesterday – they must have been up and about very early to return them?'

Ivy ceased the cleaning of her sugar-coated paws and twitched her nose. 'Something like that, dear. I've only one of everything here, nothing held back apart from a few bits and bobs in boxes on the landing.'

'That's a shame - they are rather nice; I'm sure they won't remain unsold for long.'

Ivy smiled, taking out a rag to polish the cash register. 'I'm sure they won't once the mizzle clears. I could sell those a hundred times or more - quality they are.'

Tracing a hand over a glittering, glass-blown paperweight Sarah frowned. 'There was a lady in the tea room yesterday with one of these – were they part of a pair?'

Ivy hesitated, rubbing her hands with the cloth. 'Must have been. My memory is getting so bad these days.' Her eyes fidgeted as she looked away, absently dusting a stuffed parrot perched upon the pelmet of a carved oak armoire.

Sarah glanced at her brooch. 'I'd never return this unless you asked me to. I'm glad this is one of a kind.'

'Like the girl who's wearing it,' said Ivy. 'I'm glad you think that way. No reproduction items here, in a manner of speaking.'

Sarah blushed, peering through the steamed glass in the tea room. 'I'd best be getting back in case any hardy adventurers have made it this far and need recovering by the stove.'

'Thank you for the bun, dear,' said Ivy. 'You are very kind.'

In the days that followed, tourists from all over the district and beyond flooded the village in search of fresh sights and experiences after a break in the cloud cover revealed a stunning blue sky. The village was so busy that Sarah could barely keep up with the demand. Across the street, Ivy seemed to draw the crowds as motorcars, carts, and lorries were packed with furniture, sculptures, and ornate bronze planters that customers had purchased from the bric-a-brac shop. For a moment, Sarah wished she could go with them on their journeys. With both shop doors open, Sarah heard the cash register ringing like an automaton song thrush while burly men carried out the dark armoire—minus its parrot—for the new owner to take to its new home. After much effort and coaxing, they loaded it into the waiting truck and drove off as the gentleman paid his bill, setting off one last jingle from the till's drawer.

Sarah flipped the sign on the door of the tea room and rubbed her exhausted eyes. She took a walk, glad to escape the confines of the closed shop, and spent several pleasant hours unwinding among the wood anemones and wild garlic of Westercombe woods. It was already dark as she wandered back through the window-lit cosy lights of the village, and a full moon rose above the downs setting the cobblestones glittering with the threat of a late frost. She looked through the dim window of the Bric-a-Brac to see a much-emptied display. The register sparkled in the moonlight, a beacon of exotic commercialism that set her heart racing with its lustrous beauty. A distant church bell chimed eight bells, breaking the reverie for a moment and she looked back at her own enterprise wondering if she had made the right choice. When she looked back through the Bric-a-Brac window, she blinked twice, not believing her eyes.

The contents of the shop had changed, reverted one might say, to the previous morning. All the items Sarah could remember being dragged or carried into the street, and many others she had not, were restocked in their exact spot within the cluttered showroom. Even the parrot stood perched, roosting on top of the heavy oak armoire in the sleepy darkness. A light came on in the corridor beyond, backlighting the curiosities and Sarah tip-toed away to return to her upstairs room to toss and turn pondering what she had witnessed until little owls hooted their laments and lullabies, allowing her to finally drift off into a dreamless slumber.

In the warm days that followed, Sarah noted the same objects being sold time and time again only to be returned or reproduced as though in an instant once darkness fell. Ivy certainly never ventured out far, and being a light sleeper, Sarah had yet to see a delivery lorry bring more than a few sacks of coal. It seemed to be a one-way arrangement - goods only ever came out of the shop.

Ivy remained closed one morning and grew ill. Spending what little time she had, and closing early, Sarah cared for her as she grew more infirm. A doctor shook his head sympathetically a few weeks later as she settled his bill, handing over medicines and tinctures to ease Ivy's failing lungs.

'My father gave me that,' said Ivy, weakly pointing at the

brooch pinned to Sarah's dress. It shone in the warm light of the candle. 'You've earned it, my dear, these past weeks looking after me. My relatives in India won't be needing to visit me this autumn now - I have a grandnephew about your age whom I haven't seen for twenty years or more; supposedly, he's quite driven.'

'You can't live with men...' began Sarah as she handed her a spoonful of bitter balsam syrup.

Ivy grimaced with the bitter taste, but smiled at the reminder. 'True enough, but there is always hope. Before I go, here is my last piece of advice: never give away anything you can't afford to lose, even your heart.'

'I'm not sure what I have left is worth anything, even that,' Sarah said sadly.

'As long as you bear that brooch I'll be with you in a manner of speaking. Let it fill you with hope.'

Ivy slowly leaned her head back onto the crisp white pillow, letting out a deep sigh. Her snow-white hair fanned around her head like a halo. 'You did well to come here,' she said in a weak voice. 'It's a shame I'm too old to spend more time with you.'

'You'll live a while longer,' Sarah lied, unable to hide the tears welling in her eyes as she sat beside the bed. She clasped Ivy's hand in hers, noting its frailness beneath her own.

'What is it you want most from the world?' said Ivy softly.

'That you would be well again,' Sarah said gently, forcing a smile on her rosy cheeks. 'And perhaps certainty that the future will be safe and secure.'

'Ah,' Ivy sighed, her chest slowly rising and falling as she spoke. 'Don't we all. Once upon a time, I wished for something similar when my beloved failed me.'

Sarah smiled at her kindly. 'But your wish has come true – you've lived a good life and had much success with your business.'

'Indeed, I have,' Ivy murmured, drifting off into a final sleep. 'You'll do the same, my dear.' Her last words hung in the air like a promise as morning light trickled through the window, its soft rays bathing the old woman's face in warmth. A single tear rolled down Sarah's cheek and glimmered on the green-stoned brooch at her breast.

And then Ivy was gone.

Sarah's grief joined with the collective sorrow of the village as they mourned the loss of Westercombe's oldest inhabitant. A small funeral was held with many donating food for the wake in the tithe barn. Not long after the burial, a series of lorries came in droves to gather up all the bric-a-brac from the old shop; an auction was held and attracted eager purchasers looking for treasures that had been neglected. Some of those in attendance were surprised to find items identical to ones they'd purchased during previous trips to the village.

Sarah was surprised when a man knocked on her window, and then nodded towards the cash register on a hand cart. 'It's got your name on it,' he said. 'It wasn't included in the auction.' She thanked him with a piece of Bakewell tart for his considerable efforts in finding space for the hefty object and then placing it on her countertop. She admired its embossed silver and brass panelling before pressing 'No Sale' – which opened the drawer with a melodic chime and released a nostalgic scent. Beneath one clip was a note – *'Never sell something that has more value as a gift.'* It was signed *'Ivy'*.

'Isn't it lovely to behold?' remarked a woman, poorly dressed and holding the thin, pale hand of a barefoot child.

'It belonged to the lady who used to have that store across the street until she died,' said Sarah.

The woman's gaze softened with a sad understanding as the rumbling of the little girl's stomach caused her to squeeze the hand a little more tightly. 'Terrible luck, I was looking for work,' she said while pushing the small girl away from the cakes on the counter and pulling her worn coat around her body, embarrassed by her frayed garments underneath. 'I had been working in a department store in Salisbury until things went wrong for me. We were looking to make a fresh start.' She rubbed at the base of her left ring finger and saw an outline of where a ring had once been worn.

'The war?' Sarah asked quietly as the woman self-consciously put down her hands.

'No,' she answered modestly, getting ready to leave. 'Something else—I had to sell it to make ends meet.'

'Wait,' said Sarah, motioning them towards an empty table. 'Please sit here for a moment. I can offer you some tea and cake while you tell me more about what it is you were looking for—I had been thinking of hiring help for the rest of the summer, or even longer.' With the mention of cake, the little girl peered out from behind her mother's coat sleeve, eyes wide with anticipation.

'And may I ask your name?' Sarah inquired.

'Ivy,' murmured the child, ogling the Victoria sponge. 'Has that got strawberries in it?'

Sarah smiled warmly. 'Well, I never. Yes, it does, so go sit down over there and I'll bring you both a slice and some milk for you. Then I can talk with your mummy.'

That evening Sarah peered through the dark window at the sad, forlorn space, devoid of purpose, half expecting to see the shop magically refilled. The bric-a-brac remained empty, which was more than could be said for the tea room on the following morning.

When Sarah lit the oven for the day's baking, she was met with a puzzling sight in the early morning light. Every cake, tart, and scone that had been sold the previous day had returned in its entirety—except for one Victoria sponge missing a healthy wedge.

It wasn't a one-off.

The following morning the bakes returned, minus several savoury pies donated to the village picnic, and a sausage roll secretly donated to a friendly terrier whose owner had popped across the road to look at the empty shop. Every cake, biscuit, and loose tea by the ounce sold from every halfpenny, shilling or farthing put into the cash register, returned the following day.

Sarah took out a cloth and polished the miraculous object. 'Thank you,' she whispered to whatever magic it contained.

One day, the old Bric-a-Brac sign outside the tea room was taken down and replaced with a new one.

'They're putting up a brand new sign, Sarah,' said the woman standing beside her. She had been employed at the tea room for just a few weeks and already looked much healthier and happier.

'What does it say?' Sarah asked, distracted by the brand-new china plates.

'Watchmaker Jeweller,' she replied, elbowing her employer, 'and a handsome fella is giving out orders. Why don't you introduce yourself before I do?'

Sarah shook her head and pushed lightly back, causing both of them to giggle. The man outside heard the laughter and wandered inside.

'Now look what you've done,' Sarah whispered as he stepped through the door. She quickly fixed her hair as he crossed over.

'I hope I'm not interrupting,' he said with an honest smile

on his bronzed face. 'My name's Michael Billingham; I've moved into my great aunt's place across the street.'

'You are Ivy's great nephew?' asked Sarah, coming round to greet him.

'Yes,' he said. 'I'm honouring the family tradition and going into business. I wasn't able to see her before she left—'

He stopped, his attention drawn to the green brooch pinned to Sarah's dress. 'My goodness,' he said, 'an Arabian emerald—I wouldn't have expected one of those in an English tea room, especially on someone who looks so beautiful wearing it. May I?'

Sarah blushed and handed him the brooch. 'You must be mistaken; I was told it was paste—just costume jewellery.'

The man examined the stone and shook his head. 'There's no mistake; this is real, or at least from what I can tell with a quick look over. I have all the proper tools in my shop if you'd like to come by for an appraisal once it's open for business.'

The woman behind the counter cleared her throat and Sarah answered, hesitantly. 'That would be very gracious of you, Mr Billingham.'

'Please call me Michael,' he said before turning his gaze towards the Victoria sponge cake, missing a sizeable wedge. 'Looks like that's popular already—and you've only been open a few minutes. Never had it for breakfast before, not in India at least.'

'I'll bring some over for you to have while you do the valuation,' Sarah offered.

The man smiled, giving a curt bow. 'I'll look forward to it.' He paused at the door.

'In India,' he said. 'Emeralds are a token of hope—,' his eyes lingering on the ornate cash register, '—hope and security for the future.'

GET EXCLUSIVE CONTENT

Thank you for reading *Bric-a-Brac*.

Building a relationship with my readers is the very best thing about writing. I send monthly newsletters with details on new releases, special offers and other news relating to my books.

Sign up to my readers' group at www.jtcroft.com or by scanning the QR code below, and I'll send you further stories in my collection, *Free Spirits,* exclusive to my reader's group– you can't get this anywhere else.

ABOUT THE TALES

THE EXCHANGE

An unashamedly romantic ghost story whose ending or twist, as with many of my tales, was conceived first. There must always be something that keeps a couple apart in romantic fiction, and what better barrier than death? Bringing them back together was easy, at least for the author, but I wanted to ensure the reader was kept guessing until the very end as to which side crossed over. A sudden catastrophe with heroic consequences was needed – a time and place. The East End of London was filled with such examples during the Blitz and several figures came to mind after hearing recounted stories of ordinary men and women going about their daily lives and evening rituals during this time. One man recalled coming back from an air raid shelter to find his beer still standing where he had left it, the dominoes of his hand flattened by the blast of a doodlebug a few streets away. Strong and endearing relationships are forged in difficult circumstances, and this guided me through the writing. I wonder what it would be like to be able to talk with those now gone, within finger touch, but out of reach, and whether that would make things easier or harder in the end.

Several mirrors have been featured in stories I have written over the years, and I put this down to a fascination with a story I once read about the folklore of witches. 'Scrying' (using mirrors partially submerged in running water to divine the future) captivated my young imagination, so much so, that I tried it in the bath. It didn't work, but I put that down to the overuse of bubble bath.

GLOW

A story that almost wrote itself after researching Ganser Syndrome for my second novel, *Maiden Point*.

Sufferers have short-term episodes of odd behaviour similar to that shown by people with other serious mental illnesses. The person may appear confused, make absurd statements, and report hallucinations such as the experience of sensing things that are not there or hearing voices. They can also feel compelled to act if they believe that something bad will happen without their intervention.

I imagined a 'what if' scenario, based around a sixth sense instinct, and what that would do to someone over time. I imagined it would be difficult, always being on guard, forever ready to save or protect, and the guilt that might never leave you for those you were unable to save. What I needed was a positive ending and an endearing character that would enable the protagonist to learn to live with the ability. I needed someone invisible, anonymous, always there but never regarded as we go about our daily business; the pigeon-feeding, 'bag-lady' with hidden depths seemed worth pursuing, watching over 'her spot' on the bridge as the river of humanity flowed past, ready to save those souls drowning in despair.

The bridge in in mind is Worcester Bridge, an eighteenth-century multi-arched sandstone crossing over the River Severn, and I now have a different perspective when I see lone figures on its wide pavements, watching, waiting.

I'm sure they are just looking out for the swans...

REFLECTIONS

One of the more personal and bittersweet moments in my writing that echoes something of my transition away from childhood, and the weaning away from imaginary things. I like to think I've held on to my inner child, and that my imagination has never fully embraced any restrictions imposed by adulthood, but I do recall having someone to talk and play with, that only I could 'see'. To my great sadness, I can't recall what name I gave him, her, or them, and I'm sure that the time we spent together was formative, fun, and ridiculous.

I feel strangely sorry for not remembering someone who wasn't really there, and this story hopes to make amends by telling another inevitable parting from the perspective of the one who has the most to lose. I am reminded of a lyric by Steve Hogarth (Marillion) in the poignant and heart-tugging, '*Estonia*':

"*No one leaves you when you live in their heart and mind.*"

Wherever my imaginary friend ended up, I hope they found someone new to remember them.

NIGHTINGALE

A passion project I have been trying to do justice to for some time whose genesis came from the question: 'What if the only way to save oneself from certain death (a second time!) involved confronting one's killer with a kiss?'

My work generally begins with a question, and now, how to answer this riddle became the focus of this story. I am drawn to characters whose actions come into conflict with their nature, and this novella is very much open-minded about whether the end justifies the means, and the impact it has on those individuals. From the beginning, the notion that our protagonist would have to face the full consequences at the end of a door knocker burned uncomfortably bright as I approached the end of the writing tunnel.

I've left the door open for more, though whether this particular Nightingale will return to any cage (or page!) is a matter for more questions as I lie awake after dark. Would the pull of a once glamorous career be enough to encourage a reprise despite the danger?

In the words of Doris Day: "*Perhaps, perhaps, perhaps...*"

THE CRESSET SQUARE

A little chiller about the danger of curiosity, temptation and moral failure born from an obsession with the pursuit of knowledge. We often don't realise we are about to come unstuck until the very end, and it is the slightest miscalculation that can have the greatest consequences.

I liked the notion of a monastic community on its knees (pun intended), and its salvation coming at the expense of personal loss, though whether the emboldening of faith and a fleeting vision of heaven compensates for a lifetime without earthly vision is a question I have yet to answer.

SLEEP NOW, ADELARD

A love letter to my beloved Isles of Scilly. I have always wanted to set a story in this archipelago, 28 miles southwest of Cornwall, but wanted something profound but hopeful as a story arc. The fabled land of Lyonesse, the hundreds of small rocky islets are responsible for a veritable graveyard of ships so that was a starting point, as too was the recurring motif of grief.

"Never use love in the past tense" is a phrase I heard many years ago and it has stuck with me – I forget to whom it should be attributed. It speaks to me when I think of those people who have gone before their time and brings me some consolation. You don't stop loving, you just can't be loved back but as this should be unconditional, does that matter?

At its heart, this story encapsulates what my writing is all about – human feelings and actions triggered or helped on their way through supernatural agency, usually with a few heart-tugging moments in between.

The presence of gig racing is an important part of island life so forgive the indulgence – if you ever are lucky enough to witness the courage and fortitude of those who continue their traditions in bi-weekly regattas then you might find your own troubles and challenges seem a little less significant; at least that is what Jane discovered.

The lighthouse, and rocks of Hellweathers really are a forbidding and dangerous place at the edge of the world.

Don't take Adelard's word (or drawings) for it — I've been there, take mine.

BRIC-A-BRAC

An idea from my father, who dreamed the plot device!

As you can imagine when a parent tells you to "sit down because they have something to tell you", you don't think it's going to be a dream they had that they would like to be put into prose. Relieved to hear it was nothing more serious, my father repeated what he could remember regarding an antique shop whose stock refilled 'magically' overnight. His frustration came from not being able to account for its meaning or resolution.

Welcome to my world, Dad.

A man of machines and metal, he often reminds me that I did not get my creativity from his side of the family. I hope you will agree with my rebuttal, and that he really should keep a pen and paper next to his bed to save me time concocting an ending to stories I did not begin.

J.T.Croft
October 2023

ALSO BY J. T. CROFT

Firelight and Frost
Maiden Point
A House of Bells
Midnight's Treasury
High Spirits

"Dead Brilliant"

"Well written. Fascinating and original"

"Beautifully dark and bittersweet"

ABOUT THE AUTHOR

J. T. Croft is an award winning author of bittersweet and sentimental Gothic fiction, supernatural mystery and ghostly tales. He doesn't believe in spirits, but that doesn't mean they don't believe in him.
For more information:
www.jtcroft.com

I hope you enjoyed reading this book as much as I loved writing it. If you did, I'd really appreciate you leaving me a quick review on whichever platform you prefer. Reviews are extremely helpful for any author, and even just a line or two can make a big difference. I'm independently published, so I rely on good folks like you spreading the word!

- facebook.com/jtcroftauthor
- twitter.com/jtcroftauthor
- instagram.com/jtcroftauthor

Milton Keynes UK
Ingram Content Group UK Ltd.
UKHW011819241023
431263UK00004B/39